The Devil's Kiss

John had kissed Isabelle before, gently showing his affection for the beautiful innocent who soon would be his bride.

But now he felt as though he never had kissed Isabelle before, just as he never before really had known this young woman who came to his room without invitation or warning tonight.

Isabelle's lips were on fire as they opened beneath his. Her body was soft with intoxicating invitation as it pressed against his. Her slender arms were startlingly strong as they drew him to her.

It was more than a man could understand . . . and more than he could resist . . . as John felt all barriers melt in the flames of passion rising to consume him and the woman he now so desperately feared to love . . .

#22
KATHERYN KIMBROUGH'S
Saga of the Phenwick Women

ISABELLE, THE FRANTIC

POPULAR LIBRARY • NEW YORK

Published by Popular Library, a unit of CBS Publications, the Consumer Publishing Division of CBS Inc.

June, 1978

ISBN: 0-445-04238-9

Dedicated to
Greg Gelesko
and
Antonia Leonard

CAST OF CHARACTERS

GREGORY PHENWICK	A prominent London businessman and a substantial member of the notorious Phenwick family.
ILENE PHENWICK	His lovely wife, the Phenwick woman of whom he is proud.
ISABELLE PHENWICK	The lovely firstborn of his twin daughters. Shy and fragile, she is sedate and demure, but a picture of lovely elegance.
ELENA PHENWICK	The other twin. Outgoing and provocative, Elena is identical to her twin in appearance, not in disposition.
ALEXANDRIA PHENWICK	The third daughter, who is more like Elena than like Isabelle. A year younger than the twins, she is often mistaken for a triplet.
ALBERT PHENWICK	Gregory and Ilene's only son. As a child he was a toy in his sisters' hands.
JOHN PHENWICK	A distant Phenwick cousin who lives in Boston, where he is a promising young attorney.
JOANNA PHENWICK	John's much older half sister. She is a reigning actress on the London stage.

JOSHUA PHENWICK	Joanna's younger full brother, co-head of Medallion Enterprises in London.
Olivia Phenwick	Joshua's wife.
DAVID PHENWICK	Joshua's youngest son.
Daniel Louis Phenwick	John's youngest brother, a playboy about Boston.
MOORDUKE	A wee acquaintance of Ilene.
STUART PHENWICK	The eldest son of John's oldest half brother, Augustus. Several years older than John, Stuart is the head of the Medallion Company in Boston.
Ruth Phenwick	His lovely wife.
DANNY PHENWICK	Stuart's son by his first wife, Marcia.
ANN MARIE PHENWICK	Stuart's daughter by Marcia.
Richard Polly Donald Phenwick	Stuart's three children by Ruth.
ALEXANDER PHENWICK	Stuart's son by Barbara, conceived out of wedlock while she was married to Stuart's Uncle Prentise.
MILLIJOY PHENWICK	One of the more notorious of all the Phenwick women, she is the widow of Stuart's only brother, Gordon. Extravagantly wealthy and flamboyant, she lives like a queen in opulent Triumph House.
THOMAS PHENWICK	Millijoy's seventeen-year-old son. Strangely handsome, the young man is a musical prodigy of enormous talent.
DERRICK MOLDEN	A servant, carriage driver and all-around handyman for Gregory Phenwick and his family.

Melvin Ferrett	A bookkeeper for the Medallion Enterprises.
ALISTER CROOK	A stoic inspector at Scotland Yard.
Wilfred & Pauline Quigly	A society couple in Boston.
Maribelle Wilson	A lovely young lady who is interested in John.
BREWSTER MARTIN	John's business partner and friend.
Captain Lemuel Keswick	Captain of the *Twin Dolphins*.
CURTIS TINKERSLY	First Mate aboard the *Twin Dolphins*.
VICTOR SAMSON	Millijoy's impressive butler.
Clara Whiteside	Millijoy's housekeeper.
Ryder Boxer Crisp	Seamen aboard the *Twin Dolphins*.
SADIE CARNE	A rag woman of the London streets.
Mrs. Edna Stout	A landlady.
Thane O'Reilly	A derelict at Carrickfergus, North Ireland.
Patsy	His dog.
Mr. & Mrs. Patrick Duffy	Innkeepers at Carrickfergus.
	AND
ADAM TRUFF	The handsome, lovable, astute, enigmatic long-time family friend of the Phenwicks. He is a man of charm, wit and knowledge, a catalyst and a confidant. An air of mystery and intrigue surrounds him, and he appears to be attracted into similar situations.

GENEALOGY

THE PHENWICKS

*AUGUSTA

Founder of the family, married to Barrywell, then to Joshua Phenwick. The three children by Barrywell were murdered by their father; DANIEL CHARLES was the only son of her marriage to Joshua. She later adopted EDWARD and JANE MUNSK, whom she raised as PHENWICKS. Augusta maintains an eerie hold over the surviving members of her family.

DANIEL

Augusta's only son who lived to adulthood. Father of Elias (by Kate Mumford); married to *Margaret O'Plaggerty; father of Alexander, Peter, and *Rachel.

Elias

Married to *Patricia Kelburn; father of *Rebecca.

*Rebecca

First married to Johnny Ornby; second marriage to Robert Cathcart; mother of Kate Phenwick.

*Kate

Married to John Collier. Mother of *Nellie, Elizabeth, George, and Rupert.

*Nellie

Married to Thadius Phenwick.

Alexander

Married to *Susannah Phenwick; adopted two children: Marcia and Gregory Wing.

*Marcia

Married to Stuart Phenwick; mother of Daniel Charles II, and Ann Marie.

Gregory

Married to *Ilene Dumphy. Father of *Isabelle and Elena (twins), Alexandria, and Albert.

Peter

First married to Helen Barnfather; father of Augustus, Joanne, Prentise, and Joshua. Second marriage to *Nancy Cox; father of Thadius, John, Paul, and Daniel Louis.

*Denotes Phenwick women about whom books were written.

AUGUSTA (con't)
DANIEL (con't)
Peter (con't)

Augustus	Married to Lillian Webb; father of Stuart and Gordon.
Stuart	Married to *Marcia Phenwick; father of Daniel Charles II, and Ann Marie. Second wife, *Ruth; children: Peter, Polly, Donald.
Gordon	The strange dual-natured son. Briefly married to *Millijoy Gray, father of Thomas.
*Joanne	Only daughter of Peter. Unmarried actress.
Prentise	Married to *Harriet Pettijohn; father of James, Frances, Louis, Martha, Patrick, Sam, and Tom.
Joshua	Married to *Olivia Pritchard; head of Medallion Enterprises in London; father of *Ophelia, Arnold (Leo), Ruth, Carrie, Elizabeth, and David.
Thadius	Eldest son of Peter and Nancy. Married to *Nellie Collier.
John	The lawyer son.
Paul	Married Lottie Wells. Father of John Adam.
Daniel Louis	Youngest son of Peter and Nancy.
*Rachel	Daniel's only daughter. Died in her teens.
EDWARD (Munsk)	Adopted son of Augusta; married to *Patricia Kelburn; father of David and *Susannah. (Actual son of John and Lydia Munsk.)
David	Edward's only son, killed War of 1812.
*Susannah	Edward's daughter; married to Alexander (Lex) Phenwick; foster mother of *Marcia and Gregory. (See under Peter's children.)

*JANE (Munsk)	· Adopted daughter of Augusta; married to Jeffrey Ornby; sons: Frederick, Johnny, and Andrew (Actual daughter of John and Lydia Munsk.)
THE ORNBYS	
Frederick	Jane's eldest son; married to Henrietta Ellsworth; sons: John and Edward.
John	Married Dorothy Wren; children: Millicent, Crandall, and Virginia.
Edward	Married Sarah Hadley; children: Thomas, Mary, and John Frederick.
Thomas	Married Zelda Casey. No children.
Mary	Died in teens.
John Frederick	Married Sally Battell; children: *Ann Rose and Frederick.
Johnny	Father of Adrianne and Lydia by his first wife; second marriage to *Rebecca Phenwick. No children.
Adrianne	Murdered in England.
Lydia	Unmarried.
Andrew	Married to Livinia Hendricks; father of Jane Augusta, Daniel, Theodore, Angela, Bertha, and Jeffrey.
Jane Augusta	Married to Eustace Clark, no children.
Daniel	An attorney. Wife: Mellissa Kesler; children: James, Henry, Thomas, and Sarah.
Theodore	(Dr. Ted.) Wife: Louise Lacy; children: Joseph, Augustus, Collin, Mary Rose, and Ruth.
Joseph	A physician. Wife: Sheila Dumphy.
Augustus	A physician. Wife: Nell Willet; children: Charles and *Louise.

PROLOGUE

Greed. Jealousy. More and more I see those elements creeping in among my family. Basically the Phenwicks are loving, with honest concern for others of my descendants. Yet occasionally there will be one or two, like my great-grandson Gordon, who overstep and attempt to usurp power. It is bad enough when someone from outside the family tries such a wretched deed, but when it comes from within the family itself, well, then it is unforgivable.

I have a kind of pride—if it can be called that, in my condition on this side—in the Phenwick women. I even have great admiration for Millijoy, who, I must confess, holds a special place in my esteem. Nancy is very dear to me, as are Nellie and Ann—and dear, sweet, innocent Ilene. There are the others, too, of course.

Ilene. Well, now that I've brought her up, I suppose I should get directly to the matter at hand. She met Gregory Phenwick in Boston, fell in love with him, and married him; then she returned to London with him. In time she bore him three daughters and one son. The eldest two daughters were identical twins, with exotic dark beauty like Gregory's late sister, Marcia. By the age of eighteen, physically they had become two lovelies. Their third daughter, Alexandria, only a year and a few months younger than her twin sisters, was developing into even more of a beauty. Her slight resemblance to her mother distinguished her enough so that she was only rarely mistaken for being one of triplets. Ironically, with three such young beauties in one household, only one was destined to become a Phenwick woman.

I must tell you that it is generally believed that I or one of the living established Phenwick women choose those who are to have that title. I even had that misconception at first, before I realized many things of which I have been made aware over here. There is a master plan; and try as one may, it cannot be altered to suit individual greedy purposes.

After leaving Nellie and Thadius in Greenfield, after a wedding ceremony the likes of which Greenfield had never before seen, I found that I was drawn again to London, and finally to Carrickfergus, Northern Ireland, where Ilene Phenwick had taken the twins, Alexandria and Albert for a holiday, while Gregory remained in London to look after Medallion business in the absence of Joshua, who was enjoying a lengthy visit in the United States after attending Nellie's wedding.

I must say I was never partial to Ireland or Northern Ireland. Still, I often find myself in the most amazing places. Invariably I go to where the next Phenwick woman is undergoing the preparation necessary to follow in my footsteps.

CHAPTER ONE

The cheerless gray stones of Carrickfergus Castle stood like sentries gloomily facing Belfast Lough. The dark harbor water reflected the thick outlines of the ancient edifice and the gray skies overhead. Noisy gulls with ruffled feathers stalked the quay, necks pulled down, observing.

When the carriage had earlier left the quiet inn a short distance from the castle, dogs had given chase to it. That was the most excitement that had happened in the sleepy seaport borough in County Antrim in Northern Ireland that day.

The mother, daughter and son had browsed about the uninteresting shops for nearly an hour. Ilene was as lovely as the day she had married Gregory Phenwick twenty years before. Both her daughter Alexandria and her son Albert bore a remarkable resemblance to her. The twins, a year and a half older than Alexandria, favored their father. They had left in the carriage for a ride in the countryside.

"I don't know why I couldn't have gone along with Isabelle and Elena," Alexandria stated as she fingered a piece of delicate lace. "It seems most unfair, don't you agree, Bertie?"

Albert wrinkled his nose, smirked, and ignored his sister.

"Bertie is in a mind today, isn't he, Mother?" Alexandria continued. She was the compulsive talker of the family.

"Never you mind, Bertie," Ilene rejoined. "And I do wish you would stop calling him Bertie. His name is Albert."

"The Prince was called Bertie, wasn't he?" Alexandria said.

"Your brother isn't a prince," Ilene commented, glancing up to see that her fifteen-year-old son did not wander off. "I have a feeling, Alexandria."

"A feeling, Mother?"

"I've gotten all edgy," Ilene replied. "Something's wrong, something's happened! I think it would be best if we were to get back to the inn. Do be a dear and get Bertie—that is, Albert—while I pay for this linen."

Parasols up, Albert a respectable few steps behind, Ilene and Alexandria processed down the cobblestone walk. A light drizzle was in the air, making it feel heavy and oppressive.

"Did you know that Carrickfergus means *rock of Fergus*?" Alexandria asked.

"Yes, dear. I was born and raised in Carrickfergus, you know."

"It was named for King Fergus, who was shipwrecked off the coast near here in—I believe the year was 320 A.D.—or thereabouts," Alexandria continued. "And I was told by a very nice-looking young man that Carrickfergus castle is practically perfectly preserved as a notable relic of the Norman period. It was once beseiged by the Scot Edward Bruce, who was later crowned King of Ireland, in the early fourteenth century. I don't recall the precise year."

"Yes, Alexandria, I'm fully aware of all that," Ilene said. "Can't you see my thoughts are elsewhere and you're disturbing me with your continual chatter?"

"Am I? Oh, I am sorry, Mother," Alexandria returned. "What are you thinking about, then?"

"She's probably thinking, I should think," Albert inserted, "that she wishes she had left you in London."

"What a dreadful thing of Bertie to say," Alexandria commented. "You wouldn't have left me in London, would you have, Mother? Not when you, Elena, Bertie, and Isabelle came here on holiday."

"No, dear, I wouldn't have left you in London," Ilene said. Then, under her breath, she muttered, "Besides, your father wouldn't have permitted me to have done so."

"What was that, Mother?"

"Nothing, dearest," Ilene chuckled, and hurried her chicks to the inn. That ominous, foreboding feeling seemed to be increasing within her.

Seven freckles in the shape of the number seven on Elena's shoulder was the only noticeable physical difference between her and her sister. Since that birthmark was in an area that was rarely if ever exposed, there was no way of telling them apart by appearance. Yet their personalities were remarkably opposite in many ways. The fact that Isabelle had been born seven minutes earlier than Elena caused her to be looked upon as the eldest of the two. She was quiet, confident, yet elegantly stately and grand when she wished to become the center of attention, or when she became it without being aware that she was attracting interest.

Elena mimicked her twin in every way. She delighted in confusing people and purposefully tried to deceive them. She, therefore, could be equally as grand as Isabelle.

Since they spent so much time in each other's company, it was predictable that they would attract attention and puzzlement.

With only rare exceptions, Ilene and Gregory could always tell the twins apart. They had individual mannerisms that gave them away. Even though, when Elena wanted to, she could trick her parents into believing that she was her twin. Neither Alexandria nor Albert could be fooled by their older sisters. For that matter, Alexandria could well mimic both Elena and Isabelle. Cousin Joanna Phenwick was convinced that Alexandria had the potential of becoming an actress, as she was. Joanna did not attempt to influence Alexandria in that direction. The actress was quite close to all of Ilene and Gregory's children.

The twins were dressed in red-orange velvet gowns, trimmed with an ivory-colored lace. Large yellow straw bonnets with high beaks were tied securely about their chins. They carried identical parasols. It was near the end of April, but the weather that far north was not predictable. They also had white-and-orange fans tied about their wrists in case there was a rise in the temperature or the humidity. Stiff-backed and queenly, they sat side by side on the forward-riding seat, each observing the passing scenery on her side of the carriage.

Periodically Elena glanced over at her sister. A faint smile was etched at the ends of Isabelle's lips. Her sister was curious about her thoughts, but she knew she would share them if she really wanted to.

Elena adjusted her position and reached for the strap as the road became bumpy. "I do wish that fool would be more careful of where he's going!" she exclaimed. "Derrick! Will you be careful!"

"I doubt if he can hear you, Elena, while the carriage is moving," Isabelle uttered, not turning her attention to her sister.

"I'll give him a crack of my parasol when we stop," Elena said, "and see if that doesn't improve his hearing any."

"If you hit him across the ear, it is liable to make him stone deaf," Isabelle commented.

"Oh, you're always so wise, aren't you?"

"Papa says I'm practical," Isabelle returned. She smiled at Elena.

"Is that meant to imply that I'm impractical?" Elena fired.

"Not in the least, dearest Elena," Isabelle remarked. "The truth is, we're quite opposites, don't you know."

"I didn't know." Isabelle smiled and returned her gaze to the passing scenery.

"Oh, yes. We must be opposites," Elena persisted. "You're meant to be a Phenwick woman, I'm not. Mother has said that for years."

"But that's perfectly silly, Elena," Isabelle returned. "We're both Phenwick women *now*."

"But we won't be once we've married, unless we marry Phenwick men," Elena stated.

"Then it's illogical to think that I'm to be *the* Phenwick woman, if a Phenwick woman at all," Isabelle responded. "It's you who are attracted to David Phenwick, not me."

"And who do you suppose David talks about—practically constantly—when we go out together?"

"Not me, I should think," Isabelle said.

"Oh, no? You should hear him sometime."

"Well, rest assured, sister, I'm not in the least bit interested in Cousin David—or any other Phenwick that I know," Isabelle expressed. "Papa seems to be of the opinion that we should consider the hands of the Cartwright twins. But if you ask me, that would be asking for trouble."

"I can't abide either Malcolm or Martin Cartwright," Elena declared. "They bore me."

"I couldn't agree with you more," Isabelle commented. "The Cartwrights are terribly dull, and I suspect they're opportunists."

"Papa's naïve to think they're not out to get their fingers into the Medallion business," Elena added. "But I'll tell you this, I'm not at all that impressed with David Phenwick. He is nice enough, I suppose, but he doesn't affect me—"

"Affect you?"

"You know, in a romantic way."

"David is quite handsome."

Elena glared. "Then *you* go after him. You're meant to be the Phenwick woman, not me!"

"Elena! Elena, what's come over you? You're not yourself."

"Aren't I?" Elena breathed deeply. "Oh, Isabelle, sometimes I wonder what it would have been like if I could have had a life of my own."

"But you do have a life of your own."

"No, I don't. I've always been and always will be *your* twin sister," Elena remarked. "Look at us, dressed alike, mirror images of each other. And there's Alexandria, independent and able to go about as she pleases. I simply pray that I will never give birth to twins."

"What a thing to say!"

"For the sake of one of them, I would eagerly drown the other," Elena continued.

"Elena! What a thought!"

Tall, redheaded, freckled, passably attractive Derrick Molden sat forward on the driver's seat. A light mist had begun to fall. His blue eyes scanned the surrounding area as he squinted and pulled the bill of his hat lower on his brow. Up ahead was the wooden bridge. He could not hear the roaring rushing of the water beneath, but he knew it was there. No sign of anyone. No houses. Only

18

distant smoke curling above a hillock in a slender thread to vanish in the gray of the clouds.

Periodically Derrick could hear the faint sound of the sisters' voices. He had worked seventeen months for Gregory Phenwick as driver and general handyman. The work was pleasant enough, but it was confining and not appropriate for a man with ambition.

The bridge was less than a quarter of a mile ahead. A chilling sense of anticipation came over the man. He liked to gamble.

"You do have a life of your own," Isabelle argued. "While it's true that we spent much time together in years past, we have gone our separate ways on many occasions."

"Our separate ways?" Elena echoed contemptuously. "We'll always be twins. Even if we go to opposite ends of the earth, we cannot change our status. And even after death, I suspect, we will still be closely tied by an invisible bond. We were born twins for a reason. Whatever that may be, we can't escape our destiny."

"I will always love you, Elena," Isabelle said. "I agree there must be a definite reason why we were born twins. Perhaps someday we'll know why."

The boulder had been methodically placed on the wooden bridge. The rain had made the boards slippery. By the time the horse saw the boulder, her reactions were ill timed. She swerved to miss it; instead, the wheel was directed immediately to it. The horse's front hoof overstepped the edge of the bridge. Startled as she lost her balance, she lurched. To the animal's surprise, the traces binding her to the carriage had snapped, freeing her to fall clear of the vehicle, which fell directly behind.

Derrick jumped clear as the carriage began to tip. It was several desperate moments later before he was able to swim away from the rushing rapids. By the time he regained his awareness, the carriage was a hundred yards or more beyond where he was. It was being swiftly carried on the current. His one hope was to go ashore and run in the direction it was going.

The carriage doors had opened when the wheels hit the boulder. Elena was on the far side, and had been thrown against Isabelle as the coach fell. The carriage turned over, but moments later bobbed right side up.

When Derrick reached the bridge, he realized that it would be impossible for him to get to the carriage. Spying the horse struggling to get to the shore, he went after her. Holding her by the reins, he managed to calm her and led her back over the bridge. He stopped at the boulder and pushed it over the side before some other carriage got thrown by trespassing over it.

Both Albert and Alexandria had picked up their mother's sense of anxiety. Alexandria paced in her room while Albert stood at the window and stared out through the streaks of rain that distorted his view. Ilene sat uneasily and tried to concentrate on her embroidery. Her fingers were trembling, and twice she pricked herself with the needle.

"Can't you children find something to do," Ilene asked, "instead of standing about making me more nervous than I am?"

"Do? Like what?" Albert asked, not budging from the window.

"There are playing cards in the drawer," Ilene suggested. "Why don't you have a game of—"

"Oh, Mother!" exclaimed Alexandria. "We can't concentrate on a silly card game at a time like this!"

"A time like *what?*" Ilene asked. "Why should we all feel so queerly?"

Albert pushed the window open as he saw the drenched rider approaching the inn. Because he had developed a friendship with Derrick, he instantly recognized him. He glanced back at his mother. Instinctively the boy knew there had been an accident. For what other reason would Derrick be riding back on the carriage mare? Subtly, Albert excused himself and hurried through the corridor to the entrance toward which Derrick appeared to have been headed.

"There was an accident," Derrick said solemnly. He was dripping water. He explained as best he could. "It all happened so suddenly, I didn't know what to do. There was no way I could have gotten to that carriage. . . . No way, lad."

Tears had come to Albert's eyes before he reached the door to his mother's room. Derrick was directly behind him, carrying a bonnet he had found. The boy looked back at him, and appreciated the hand that was put to his shoulder.

Ilene took the news as calmly as she could, but Alexandria became hysterical. Albert did what he could to control his sister; it was an impossible task.

Alerted to the excitement, the manager of the inn went immediately to encounter Ilene. When the situation was explained, he took it upon himself to notify the constable. Within half an hour a group of men was gathered together to form a searching party.

Albert insisted on going with the men, proclaiming that they were his sisters and that he was a Phenwick man and must be responsible. A doctor was sent for, to administer strong sedation to Alexandria and a weaker portion to Ilene. She wanted to be fully conscious and aware of what was happening, but she did accept enough to ease her nerves.

Once Alexandria was asleep, Ilene sat by the open window and stared blankly out. "Oh, m' wee one, where d'ye be now, when I need ye th' most?"

"I beg your pardon, Mrs. Phenwick," the manager's

wife said as she softly entered the room. "Miss Phenwick is a-sleepin' now."

"Oh. I thought I was alone," Ilene said, swallowing the old brogue that had slipped out.

"Ay, 'tis a terrible thin' that's happened, missus," the woman commented, feeling awkward and inadequate to the situation. "Is there somethin' I kin git for ye?"

Ilene shook her head.

"Ye're not a Catholic, are ye?"

Again Ilene shook her head. "My mother was Catholic, but my father was an Orangeman. We were raised without religion."

"Ay, 'tis a pity. Perhaps I had better run and git th' vicar. He kin give ye some words o' peace."

"That won't be necessary," Ilene uttered feebly. "I must get word to London. My husband must know what has happened."

"Ye write down what ye want sent, an' I'll take it over t' be wired."

When the manager's wife returned after sending word of the tragedy to Gregory Phenwick in London, the vicar accompanied her. Ilene was grateful for his presence.

The men searched until night fell and it was too dark to see anything. By then they had pretty much covered the ground five hundred yards on either side of the creek.

Albert had bravely kept a stiff upper lip throughout the search. When it was decided that the hunt was futile, the youth began to sob. The men comforted him as best they could. Then Derrick sat with him on the seat of the constable's carriage and did what he could to help the saddened lad.

CHAPTER TWO

That same afternoon a ragged derelict made his usual rounds in Carrickfergus. There were specific places where he was certain to get handouts, other places he knew where items of value were sometimes discarded. He had a routine. Not making a daily pest of himself, he had a schedule of areas to hit at certain times.

A black mongrel of disputed backgrounds was his constant companion. The dog was called Patsy.

Twice that day the derelict had dodged the constable. He was just superstitious enough to realize that two such near encounters were an omen. He would carry his sack of miscellaneous items and head to his hideaway in the woods.

When asked his name, the derelict would probably explain that he was Thane O'Reilly and both his father and uncle were prizefighters of erstwhile fame. He often talked to himself or to Patsy. A man of thirty-four years, he had traveled around most of his life, living as best he could. He was accustomed to that way of existing. He had no idea what had ever become of his famous relatives. Probably, he often thought, they had each lost fights and had fallen from notoriety.

"Ay, Patsy, 'tis a sad state o' affairs," Thane commented as he sat on the riverbank and gnawed on a lamb leg bone before he tossed it to the dog, "Ye an' me bein' out in th' bloody open wifout th' slightest hint o' a umberella. Well, ye kin't have ever'thin', now, kin ye?"

Patsy barked and caught the tossed bone.

Thane turned to a small jug of Irish whisky he had traded a broken mirror for. After a substantial portion of the liquor, his attention went to the dog, who had lost interest in the bone. The dog growled.

"What is it, Patsy?" Thane questioned.

Patsy was quickly to his feet, abandoning the bone and racing toward the creek.

"Where ye runnin' off to?" Thane called, before he took another drink from the crockery jug.

Patsy had reached the shore. His barking became more frantic as he leaped about and periodically glanced back to see if Thane was curious enough to come and investigate.

After a third swig from the jug, Thane balanced to his feet and lurched his way through the boggy soil. He stopped short, teetered slightly, and took another drink before he went to get a closer look at the body that had been caught among thickets just beyond the edge of the water.

"Ay, 'tis a lass, ain't it, Patsy?" Thane said, one eye closed. "D'ye reckon she's dead?"

Her bonnet was gone and her hair flowed like spokes of a wheel around the back of her head. She was caught in the thicket, which held her head from the water.

As Thane stared, she heaved a deep breath, which caused her bosom to rise. Then she sagged down and her chin submerged nearly to her mouth.

Quickly Thane gathered his wits. "Ay, she's alive. I'll

have t' fish her out, I will." He waded down into the creek, caught hold of her, and, with enormous effort, managed to free her from the barrier that had kept her from drowning. She was wearing only her underskirts, and she was shoeless.

"What'll we do wif her?" Thane questioned. "Wif all this wet, it's no place for a lass th' likes o' her."

Patsy sniffed around the girl's face, while Thane emptied the jug of whisky. "There's always th' ol' mill. We could carry her there, couldn't we?" He rose. "Ay, that's what we'll do. Then, once she's safe an' outa sight, we'll go back into th' village an' open our ears. That underskirt is trimmed wif pretty lace, an' ye kin tell by her hands she ain't done a might o' work in her life."

Ilene was in a daze when Derrick returned with Albert. She opened her arms to her son and gathered him to her.

Derrick asked if there was anything more he could do.

"There's nothing anyone can do now," Ilene said. "Just leave me with my son. We'll wait here for Mr. Phenwick. I'm sorry I ever returned to the place of my birth—or that I wanted my children to come see it."

Derrick quietly excused himself. Ilene presumed he would go to a tavern. Albert held to his mother and wept.

It was the manager's wife, Mrs. Duffy, who interrupted with a light rap on the door. "There's a man here what says he wants t' speak t' ya."

"It can't be my husband so soon," Ilene said, shaking herself out of grogginess akin to sleep.

"No, missus," Mrs. Duffy replied. " 'Tis far from th' likes o' th' man a fine lady like ye would have for an husband."

"Well, who is he?" Ilene asked impatiently.

Albert left his mother's side and started for the door.

"He asked me t' gi' ye this," Mrs. Duffy explained, protruding the remnants of a fan toward Ilene.

Albert took the object and immediately recognized it. "It's one of their fans."

Ilene accepted the item and examined it. She nodded her head. "I'll see the man."

The man's entrance was humble. He obviously felt out of place in the presence of such an elegant lady. Quickly he explained what had brought him, relating that he was a poor—a desperately poor—man with many urgent needs. He punctuated his statement with a remarkably loud belch.

"You found only one?" Ilene asked.

"Ay, how many were ye expectin'?"

"There were two."

"Wal, this one had dark hair—"

"It will do no good to describe her," Ilene explained. "They both looked alike."

Thane's eyes widened. Ilene continued with the explanation. Then she arranged to give him a sizable amount of cash for bringing the information.

The sky was not quite dark when the young lady began to restlessly move her head from side to side. Suddenly, as if a loud cracking noise had alarmed her, she flashed open her eyes. Her hands reached on either side of her as far as she could without actually moving her body. Where was she? What had happened?

"Elena? Are you here, Elena?" she questioned, her voice husky and trembling. "Elena?" Her feet reached out as she moved her legs in either direction. Her left foot hit a stack of peat and she quickly pulled it away.

"Here now, will ye watch where ye're puttin' yer bloody foot?" The voice was tiny, but it had very definite masculine tones to it.

"Who—who's there?"

"Glory be! Here I am trying t' take me nap, an' there ye are kickin' me bed out from under me. D'ye mind?"

"Please help me," Isabelle said. "I don't know where I am."

"Ye're in th' ol' mill, that's where ye are."

Suddenly a tiny glow of light came from the direction of the sound.

"Is that a lightning bug?" Isabelle asked.

"Nay, it's me lantern." The light came toward her. "Cor!" he exclaimed as he got a closer look at her. "Ye're no fairy, are ye?"

"I—I don't believe I am," Isabelle said skeptically. "Are you?"

"Nay. I'm a mite on th' wee side," the voice explained, "but I ain't no fairy. What're ye starin' at? Ain't ye never seen a leprechaun before?"

"A *what*?" With effort she pushed herself up to lean on her elbows.

"Nay a *what*, a leprechaun! Sure and b'gorra, ye're a mortal, aren't ye?"

"I think I *still* am. I'm not certain."

"Ye're not Irish, are ye?" The light blazed up.

"No. I'm mostly English. My mother was Irish—I mean—well, she once went to America and became an American," Isabelle related.

The leprechaun laughed. "I once went t' America, meself. An' me human up an' fell in love with a bloody Englishman. But I was glad she did, because I was able t' come back over th' sea wif her."

Isabelle was amused, but she could not bring herself to laugh. She tried to analyze the situation, and at that point she believed that she was asleep or dead, and that the peculiar little creature was somehow part of a dream.

"Ye know," the leprechaun said, "it's only once in a blue moon that I let myself be known t' humans. Ye caught me off guard, ye did. What a pretty kettle o' fish this is!"

"I beg your pardon."

"Well, it was only because Ilene Dumphy kicked over the toadstools in me fairy circle that I ever made meself known t' her in th' first place. She tricked me."

"*Ilene Dumphy,* did you say?"

"Ay, that I did. Ye wouldn't know her."

"Did she marry a Phenwick?"

The light blazed even brighter. "Ay. How d'ye know that?"

"Gregory Phenwick?"

"Ay. An' he himself was—ah-ah—ye tell me."

"He was a partner in Medallion Enterprises?"

"That may be, but it ain't what I want t' know."

"That he is very handsome."

"Why should I care about that?"

"That he was—that he was adopted by Alexander and Susannah Phenwick along with his sister, Marcia?" Isabelle questioned.

"Ay! How'd ye know that?"

"My name is Isabelle Phenwick."

"Here now, let me put meself into better focus." The light became brighter and Isabelle could perceive the figure of a small man no larger than her hand. She quickly explained what had happened that afternoon, and how she suspected that her sister had drowned.

" 'Tis a sad tale, lass. Ye know, there's a legend an' a warnin' among us wee folk concernin' mortals. Once we befriend one o' them, we kin expect t' to be plagued wif them for years t' come. First, it's th' mither, then th' daughter, then th' granddaughter—it goes on like that. 'Tis a sad curse. That's why we never show our faces. Ay, but when yer mither kicked over me fairy circle, I could nay take that lyin' doon. I had t' say somethin'."

Sadness had come over Isabelle. Her body ached, but the deepest pain was within her heart as she thought of Elena. She wanted to fall back down and close her mind to all thoughts. Poor Elena. Tears came.

"Sure now, what're ye doin' that for? D'ye know what a human tear could do t' th' likes o' me if'n it were t' splash on me?"

Isabelle shook her head. "What?"

"It could well dissolve me, that's what!"

"I can't help myself," Isabelle explained.

"In which case," he replied, "I'll just have t' leave ye be. I'm nay in th' mood for a salty tear bath."

"Will you tell me your name? That is, if you have one."

"It's Moorduke. Ye might as well know. An' good night. I'm bound t' dance in th' fairy ring at midnight, an' I'll nay miss my sleep an' be drenched wif tears. I get a crick in me leg when I try t' dance after I don't git enough sleep. Ye'll excuse me."

"Moorduke?" Isabelle questioned as she watched the tiny glimmer of light fade into darkness. What a strange experience, she thought. She recalled tales her mother had told about leprechauns when she and Elena were just children. Alexandria had always been particularly fond of such stories.

Isabelle shook her head. The vision of the little person could only have been an illusion, a trick being played by her imagination. Once while visiting eccentric Cousin Joanna Phenwick, the famous actress, the subject of leprechauns had arisen and her illustrious cousin had been quick to pooh-pooh the notion of such creatures existing. Isabelle was basically practical, and the idea of little people struck her as being odd. Still, what she had just experienced, if it was not part of a dream, had been mighty peculiar.

A brief period after the "illusion" disappeared, Isabelle became aware of the sound of voices, men's voices. She wished to rise to her feet, but she was desperately weak. When she nearly reached a sitting position, her spine felt as if it collapsed and she fell backwards, easing her fall with her elbows. That was the first time she became consciously aware that her clothing was wet. A picture of the accident flashed into her mind and she relived the impact of her sister's body being pitched on top of her. Elena. Tears came to her eyes and her head rolled backwards and to either side of her.

Thane O'Reilly stood at the doorway as the men with lanterns entered the old mill. A middle-aged doctor quickly rushed to examine Isabelle. He made noises of concern as he checked for broken bones.

"Can ye sit up, lass?" the doctor gruffly asked.

"I don't believe I can," Isabelle replied. "I tried to raise myself a few moments ago, but I was unable. I feel very tired—exhausted."

"Ay, I kin see that. Wal, t' me discernin' touch, there isn't anythin' broken," the doctor said, and got to his feet.

Isabelle looked up into a ring of men's faces, all of which were wearing curious expressions of concern. "Did you find—"

The doctor gave a jerk of his head, which seemed to indicate instructions before he moved out of the old mill.

"—my sister—my twin?" Isabelle managed to say as she felt herself being hoisted onto a stretcher. A blanket was put over her and tucked in about her to keep her warm. "—Elena?"

Nobody seemed to know Elena, nor did they care about her.

"B'gorra, this is th' bumpiest ride I've ever taken," a tiny voice said at Isabelle's ear as she was carried into the fresh air. "I hope ye don't mind if'n I hang onto yer hair, lass. I'm a-clingin' fer me life, I am."

Without really rationally thinking about the matter, Isabelle accepted the presence of a somewhat familiar voice and almost immediately thereafter lost consciousness.

CHAPTER THREE

The handsome man had a long, slender body. At forty-four, he moved with the ease and grace of a young athlete, yet his bearing and his attitude were those of a man who had progressively reached the maturity of his chronological age. The once yellow hair had turned to a satiny, dusty texture. Warmth radiated in his eyes. The thick lower lip quivered with a smile, and teeth flashed in reaction. The world had basically been good to Gregory Phenwick up until the recent tragedy. He had been in the company of David Phenwick at the private men's club in London, where he had inherited membership from his foster father, Alexander Phenwick.

Bitter tears had come when Gregory read the announcements from his beloved Ilene. A second telegram had arrived at the same time as the first, telling that Isabelle had survived. Young David had caught his cousin in a tight embrace as Gregory scanned the words, tears dimming his eyes. David, the youngest son of Joshua Phenwick, possessed that remarkable beauty that seemed to pass from Phenwick man to Phenwick man. His attractiveness was far different from that of his older brother,

Leo. Leo somewhat resembled his mother, while David's likeness could be seen in the portrait of his great-grandfather Daniel.

David remained with Gregory in a quiet corner of the club parlor, a vast room with enormously high ceilings and huge beams. The walls were paneled part way up and had a deep maroon wall-covering above them. Ancient portraits of long-gone members stared down at the present associates of the organization. A faint haze of smoke occasionally curled up from a large winged chair, so enormous that the occupant appeared to be buried within it.

"What more can I say, Greg?" David asked. "Words are so ineffectual at this time."

Gregory glanced up, his red and swollen eyes attempting to penetrate beyond the brightly flashing eyes of David. He shook his head and swallowed. "You might tell me one thing, David."

"What is that?"

"Why you seem to have so little emotion at hearing about Elena," Gregory commented. "I was under the impression you were practically betrothed to her."

"That isn't true, Greg."

"Why, only less than two weeks ago," Gregory continued, "Elena and I had an intimate chat. At that time she confessed she was deeply in love with you and hoped, since you were not related by blood ties, that you and she would be married one day."

David laughed awkwardly. "Dear Greg, I admit that I have had enormously good times with Elena—especially when Isabelle wasn't around—and we had jolly good sport. Still, I was under the opinion that I was a convenience to be with, I was her cousin and accessible when a social impression was to be made. But, as Aunt Joanna would say, I had the feeling that someone else was always lurking in the wings."

Gregory blew his nose. "Someone else in the wings? Preposterous nonsense! Who else did Elena know?"

"That, of course, was it, don't you see?" David questioned. "There may bloody well have been nobody else, but damn it, she made me think that there was."

"Did she say she had another interest in so many words?"

"No, I can't say that she did. Blast it, this is awkward," David stated. "I know I must sound a stupid ass for speaking this way, with nothing to substantiate my feelings, but I cannot deny my suspicions."

"Peculiar. Most peculiar," Gregory remarked. "David, will you do me the kindness of making the trip to Northern Ireland with me? I believe that with your strength and support behind me, I will manage much better. I'll have my hands full with Ilene alone, much less with the other—the other children."

"I should imagine this would be especially difficult for Isabelle," David interjected. "It would be a bloody shock to lose one's regular brother or sister, but to have a twin—I mean—well, you *do* see my point, don't you?"

"Yes, I've thought of that myself. Poor, dear Isabelle." Tears came again and David reached to touch him.

"Yes, I'll go with you," the younger man said a short while later.

"I appreciate that." Gregory managed to pull himself together.

"I'm frantic with grief," Isabelle explained when her father arrived at the bed assigned to her in the small Carrickfergus Infirmary. She appeared pale and weak. Her eyes were puffy, yet dark circles outlined them. A brace was tied about her body to support her spine, which apparently had been whipped about either during the actual accident or at the time she was tossed among the rapids in the rushing creek.

"Frantic, my dear?" asked Gregory as he hugged and kissed her.

"Please take me home, Daddy, please. I want to be away from this terrible place as quickly as possible," she whined.

"The doctor assures me that it will be no difficulty to move you," Gregory explained. "You have no broken bones, just a few bruises and twists that can be uncomfortable. They'll go away."

Isabelle controlled tears as she clung to her father.

Because Ilene often burst into distressed crying, it was decided that Gregory would occupy a train compartment with her and Alexandria, while David sat with Albert and Isabelle in the nearby cubicle. David was ill at ease, but fortunately he had Albert with whom he could converse. Since he had recently received a letter from his brother Leo in Portland, Maine, David passed the time by relating the contents of the epistle and giving him his impression of America from the two times he had visited it. Albert had heard some of the tales before, but he enjoyed hearing them again. To the boy, his cousin David was a man of the world, an adventurer—and sometimes a liar. The latter really did not matter to the boy as long as David kept him amused.

Isabelle only half listened to the conversation. Her own reflection in the train window made her think Elena was watching her. Would she be haunted for the rest of her life by the memory of her twin sister?

When the conductor called that luncheon was being served in the dining car, Isabelle asked her brother and David to excuse her. She preferred to remain in the compartment, since she had no appetite whatsoever.

Surprisingly, Ilene desired to partake of nourishment and leaned heavily on Gregory as they made their way to the dining car with Alexandria directly behind them. They joined Albert and David, but Albert had to sit at the table behind the others.

The *clickity-clack, clickity-clack* of the rail wheels droned on and on in a hypnotic meter. Isabelle sat staring out the window at the rolling English countryside, the farms and meadows filled with grazing sheep. Suddenly the train jerked to a much slower speed, although it did not go to an abrupt stop. The jolt caused her hatbox to fall from the rack above. After identifying what had fallen, she ignored it, deciding to wait for David to return to put it back in place. Nothing, no physical thing, seemed important to her.

Her attention returned to the passing countryside and the momentum that the train was beginning to generate. She saw a hay wagon moving down a side road, and speculated that it must have been it that had caused the train to slow up for awhile.

Isabelle began to feel drowsy. She closed her eyes, but she was far from falling asleep. Then her attention was attracted to a singular sound coming from the area of the floor. At first she tried to ignore it. But when she began to hear muffled words, and those with a blasphemously profane quality, she turned her attention to the floor of the compartment and directly to the hatbox. Moments later she unlocked the clasp and lifted the lid. Her favorite hat with four frilly ostrich plumes was inside. She readjusted the hat in place and was about to close the box again, when the plumes parted and she thought she beheld the figure of a small man.

"What th' divil d'ye be doin' up here, lass?" came the small, but masculinely sounding voice. "I've bin thrown from better places, but at least I could git t' me feet an' scamper away. But I was trapped, I was. Eee, glory be, I mighta busted somethin'—like me skull."

Isabelle stared incredulously at the little creature. At the old mill, she had merely perceived a tiny lantern light and a mysterious voice. To see such an animated little thing in broad daylight was quite another experience. She swallowed hard, but could not force herself to speak.

"Oh, 'tis ye, is it? Wal, a fine kettle o' crickets this turned out t' be!" the little one exclaimed. "B'gorra, an' we're a-ridin' in somethin', too, ain't we?"

"Yes, in a train," Isabelle managed to say.

"Glory-glory be! Let me out o' here!"

"I'm afraid that's impossible," Isabelle explained. "You see, the train is moving. And if I were to pull the emergency cord, I fear I would have a dreadful time explaining why I had done such a thing."

"Where are we headed?"

"Why, to London," Isabelle replied, somewhat amused by the little fellow, who had climbed up and was clinging to the side of the hatbox. "I confess I don't recall your name."

"Ay, an' that's an even finer kettle o' crickets, it is. Me name's Moorduke, an' don't ye forgit ag'in."

"Moorduke. Yes, I'll remember that now. But tell me what you're doing in my hatbox."

"I climbed in where it looked t' be a nice comfy place t' snooze," Moorduke replied. "I'm a nocturnal creature, ye know. All th' wee people are. It's th' only way we keep from gettin' trampled t' death. We avoid th' mobs. I'll confess somethin' t' ye. I rode on th' stretcher wif ye t' th' inn. I jumped off before they decided t' take ye on t' th' infirmary. It was a lovely peaceful day, too."

"Why did you follow me?" Isabelle asked.

"Because I wanted t' see fer meself if'n th' Ilene Dumphy who was yer mither was th' same Ilene Dumphy I knew when she was a girl—th' one who kicked over th' toadstools in me fairy ring," Moorduke explained. "Ay, an' t' tell ye th' truth, there's no denyin' she's one an' th' same."

"Now that you've satisfied your curiosity," Isabelle asked, "what do you propose to do?"

"Sure now, I would dearly love t' go back t' th' fairy glen o' Carrickfergus," was the reply. "But d'ye know, I fear I kin't for th' moment. Ye see, it has t' do wif that silly legend about th' likes o' me fraternizin' wif th' likes o' ye. Legends do be one thin' among mortals, an' quite another thin' among fairies. We don't have legends unless there is a morsel o' truth to 'em."

"I confess you have me confused," Isabelle responded. "The fact is, I'm in a dreadful state of mourning over the death of my sister—my twin sister."

The little man removed his hat. "It's bin decided then that she's dead?"

"Her dress was found on the shore this morning, just before we left Carrickfergus," Isabelle explained. "And a fisherman had discovered her body, shortly after dawn. She was wearing nothing when she was found, and my father went to identify it."

"I sense a grain o' doubt in yer voice, lass."

"Some animal or sea creature had got to the body before the fisherman did. It was mutilated." Isabelle cried.

Moorduke hopped up onto the seat beside her. "Here now, I tol' ye once about tears an' we little people."

The door to the train compartment slid open and David appeared. He gazed compassionately down at Isabelle. Then his devilishly handsome face glowed with a radiant smile. "Dearest Isabelle, I know the grief you must feel, and I am helpless to lessen your unhappiness. Do you mind if I sit beside you?"

Isabelle looked up through teary eyes. She nodded. As David moved to the seat, she exclaimed, "No, not there!"

"Not there?" David questioned. "I can't very well sit beside you if I don't sit there, Isabelle."

She wiped her eyes and casually moved her hand over the section of the seat beside her.

"Did you lose something?" asked David.

"I—I hope so," Isabelle replied.

"I beg your pardon."

"It's nothing, David. Come sit down."

As she felt her handsome cousin's presence beside her, Isabelle wondered what had become of Moorduke. Almost immediately she realized that the leprechaun, if that indeed was what he was, had come at an emotional time of crisis, and chances were that he was no more than a figment of her distraught imagination.

"You surely must miss Elena as much as I do," Isabelle said during the sullen silence that followed. She started to put her gloved hand to his, but hesitated and returned it to her lap.

"I liked Elena well enough," David admitted, "but I can't say I was—well, after all, she was my cousin. I mean—well, we had a kind of understanding. I know people, even you, must have thought there was something romantic between us. There were times when I had hoped there might be such a relationship. At other times I was convinced it was a complete impossibility. Naturally I'm grieved at her passing, too."

"Isn't it peculiar," Isabelle suggested after she had gained control of her emotions, "that you and Elena became so close to each other, and here I, her twin, have remained singularly remote from you?"

"There was a difference—a noticeable difference between—I mean—"

"Between Elena and me? Yes, I know. But very few other persons were perceptive enough to see it," Isabelle said. "However, dearest David, supposing it was not Elena's body that was found."

"Not Elena's?" He turned in the seat to face her.

"Supposing it was Isabelle's."

"Is that the case?"

Isabelle laughed. "No. But would you have known the difference?"

"I suppose not, if you were Elena and had adopted Isabelle's ways and attitudes," David replied. "I doubt that that would be possible."

"Would it?" Isabelle questioned, and turned her attention to the passing countryside.

Shortly after arriving at Charing Cross station in London, Gregory Phenwick sent his family home. Calling Derrick Molden aside, he explained to the man that he felt it would be advisable to terminate his service with the family. A sizable cash settlement was made, and Gregory explained that he would have Derrick's few things gathered at the house and sent to an address where the man would be staying.

CHAPTER FOUR

Flamboyant, grand and pretentious Joanna Phenwick had become more eccentric than ever by the time she had reached her sixty-first birthday. As she approached her sixty-second, she decided to accept her fate as being a character actress and no longer a leading lady. However, due to her enormous wealth and influence, she made a practice of hiring young writers to create new stage plays for her to star in. That was her life, and she intended to breathe her final gasp on stage. Whenever a new play would appear in a London theatre, Joanna would make a point of viewing it and reading the critical reviews of it. If the play were a success, she would instantly make arrangements to meet the playwright, wine and dine him, and proposition him to create a vehicle for her. Hence, she was regularly seen in the company of such men as James Barrie and Oscar Wilde. She even toyed with the notion of wooing Arthur Sullivan after his partner William Gilbert rejected the proposal that she appear in one of their operettas.

Joanna considered it proper to close her current show on the day of the memorial service for Elena Phenwick.

While the actress was not particularly close to the children of Gregory and Ilene Phenwick, she felt it her duty as eldest living Phenwick woman in England to make an effort toward grief. It would please Gregory, and that was all she felt was necessary. Nor had the aging actress been as close to David Phenwick, her nephew, not as close as she had been to his older sister, Ophelia, and her dearly beloved Leo, the second child of her brother Joshua. When she arrived at St. James's, she was dressed in heavy black attire and braced herself against the youthful arm of an aesthetic young actor, who had become convinced that winning fame and fortune in the theatre came through patronizing the likes of Joanna Phenwick. He, like so many of the others that had impressed Joanna's passing fantasy, was disillusioned.

Joanna had arranged to have the family and friends of the deceased adjourn to her home in Kensington for light refreshment. It was a considerable distance between St. James's and Kensington, so many of the mourners declined the socializing following the solemn event.

At Joanna's, David tried to draw Isabelle aside and into conversation. The grieving young lady was too upset to show more than passing interest in her cousin. He soon became discouraged and went to console Gregory and Ilene.

Isabelle retired into the privacy of an upstairs fitting room, a room in which Joanna permitted seamstresses and costume people to work on special creations for her. A treadle sewing machine was in one corner and a cutting table had patterns neatly stacked in the other. A dress dummy in the likeness of the actress's body was bare near the window. The shadowy afternoon light called attention to it.

"Well, well, what have we here?" exclaimed Joanna as she entered the chamber on the pretext of fixing a strap that had broken. Her arms flew up dramatically, extending an invitation for the girl to come to them. Isabelle held her position. "My dearest Isabelle! How grieved I am for you. And all these years I couldn't tell you and your sister apart. I should think it would be a terrible burden to one's self-esteem to have an exact duplicate following her about."

"I was used to being a twin."

"And now you must become used to being an individual," declared Joanna in her best stage voice. "Do be a dear and help me with this strap." She stepped to the girl. "David tell me that you have aspirations of becoming an actress."

"Not me," Isabelle quickly denied.

"But David said Elena's sister—"

"No doubt he was alluding to Alexandria," Isabelle explained.

"Ah, yes, dear Alexandria, of course! It just naturally occurred to me that *you* were the sister to whom he was referring. I must have a word with dear Alexandria before she leaves."

As breezily as Joanna had rushed into the room, she left it, after Isabelle had insisted she wished to remain with her thoughts a short while longer.

"Cor blimy!" a small voice declared as Joanna firmly closed the door behind her. "She nearly stepped on me. I leapt aside in th' very nick o' time."

"Moorduke?" Isabelle questioned.

"Ay, lass."

"What are you doing here?"

"Where else would ye expect me t' be?" he asked, showing himself on the cutting table as he dusted his cap over his knees. "I've reached th' unalterable conclusion that ye are destined t' be me human an' there's little or nothin' else I kin do about it. I accept."

"But I don't want a leprechaun."

"An' why not?"

42

"In the first place, I'm not Irish."

"Ay, but yer mither was, an' that's good enough—I reckon."

"But how would I explain you to my friends."

"They don't even need t' know about me. I'll remain invisible t' 'em." He took in a deep breath and appeared to increase to about three times his original size. "Even when I swell meself up like this, no one will see me if'n I don't want them to. So ye see, ye needn't tell a soul about me."

"What do you want of me?" she asked, becoming annoyed.

"T' cheer ye up," he replied merrily. "I kin do all sorts o' tricks, like makin' thin's appear an' disappear. Fer instance—" He snapped his fingers and a small bouquet of flowers materialized in his hand. "Here, this is fer ye. Take it, go on. It's real—*now*."

Reluctantly Isabelle held out her hand to Moorduke, who placed the bouquet in it. Again he snapped his fingers, and it expanded in size to that of a customary nosegay.

"Violets?" Isabelle questioned. She held them to her nose. "They not only look like violets, they smell like violets."

"An' they should cheer ye up " He danced a whimsical jig. "D'ye know, I was at th' funeral. I rode there in th' veil o' yer bonnet. Then me curiosity got up an' I slid down th' veil an' went t' have a look in th' coffin. I don't know about such human thin's as funerals, so I jus' let me curiosity carry me away. They dang near carried me away in th' coffin. I escaped jus' in th' nick o' time as they was about t' seal th' lid in place. I almost made meself visible t' 'em so as I could tell 'em a piece o' me mind. Sensibly, I scampered after ye an' never even turned back t' thumb me nose at th' blokes. It was a close call. Don't that amuse ye, Isabelle?"

"I'm afraid nothing would amuse me today, Moorduke," Isabelle replied. "Now, I think you had better excuse me. My parents will be looking for me."

Moorduke snapped his fingers and disappeared.

Dreading the ascent to the first-floor parlor, where only a few mourning guests remained, Isabelle moved slowly. As she passed a mirror in the hallway and caught a glimpse of her reflection, she gasped. For an instant she was certain it was Elena. She moved to the glass and examined her face. Cousin Joanna was right. Now the likeness only belonged to her, not a likeness she was forced to share with her sister.

"Isabelle?" Ilene questioned as she came from the parlor. "There you are."

"Mother!" Isabelle ran to her mother and hugged herself into Ilene's embrace. "Oh, Mother, you can't know how horrible this is for me."

"Yes, I should imagine it is terribly difficult for you, my darling Isabelle," Ilene replied, stroking her daughter's head as she pressed against her. "We will all greatly miss Elena, but I suspect you will miss more than the rest of us. Come into the library for a moment. We must put our tears away, dearest child."

Isabelle went where her mother led.

"There now, let me see how you look," Ilene stated after adjusting Isabelle's attire and wiping her eyes with a lace handkerchief. "In time this will fade away and we'll look happily back on the years Elena was with us and—" She stopped as her attention went to the nosegay in her daughter's hand. "Are those violets?"

Isabelle glanced down at them and instinctively tried to hide that hand behind her. "I—ah—"

"Violets?" Ilene stepped nearer. "Don't hide them. Why, where did you get violets this time of the year?"

"I—I don't know," Isabelle stammered.

"Why, surely, you must." Ilene embraced the girl again. "Oh, my dear, I had a premonition about you from the day you were born."

"A premonition about me?" Isabelle felt herself trembling.

"Hours before I started to go into labor," Ilene explained, "I thought I was visited by Augusta Phenwick, and she told me that my firstborn was destined to become a Phenwick woman. And as the birth pains came, and I wanted to shriek out, I felt myself surrounded by the scent of violets. You were born with great ease. Then the pain again came and the doctor explained I had a second child within me. The pain was so terrible that I lost consciousness. I wondered why the scent of violets hadn't come with the second child. Then I realized that only my firstborn was meant to be a Phenwick woman. I recall I explained this to Elena two or three years ago. I didn't like to have to disappoint her, because at that time I felt she was very much interested in David Phenwick."

"I like David very much, but I'm not romantically interested in him, nor have I ever been," Isabelle countered. "Besides, wasn't I born a Phenwick woman?"

"Only in a sense, my dearest," Ilene replied. "Oh, but this isn't the time to speak of such things. Still, I am curious about the nosegay of violets and where you obtained it."

Isabelle braced herself and crossed away from her mother. A shiver of excitement seemed to spout up from her toes. He jaw was trembling and she did not believe she could control it long enough to project the word. A second deep breath. "Moorduke gave it to me."

"What was that, my dear Isabelle?"

"I said, Moorduke gave me the violets."

"Moorduke?" Ilene gasped and clutched to her bosom. She swayed and caught herself against the back of a chair.

"You don't mean to tell me you have met a man by the name of Moorduke, do you?"

"Not exactly a man, Mother."

"Not a—oh, dear, I can't say it. Not a wee—"

New strength and courage seemed to come to Isabelle. "He told me he was a leprechaun. Did you ever know of such a creature by the name of Moorduke?"

Ilene sat in the chair. "Saints above! I thought when I last saw that little imp—I mean Moorduke—that that was the end of it."

"Moorduke says there's a fairy legend about once a leprechaun shows himself to a mortal, that he's bound to also reveal himself to that person's children and to their children. I naturally, didn't believe him when he first told me; but now I can see in your face and expression what a thousand words couldn't explain."

Ilene looked away and began to scan about the room. "He isn't—I mean—he's not—that is—"

"If he's here, he's made himself inconspicuous."

Ilene rose and embraced her daughter again. Of all her children, Isabelle had always been distant and hard for her to reach. In a way, she reasoned, it was because Elena had had much more of a dominant personality, more aggressive and determined to have her way, while Isabelle demurely stood back and observed. There had been times when the mother suspected that her twin daughters had been wrongly identified at the hospital and that the one she had known as Elena was really her firstborn. Now here was Isabelle left, acquainted with Moorduke and in possession of violets, which were out of season. With all that, she reasoned that Augusta must have been right about Isabelle after all.

In the days and weeks that followed, the Phenwicks adjusted to their loss and soon began getting back to their usual routines. There was an empty space without Elena, but the others quietly worked around it. Only Isabelle lapsed into long periods of depression.

Of course it was her face, Isabelle told herself as she stared into the mirror. It was her *own* face. Yet each time she viewed it, she was reminded of her sister.

Alexandria attempted to become closer to Isabelle. But the younger sister's constant chatter got on Isabelle's nerves. She could tolerate her presence just so long before she felt she had to flee from it.

Albert, too, tried to make Isabelle feel at ease. He did a better job of it than Alexandria. Still, he was quite immature and obviously unable to perceive the depth of his eldest sister's problem. True, he, too, had lost a sister, but it was not the same as losing a twin.

"Bertie, I love you dearly," Isabelle exclaimed, "but do leave me alone with my thoughts."

"But Father said I was to come to cheer you."

"You only depress me, Bertie," Isabelle said. "When you return to Father, thank him for his kind interest."

During those days, as snow came with winter, the only one that appeared to cheer Isabelle in the least was Moorduke. His periodic presence amused her. But the leprechaun would not put in an appearance sometimes for several days. He explained that he had found a marvelous Irish tavern where he could get his fill and more of Irish whisky—his favorite. The effects of his imbibing often caused him to sober up in curious out-of-the-way places around London. And one time he had lost consciousness on a hay wagon and had gone all the way to Cambridge before he gained his bearings. His tales were outlandish. Isabelle was certain they were contrived to make her laugh, although the leprechaun stoutly denied it. And she did laugh, but only in private behind closed doors.

David Phenwick became interested in another young lady and all but neglected calling on the Phenwicks of Hyde Park. Only Alexandria, who had romantic imaginings about her distant cousin, kept David's name in conversation. The sound of it more disturbed Isabelle than pleased her. David's preference had been Elena; Isabelle did not wish to step into her sister's shoes—not now.

CHAPTER FIVE

The Joshua Phenwicks arrived from America three weeks prior to Christmas. Olivia had returned with a severe cold that kept her in bed and complicated plans for the usual round of holiday affairs. Since her husband, Captain Henry Ashton, was away at sea, Ophelia Phenwick Ashton accompanied her father to social engagements. Joshua and his daughter made a handsome couple and attracted great attention.

Although David maintained a room in his parents' home in the Belgravia section of London, he had also set himself up in an apartment in Soho, only a short walk from Trafalgar Square. He often attended the same parties as did his father and sister, but he was usually preoccupied with one lovely creature after another and rarely spent much time in conversation with either Ophelia or Joshua.

Two days before Christmas, a party was given by Joanna Phenwick. She had hired a hall for the occasion and had the entire affair catered. Gregory, Ilene, and their children were invited to attend. Alexandria looked forward to the occasion with great anticipation, and with the assistance of Joanna's favorite dressmaker, Alexandria was certain to have the most attractive gown of the evening.

Albert cut a handsome impression that instantly captured the attention, if not the hearts, of several young teenage ladies. There was no doubt in his parents' minds that he was destined to be quite a man-about-town.

An hour or so into the party, Joshua, whose hair had become snowy white, but who showed little other signs of age, caught Gregory's attention and motioned to him for a private word.

"Enjoying yourself, Josh?" Gregory asked as he arrived after leaving Ilene to chat with Ophelia and two actress friends of Joanna.

"My sister's parties are always the most lavish of the season," Joshua explained. "She knows how to entertain. I suppose I will always be Joanna's little brother and be included at all of her affairs for as long as I live. Joanna, of course, has full intention of living forever." He laughed.

Gregory joined the laughter. "There seemed to be an urgency in the way you beckoned to me, Josh. I say, is something up?"

"To be perfectly blunt, there is," Joshua explained. "Emeran Hoskins called my attention to a matter late this afternoon."

"Emeran Hoskins the accountant?"

"With a name like Emeran, who else do you suppose I might be referring to?" Joshua returned playfully. "Well, the fact of the matter is, Hoskins has discovered a discrepancy in the books."

"A discrepancy?"

"Yes, of several thousand pounds—perhaps more," Joshua replied. "He is spending his entire holiday going over the figures again."

"You don't suspect Hoskins himself, do you? I say!"

"No. Not Hoskins," Joshua said. "It seems the finger of suspicion is directed toward one Melvin Ferrett. You know which one I mean?"

"Yes, quite," Gregory replied.

"Well, we must keep our eyes on the chap," Joshua stated. "There's no evidence that he is the culprit, only an indication. The other matter I wished to discuss with you has to deal with you personally, Gregory."

"And that is?"

"It's been some time since you were last in the United States," Joshua continued. "Stuart is doing remarkably well in Boston and my son, Arnold—or should I say Leon?—has gotten the Portland organization on its feet. There are labor problems, but nothing he can't handle. It's Jim Phenwick in Savannah who is having the problem. I thought perhaps you might make a crossing in the early spring, survey the three offices, and see what you believe would assist in bringing Medallion, Savannah, up. You're the expert at that sort of thing. Jim has asked for more money, and I would gladly give it to him because he's my nephew, but I can't see putting money into a sinking ship, don't you know?"

"Precisely. Well, I suppose I can make the trip," Gregory commented. "It's still very close to our tragedy. I don't know that Ilene will be up to making the voyage. But we shall see, shan't we?"

Alexandria attended a private school for young ladies. She was seventeen, and it was the year her mother had promised that she might consider the chaperoned company of a young man, or perhaps several different young men. The thought of depriving the girl of that opportunity caused Ilene to realize it would be a mistake for her to leave London that spring. And she was determined that Albert remain in school where he belonged.

"I'll travel alone, then," Gregory stated, "unless—"

"Unless?" Ilene blinked at her husband across the dinner table. The two were dining alone. "Unless you remain here?"

"No. I was going to say, unless Isabelle were to accompany me," Gregory continued.

"Isabelle?" Ilene shook her head. "The poor child has sat and moped around the house all winter. She's lost weight and her color is bad. She's such a pretty child, too."

"Then a change of scene may be just the thing for her, don't you think, old girl?" questioned Gregory.

"It might just that, my darling Mr. Phenwick. It might," Ilene returned, her eyes wide with quiet excitement. "Her mood has been such a worry to me. I know she thinks constantly of Elena still. I should imagine when one is wearing one's dead sister's face, it would be a constant reminder."

"Ilene!"

"Well, it is true, you know." Ilene folded her napkin. "Shall I broach the subject to her, or will you?"

"If you will, my dear, I would be most obliged."

A servant entered with a calling card on a salver. The card was presented to Gregory.

"Alister Crook?" he said as he read the name.

"Inspector Alister Crook?" Ilene repeated. "What ever do you suppose he wants?"

"There's only one way to find out. Why don't you go speak with Isabelle while I greet the good inspector?" suggested Gregory.

Tall, graying Alister Crook had been shown to the library, where he waited for Gregory. He had removed his cap and stood in his black greatcoat as he drummed his fingers on the top of the oak table. At the sound of the door opening, he turned about, a movement that coincided with smoothing his index finger over his moustache. "Ah, Mr. Phenwick!"

"Inspector Crook," Gregory said as he extended his hand. "To what do I owe this honor?"

"A bit of business, I fear," Crook replied. "I rarely make social calls."

"I say, what is it my Uncle Joshua calls you," Gregory questioned lightly, "the ever-present watchdog of Scotland Yard?"

"Yes. Well, I suppose I have been called worse things, haven't I?" the inspector returned in a wry voice. He was not without a sense of humor, but it rarely was presented out in the open.

"May I pour you a glass of sherry?"

"Yes, that would be pleasant, don't you know?" Alister Crook studied Gregory as the younger man moved to the crystal decanter. "I had imagined you would have known why I've come, Mr. Phenwick."

"I can't say that I do."

"As you know, I have long been a friend of your relative, the actress," Crook commented as he accepted the wine glass. "Thank you. Yes, indeed, Miss Phenwick and I have been friends a good many years. I've been one of her fondest admirers."

"I take it, when you say *Miss Phenwick*, that you could only be referring to my Aunt Joanna."

"Quite so." The Inspector smiled broadly, caught himself and wiped his moustache to cover a flush of embarrassment. "Quite so, indeed. A marvelous actress—and, I admit, quite a woman."

"So you've come to discuss Aunt Joanna, then?"

"Not in the least," Crook denied. "That is, only to mention her in passing and to explain that she arranged for my recent holiday to Northern Ireland."

"Ah, I'm beginning to see the point of all this."

"Are you? I wonder. Very good sherry, don't you know?"

"Yes, I do know." Gregory poured himself a glass of

the wine. "So Aunt Joanna sent you north to do a bit of snooping, did she?"

"Miss Joanna has had some rather uncanny premonitions in the past," Crook went on to explain. "I shouldn't accuse her of being psychic—not out-and-out so—nor is she clairvoyant, I should think. Still, she has had some interesting thoughts. Might I tell you about them?"

"By all means. Shall I refill your glass while you take a seat?"

"You may refill the glass, but I prefer to stand, Mr. Phenwick," Alister Crook said as he extended the hand in which the glass was held. "It all started a while back, at the time your uncle, Mr. Joshua Phenwick, suspected embezzled funds at Medallion. I was called in to have a look about, don't you know. One Melvin Ferrett was suspect in the matter, he being a bookkeeper. Well, we interrogated him until our throats went dry. He had perfect alibis, etcetera. And, the fact is, we privately searched his dwellings and followed his movements about for five weeks. Either he was aware that he was being followed and made no false moves, or he was basically innocent. Nor did the man break under stiff, I might say the most stringent, interrogation."

"Yes, I'm aware of all this," Gregory commented, sitting back in a maroon leather upholstered chair. "What about Melvin Ferrett?"

"I am getting to that, sir." Crook cleared his throat. "It was your aunt, Miss Phenwick, who noted that the embezzling incident occurred, or was at least discovered, at the time your wife and children were on vacation in North Ireland. Again I wish to extend my sympathies to you and your dear wife over your loss."

"Thank you, Inspector Crook."

"I shall continue." Crook paced, setting the empty wine glass on the library table. "Miss Phenwick is of the opinion that that carriage mishap might *not* have been an accident."

"Might *not*?" Gregory sat forward.

"It's only another one of those premonitions of hers, I should imagine," Crook replied. "And what stock can one put into premonitions, I ask you?"

"So Aunt Joanna sent you to Carrickfergus to have a look around, is that it?" Gregory questioned.

"That is about it, sir." Crook braced himself against a high rolltop desk and dug in his pocket for his pipe. "Prior to going, I had had a short conversation with the driver of the ill-fated carriage."

"Derrick Molden."

"Yes, quite so. Molden related that it had been a bit drizzly that day, and when he came upon the particular bridge, narrow and I fear a bit rickety, he had not seen the rock or boulder upon it until it was too late. Being in the driver's seat, he was able to jump free of the carriage as it went over the side. Now the curious thing is that Miss Isabelle was seated on the left side of the vehicle, of that Molden was certain, and the late Miss Elena was sitting on the right. Now, at the time of impact, it would seem likely to me that Miss Isabelle—since the carriage fell to the left—would have been the one in most jeopardy. Be that as it may, it's just a curious side glance at the thing."

"Elena could have been knocked unconscious at the time of the initial impact," Gregory stated. "That is quite possible, you know."

"Quite true." Alister Crook put a match to his pipe and drew in on it. Clouds of smoke momentarily hid his face. He blew an opening through it and continued. "There is another faint possibility, you know—and I cannot take credit for being author of this theory."

"What is it?"

"This is—oh, I say—difficult to even suggest," Crook

said and took four gigantic steps toward the window. He peered out as if something had caught his attention. "Has the thought ever occurred to you, Mr. Phenwick, that Miss Isabelle, and not Miss Elena, was the victim of the accident in Carrickfergus?"

"What? What are you suggesting?" Gregory sat forward, then rose to his feet. "Preposterous notion."

"Is it, Mr. Phenwick?" Alister Crook inhaled deeply on the pipe and held the smoke for several seconds before he released it as he watched Gregory incredulously move toward him. "But then, I see you don't have the sort of diabolical mind that I have, Mr. Phenwick."

"Diabolical is right!" exclaimed Gregory. "How can you even suggest such a thing?"

"It was Mrs. Joshua Phenwick who first made the suggestion to me, sir," Crook replied.

"Olivia?"

"Yes, Mrs. Olivia Phenwick. She is of the opinion that the matter might have something to do—or might have had, had that been the case—with Miss Elena's desire to become a Phenwick woman."

"Silly! Silly, silly!" declared Gregory. His face had turned a bright red. "Yes, that would sound like the reasoning Olivia might come up with. She is disappointed, I presume, that neither of her two younger daughters acquired the title and dubious honor of becoming a so-called Phenwick woman. Oh, I know what that's all about. My mother—that is, my stepmother—and my sister were both Phenwick women. My wife is considered to be a Phenwick woman, just as Olivia and Joanna are. Well, what is a title anyway? Certainly being a Phenwick woman has no particular prestige to it."

"Except that the Phenwick women are all fairly wealthy women," Alister Crook inserted, "and appear to be socially prominent."

"Inspector Crook, I have made arrangements that assure each of my children of prosperous futures. And that was also the case with Elena." Gregory paced. "Oh, I see what it is. Yes, you've listened to the women. I know my wife on several different occasions had mentioned that she believed only Isabelle was destined to become a Phenwick woman. But Elena was a sensible girl, she would have never—"

"Was Miss Elena your favorite daughter, Mr. Phenwick?"

"What?" Gregory shook his head. "I've tried not to make a favorite of any of my children."

"Tried not?" Crook chuckled. "Ah, Mr. Phenwick, I believe every parent in the world vainly tries to accomplish that; but I am of the opinion that very few are successful in so doing. There is always one who seems to be a bit closer than the others."

"If that is the case," Gregory commented, "I must reluctantly admit that I never felt remarkably close to either of the twins—that is, with extraordinary feelings. If my affections lean toward one of my children more than another, I would guess that I am a bit partial to Alexandria."

Crook smiled. "Touché!" He put the wine glass on the table and strode toward the door. "Oh, there is one other matter, Mr. Phenwick. It nearly slipped me."

"What is that?"

"Melvin Ferrett has been found dead," Crook replied matter-of-factly.

"Ferrett *dead*?"

"In plain words, he was murdered. We, of course, have no notion at the moment who might have committed such an atrocity. My superior is of the opinion it isn't important since the poor fellow appeared to be quite alone in the world—no family, few if any friends. He lived by himself in a rooming house in Chelsea—not one of the nicer sections of Chelsea, at that." He reached into his inside coat pocket and removed a small white bone fan. "I don't suppose you recognize this *objet d'art*, do you?"

"A fan?"

"Quite so. This one, however, so happens to have the name of *Miss E. Phenwick* written on it."

"Elena's fan?" Gregory reached for it. Crook held it for him to examine, indicating the engraved name. "It can't be."

"But it is. It has already been positively identified by Mrs. Phenwick."

"Ilene?"

"Mrs. Joshua Phenwick."

"Olivia. Hmm."

"I must keep it for a while longer, Mr. Phenwick. I'll say good evening to you, then."

"Wait. One more question, Inspector Crook."

"Yes?"

"I'll see you to the front door," Gregory said, motioning him from the room and leading the way. "How long ago was Melvin Ferrett—that is, when was his demise?"

"Last week." The tall Alister Crook stared dark eyes down into Gregory's bewildered face. "Thank you for the sherry, Mr. Phenwick. We'll be speaking again soon. Good night."

Gregory had other questions, which he could not voice. He closed the door after the impressive personage of Alister Crook. Then he leaned against it for several moments. His mind was a whirlpool of confusion as a distinctly uncomfortable feeling came over him. "I say—!"

Gregory was headed back to the library to pour himself another glass of sherry when he heard a door close down the hallway. He did not wish to encounter any of his family until he had at least two drinks. He was in the midst of swallowing the first when the library door was opened and softly closed behind the intruder.

Gregory poured the second glass of wine, pretending he

had not heard the door. But before he could drink, his curiosity got the better of him and he glanced back to see Alexandria prettily standing in a pink dress at the door.

"Papa?" she questioned.

"Dearest Alexandria!" Gregory exclaimed and carried the filled wine glass with him as he went to kiss her.

"I saw you dash in here," she explained, "and thought I would come join you for a few minutes. I've only returned a few minutes from Miss Tillie's."

"What sort of a thing is Miss Tillie's?"

"Why, it's a dancing academy where young ladies learn the niceties of social dancing," Alexandria commented. "I like learning the steps. That is a bit of all right, don't you know. But I confess it seems terribly awkward when there are only three young men and eleven young ladies. I don't mind dancing with the other girls as long as I don't have to lead; but Miss Tillie claims that she believes I am so accomplished that I should be able to lead or follow with no difficulty. And to be perfectly honest, dancing with at least two of the young men is practically like dancing with—"

"I get the picture, Alexandria, you needn't be explicit," Gregory interrupted. "And how much longer do you expect to attend Miss Tillie's?"

"There are four more lessons. By then, I trust, I will be permitted to attend a few parties and demonstrate my dancing ability. After all, I am nearly eighteen. And several girls of my intimate acquaintance are already betrothed to be married."

"Married?"

"Many girls marry by the time they're eighteen, Papa. Elena—that is . . ." She hesitated, putting her hand to her mouth.

"Elena? What about Elena?" Gregory asked.

"I suppose I can tell you *now*," Alexandria said, her

eyes widening on her pretty face. "Although when I first found out about it, Elena made me swear to secrecy."

"What are you talking about, my dear?"

"Nearly two years ago, I happened into the stable one day to get the stableman to drive me into Soho," Alexandria related. "There, instead of finding the stableman, I discovered Elena and the groom. I forget his name. He was let go a short while after that."

"You discovered your sister and the groom—in the stable?"

"The stableman had been sent on an errand and wasn't expected back for nearly an hour," Alexandria continued. "I obviously had surprised Elena and groom, because once she saw me she became flushed and began fastening buttons and straightening wrinkles. The groom was a fiery red—what I could see of him—for he instantly grabbed his things and disappeared into the hay room."

"Why didn't you report this incident to your mother or me?"

"Sisters don't do that sort of thing—I mean tattle on each other—not when they're practically grown," Alexandria said. "Besides, Elena made me swear to secrecy."

"Are you—are you certain it was Elena?" Gregory asked, the words heavy on his tongue.

"I knew my own sister. I've always been able to tell Elena and Isabelle apart. When you're practically raised as a triplet, you know, you're so close you always know who is who. Besides, she was just pulling her blouse onto her shoulder when I arrived and I saw the seven formed in freckles on it. Furthermore, Isabelle would have never spoken to me the way Elena did. Elena actually threatened me."

"What did she have to threaten you about?" Gregory asked.

"She wouldn't have had to have anything," Alexandria returned. "She would have made up something—she always did. And she was such a charming prevaricator that no one would disbelieve her."

"A prevaricator?"

"I called her a liar once—*only* once."

"I've never heard any of this about Elena. You're not making it up, are you?" questioned Gregory.

Alexandria's eyes sparkled mischievously. "Would I do such a thing, Papa?"

Gregory could not help himself, he laughed. Then he put his arm about Alexandria and kissed her on the cheek. "Dearest Alexandria, we must speak only kindly of Elena, now that she's gone."

"Yes, Papa." Alexandria nestled in her father's embrace. "I love you, Papa."

"And I love you, my darling." Gregory stared out the window as he held his youngest daughter. A thought came, then a question. He did not have the courage to ask. Instead, he said, "This has been a very difficult time for Isabelle, you know. Harder than for any of the rest of us. If Elena's death was bloody awful for us, you can imagine what it must have been like for Isabelle. I trust you have spent a good deal of time with your sister since—that is—after the—"

"Accident?" Alexandria filled in. "Isabelle has always been somewhat of a private person. She seems to be even more so now. I do go out of my way to be friendly with her, but she usually gives me evasive answers and cuts me short. I know she is distressed. Should I ever have the misfortune of being the parent of a set of twins, I'm certain I would send them each to different private schools by the time they reached the age of ten, if not before. I'm not criticizing you and Mama, but I think it's very unfair for twins to grow up so dependent on each other."

"I suspect you may be right, my dearest Alexandria. Was there something special you wished to ask me?"

"It can wait until later, Papa. I merely wanted your

permission to attend a party. Mother said I had to speak to you about it. But I'll speak to you later, Papa."

"What party?"

"One that Miss Tillie is giving for her students and former students," Alexandria said. "She has promised that there will be an equal number of young men to match the number of young ladies. But it will be at night and will last until goodness knows when."

Gregory kissed her again. "Of course, my darling, you may attend the party and dance to your heart's content."

Alexandria embraced him, kissing him affectionately, and thanked him as she sailed from the room.

Distraught, anxious with questions, Gregory returned to the wine decanter and poured another drink.

CHAPTER SIX

"My decision is final," Ilene stated on the last day before the *Twin Dolphins,* Medallion's finest passenger vessel, was slated to sail for Boston. "I will never knowingly permit two of my daughters to travel together again. Nor do I intend that Bertie ever travel with either of his remaining sisters."

Gregory understood his wife's feelings. On the surface Ilene appeared to have adjusted to the passing of Elena. Still, she continuously made little remarks that indicated that a faint taste of bitterness, anger, and remorse remained. Alexandria had begged to accompany Isabelle to Boston; she had thrown tantrums and had pouted. She even had threatened going without food, a threat she could not keep, since she dearly loved to eat.

Ilene would not be swayed. "Alexandria belongs here in London at Mossweed. It's scandalous to think she would even consider not finishing her school when this is her last year."

"We won't say any more about it, my dear," Gregory said as he embraced Ilene. "You are right, of course. It's just that Alexandria has such a way about her."

"With *you*, yes, my darling," Ilene returned with a wry smile. "Oh, yes, Alexandria *is* her father's daughter, there is no doubt of that. The twins have always been well aware of that." She patted his cheek. "I know you were confused when two daughters were born the first time around. Well, pip-pip and cheerio! and all that rot, it happened. Now my precious Gregory, it would seem the time is past due that you gave as much of your attention to Isabelle as you possibly can. Think of it this way: If Alexandria were along on the *Twin Dolphins,* she would find a way to monopolize your attention."

Gregory chuckled with mock amusement. "Yes, my dearest, I shall devote as much of my attention to Isabelle as I can—or should I say, as much as she will permit me to do. I swear I will put forward a concerted effort to get close to her."

Ilene frowned. What troubled her? Was it Gregory's attitude? Certainly he was kindness itself; a more loving parent could not be found in all of London, in her opinion. "Gregory—?"

"Yes?"

Ilene flushed. "I was merely going to suggest that there must come a time in the near future when you make an effort to travel alone with Bertie."

"With Albert?"

"Your son is fast becoming a man, my dear. You don't want him growing up being a complete mother's boy, do you?" Ilene smiled sweetly, but did not wait for Gregory's reply. "I had best go upstairs and see if Isabelle is fully packed and ready to leave as early as you must tomorrow morning to catch the train for Southampton."

"One moment, Mrs. Phenwick," Gregory called as she reached the door.

"Yes, my darling?"

An instant later Gregory had his arms about Ilene. His eyes stared deeply into hers before he kissed her. Then he stood, his cheek pressed against hers. "I love you very, very much, Mrs. Phenwick. I shall miss you very much while I'm away. I'm certain Isabelle has her things completely ready. Why don't you simply come upstairs with me?"

"My dear Mr. Phenwick," she returned lightly, "the children must be looked after before the husband."

"Nonsense! Who made that up?"

"I suppose I did." She kissed him and eluded his grasp to hurry out the door. "I'll be up directly." Giggling, she dashed to the stairs and took them as if she were dancing.

Gregory watched as she disappeared into the shadows of the second floor.

"She absolutely won't permit me to go, will she?"

"What? Oh, Alexandria, is that you?"

"Yes, Papa." Alexandria poutingly moved from the shadows of the hallway. "I confess I had my ear at the door, but you were both speaking quite softly. Still, I know mother. She's bound not to relent."

Gregory put his arms about his youngest daughter and kissed her on the forehead. "Alexandria—this is your sister's trip. I can say no more about the matter. There will be other times when we can travel together."

Alexandria sobbed lightly and sniffled sufficiently loud to let her father know of her disappointment.

Upstairs, Ilene knocked before entering the room Isabelle previously had shared with her twin sister. The other bed had been removed after the accident. Shortly after Isabelle had returned to London, she insisted that she have a completely new wardrobe and that all the identical apparel she and her sister had worn were given away. It was an expensive endeavor, but the Phenwicks were an enormously rich family.

"Mother?" Isabelle questioned, glancing up from the desk where she was penning a thank-you letter to Joanna Phenwick for the gift of an ermine cape for the journey.

"You're all right, then, are you dear?" Ilene asked as she entered the room.

"Quite, Mother." Isabelle was clad in a sapphire blue dressing gown, her satinlike hair arranged in a net for sleeping. In the pale glow of a single lamp, she looked fragile and sullen.

"Is there anything I may help you with?" Ilene asked as she ventured into the room and observed the packed portmanteaus. The trunks had been shipped to Southampton two days previously.

"Everything is finished," Isabelle said. "I was just dashing a note to Joanna. Then I'm off to bed."

"There is nothing I can do for you?" Ilene persisted.

"Nothing, Mother."

"Are you excited about the trip?"

"I suppose—in a way. It will be a different experience, won't it?" Isabelle signed her name to the note. After placing the paper in an envelope, she glanced up at Ilene with an expression of surprise, as if she had not expected to see her mother still standing there. "I hope I can sleep tonight. I don't wish to take a sleeping draught. I'll never be able to awaken early if I do. Still—"

"What is troubling you, Isabelle?"

A faint smile crossed Isabelle's pretty lips. She shook her head. "It's nothing, Mother. I do pray that the dreams will not continue once I leave London."

"The dreams?" Ilene moved closer to the girl. "*Which* dreams?"

Isabelle turned to the window. Moisture was on the pane. "Just dreams." She put the tip of her finger to the glass, then caught her mother's reflected worried expression in it. Instantly she turned and leapt toward Ilene. "Oh, Mama, Mama, I don't want to leave you—and England. But I fear that as long as I'm here I'll always have those dreams. This room reminds me of her. I've been nearly driven frantic by her memory."

"Elena?"

Isabelle raised her head and stared at Ilene's face with tear-glistening eyes. Her lower jaw was trembling so that she could not speak. Again she fell to Ilene's bosom and sobbed deeply.

"Why didn't you tell me about these dreams before this?"

"I thought I had." Ilene pushed herself away to get a handkerchief. "Yet they are such unspeakable nightmares that I may have neglected telling you about them. I did tell Cousin Ophelia. And she suggested that I speak to a distant cousin of ours while I'm in Boston—a doctor, Joseph Ornby."

"Joseph may be a distant cousin to Ophelia, my darling," Ilene stated, "but he happens to be your uncle by marriage. He's married to my sister Sheila. It was through your uncle Joseph that I was introduced to the Phenwick family in the first place. You must go visit your aunt Sheila while you're in Boston. I suppose she still sounds as Irish as Paddy's pig. Dear Sheila, how I would love to see her again."

Isabelle went to warm her hands at the fire. "Mama, would you be terribly upset if I didn't come back to London?"

"Not come back to London?"

"Not for a—I mean, not to live here."

"It would sorely grieve me if you were to stay away from home," Ilene answered. "Still, I know that you must one day marry, and that marriage may take you a distance from me."

"The fact is, Mama," Isabelle stated, "I fear for my sanity. Interminable dreams about Elena while I'm asleep are quite one thing. Several times lately, I've thought I've seen her while I was very much awake. I accosted a lady on the street just the day before yesterday—I was that certain she was Elena. When I got up close, of course, I

67

could see there was hardly more than a vague resemblance to my sister. I apologized profusely. Then a short while later, I again thought I beheld Elena. I called her name. But since it was not my twin, the lady did not look back or pay heed to my cry. It was all I could do to keep from weeping. I ran to catch up with her, but she was gone in a carriage before I could get to her."

"Your imagination, Isabelle."

"I have no doubt that it is," Isabelle returned. "But what will stop it? Boston? Oh, I pray with all my soul that being away from England will diminish the memory of Elena."

"Sure now, you mustn't let the memory of your dear sister drive you frantic, Isabelle." Ilene went to hold her daughter again. "Perhaps you'll meet one of your handsome Phenwick cousins and fall in love with him. If I knew you were deeply loved and had become a Phenwick woman, it would ease my worry about you."

"A Phenwick man? Is that so important, Mama?"

"I believe it is."

"Why can't Alexandria become the Phenwick woman?" Isabelle asked.

"Because I believe it was predestined that you are to have the honor of that title. I'll not alter my opinion."

Isabelle managed a brief smile. "In that case, I suppose I shall have to fall in love with a Phenwick man, won't I, Mama?"

"You are that determined already to remain in Boston, are you?"

"Put it this way. I'm determined not to come back to live in London. I hadn't meant to mention this. I'm glad I have. It would be unkind of me to surprise you with my decision."

"I cannot attempt to dissuade you. I dare not." Ilene sighed before she went to kiss the girl again. "You must always remember that I love you deeply and that, when time permits, we will visit each other. Still, you may change your mind once you've been in Boston for awhile. Now I must say good night."

"Yes, Mama, good night."

Ilene got to the door before she stopped. Her back stiffened and she slowly turned around to gaze at Isabelle. A smile was difficult. "There is one further question I would like to ask you, precious Isabelle."

"What is it, Mama?"

"Is he—that is, you mentioned a—well—a leprechaun—"

"Moorduke?"

"Are you certain it *is* Moorduke? I thought he told me I'd never see him again," Ilene said.

"Have you seen him, Mama?"

"No—no, *I* haven't. But if you know his name—and I know you to be an honest girl, then—" Ilene looked confused. Then she smiled. "You'll be looked after if Moorduke's with you." She blinked. "Well, good night, then."

"Good night, Mama."

Isabelle prepared for bed. By that time she had become accustomed to looking at her reflection in the mirror without being reminded of Elena—most of the time. Still, there were so many memories of her sister in that house, in so many things that she did.

As Isabelle returned from washing her face and creaming it with a special French mixture that was guaranteed to keep her lovely, she stopped cold in the doorway of the adjoining room. A figure was standing at the window, her back to Isabelle. She was clad in an identical dressing robe to the one Isabelle was wearing. She might have at first thought she was seeing her own reflection in the mirror, except that the image had its back turned to her. Gasping, whimpering, unable to make a sound, she trembled in every part of her body. There was no time to reason with herself, she reacted emotionally. A few steps farther into the room, she found her voice. "Alexandria?"

The vision at the window slowly turned about, wearing an expression that was almost menacing. "No . . . Elena."

Isabelle's vision blurred, and a jab of fright pierced her solar plexus. Her knees buckled and she fell unconscious to the floor.

Sometime during the night Isabelle regained consciousness and found herself sprawled on the floor. How could it have been a dream if she regained consciousness on the floor where she remembered standing when she saw the— *was it an apparition?*

The lamp had burned low, nearly empty of fuel. Using the back of the chair to support herself, Isabelle managed to make her way to the bed, where she lit a second lamp. What had actually happened? She poured water from a pitcher on the commode and drank it as if she intended to put out a fire that was burning in her throat. As she raised the glass, her hands were trembling so that she could hardly hold it at her lips.

It was nearly an hour later before she was able to calm herself enough to consider sleep. She had thought of waking her parents and telling them about what had happened. *But what had happened?* She rationalized that the vision of her dead sister had been a hallucination; and if that were the case, might speaking of it cause her parents to believe that she was verging on insanity? The thought terrified her. That awful, frantic, helpless sensation came over her.

She decided to let the light burn until it ran out of oil. By that time, hopefully, she would be asleep. A sleeping draught was considered, but she would do her best to conquer the state of her nerves without it. After climbing beneath the covers, she stared up at the canopy above her.

The lamp contained less oil than she thought. It soon began fading lower and lower until there were only sputtered flickers and soon a shroud of darkness. Heavy-eyed despite her uneasiness, Isabelle closed her eyelids and soon found she was drifting in a state somewhere between being awake and being asleep. She had begun to drift off.

"Isabelle! Is-a-belle!" a familiar voice seemed to be calling as if it were bathed in an echo. *"Is-a-belle! Come with me, Isabelle. Come join me. It's lovely over here, Isabelle."*

Frantically Isabelle reached for a match and struck it. From the flickering matchlight, she would see that the room was empty.

"Elena? Is that you?" Isabelle questioned.

The reply was a muted sound of laughter, hollow, faraway sounding, yet nearby. Isabelle wanted to scream, but the fear that lodged in her throat made her dumb.

The voice did not call again that night.

CHAPTER SEVEN

Isabelle was sick the entire first two days at sea. She could hold nothing down. Gregory was deeply concerned over her health and was almost tempted to make arrangements to turn the ship about and take Isabelle home. Fortunately, by the third day she was able to take soft food; and by the end of the sixth day she was eating well.

Father and daughter spent many hours together. Isabelle rarely spoke, and when she did it was about some mundane matter. Gregory was of the opinion that she had built an invisible wall around herself, an impenetrable barrier meant to keep everyone out.

Gregory would find himself talking at length, seemingly to Isabelle, only to discover that her eyes held a glazed look and she was obviously not hearing a word he uttered.

A doctor, who was a passenger aboard, was persuaded to examine Isabelle. He could discover no functional ailments and considered her health to be a matter of reaction to the tossing sea. It was early in the season for crossing. Hence, the girl stayed bundled up in her stateroom, attempting to read one of several books she had brought along to occupy her time during the voyage. But she could not concentrate on the stories, nor could she seem to remember what happened from one page to the next.

"Wal, sure an' b'gorra, if'n ye ain't piled into that bunk like th' bloody queen herself, ye are," a small voice next to her ear observed one afternoon.

"Moorduke?"

"Ay, what other leprechaun was ye expectin'?" He saucily replied.

"I didn't think you were aboard."

"Not aboard? Sure now, an' how d'ye reckon I could escape me duties?" he asked.

"Where have you been all this time?"

"Catchin' up on me sleep, I have." He yawned. "An' I'll confess I've found me way t' a rum keg er two." He burst out singing. " '*Oh, the days o' th' Kerry dancing, Oh, th' ring o' th' pipers' tune . . .'* "

"Moorduke!"

"D'ye nay think I have a lovely voice? '*. . . Gone, alas, like our youth, too soon . . .'* "

"I fear I have a bit of a headache," Isabelle complained.

"Ye haven't bin in th' rum keg yerself, have ye?"

"No. I'm afraid being at sea doesn't quite agree with me."

"I kin take it or leave it," Moorduke commented.

"Moorduke, may I ask you a question?"

"Ye kin ast all ye like, but if'n I don't know th' answer, er don't care t' admit that I do, don't be surprised."

"Were you with me on the night prior to leaving England?" she asked.

"Oh, I d'nay know if'n I kin think back that far. Chances are—just takin' a fairy guess—I weren't. Ye see, I've discovered—an' quite by accident—that when a lep-

73

rechaun has hisself a mortal, he isn't obliged t' be near said mortal at *all* times. Glory be, that's a break! But rest assured, I do check up on ye time an' ag'in."

Isabelle related about the incident that happened, or that she imagined happened on the night in question.

"Wal, now, I ain't nay doctor, b'gorra, but it would seem t' me that ye are doin' th' best thin' in th' world by takin' a trip. Me, too."

"Can you explain what happened?"

"I kin. But I don't believe ye'd care for me explanation in fairy terms. Ye see, we know about thin's th' likes o' ye kin't never know."

"What sort of things?" Isabelle persisted.

"Sprites an' thin's o' that nature. Ay, ye mortals do be a strange lot. Th' fact is ye deceive yerselves by believin' in only what ye kin see. I'll tell ye this, there's far more in th' so-called invisible world than there is in th' one what ye see. Sure now, it's more than yer wee mind kin imagine," Moorduke said, lounging back on the pillow. "There do be a quare notion that when a body dies that that is th' end. Crickets almighty! What a silly superstition that is! Lor', 'tis such a misconception."

"If it isn't the end, what is it?"

"What else? It has t' be th' beginnin'. Th' beginnin' o' somethin' new, that's what it is." He laughed. "Nay only do ye right now be a mortal, but ye're also *immortal*. That what ye really are has bin goin' on an' will go on forever. Ye continue in a whole chain o' experiences, th' likes o' which yer wee mind kin nay imagine."

"Do you mean to tell me I'm actually immortal right now?" Isabelle questioned.

"Ay, that is th' truth, lass, I kin nay deny it." He laughed again. "Sure as winter comes ye'll leave that bit o' flesh ye occupy at this moment, but ye will still exist. An' no matter how many garments o' flesh an' bone ye take on, ye'll always exist wif or wifout them."

"What are you getting at, Moorduke?"

"Me? Gittin' at?" He rolled over so that he was quite close to her ear. "If'n what ye tol' me was true about what happened th' night before departure, then I expect th' fine sprite o' yer sister is still hoverin' about yer home in London."

"Do you mean her ghost?"

"Ay, that would be a clever guess, it would."

Isabelle stared, her eyes growing larger. "I don't believe in ghosts."

"Don't ye?"

"No, I think not."

"An' why not, pray tell?"

"Because they're unreal, they have no substance."

Moorduke rolled over with laughter. "What a silly little thin' ye are, lass. Well, have it yer way. I'll nay attempt t' change yer mind on such thin's. But th' next time ye see yer sister, ye might do bloody well t' remain conscious long enough t' see why she's come back t' haunt ye."

Isabelle became rigid. "To—to haunt me?"

"I kin see by th' frantic expression on yer face that ye know well o' what I speak." He leapt up to the porthole and leaned against the closed glass. "Watch me." Before Isabelle could blink, he had disappeared. "Do ye see me now, lass?"

"No."

"But ye kin hear me, kin't ye?"

"Yes."

Moorduke laughed. A moment later he reappeared, this time standing on the small desk beside the bunk. "I'm over here now."

"How did you do that?"

"It's part o' me fairy power," he related. "Ye see, I'm really a sprite myself, th' likes o' which kin make hisself visible or invisible at will. Some spirits o' mortals kin do th' same thin'."

"You mean that you're really a ghost?"

"I've never thought o' it that way, but I reckon, I am—in a way. I'm o' a breed o' sprite that was never meant t' become a human mortal. There are different kinds o' mortals, ye know."

"I didn't know. You're confusing me."

"In that case, I'll just disappear an' continue this conversation at another time." He snapped his fingers and disappeared.

"Moorduke?" Isabelle sat up. "Moorduke? Where could he have gone?" Slowly she let her head fall back to the pillow. Her thoughts were still with the little creature and his profound statements. Had her mother not recognized the name of Moorduke, or had she not inquired about him, Isabelle might have thought he was entirely of her imagination. Such things confused her.

In the hour or so that followed, Isabelle considered many different things. For over six months she had known a kind of freedom she had never before experienced. So much of her life had been shared with Elena. She had confided much in her sister. She was glad she had never confided in Alexandria to a large extent. Now Isabelle wanted to be a private person. But what sort of private person?

During her growing years, Isabelle had been somewhat introverted, drawing into the solitude of her own thoughts. Elena had been the extrovert. Isabelle was shy. Elena had been outgoing and gregarious. Isabelle often thought it strange that two such identically appearing people could be so different beneath the surface. Elena had perpetually talked about men from the time she was thirteen. She would nudge and call Isabelle's attention to an attractive young man. And if she wanted an introduction, she would blatantly take the initiative. Isabelle would become embarrassed and blush.

Still, Isabelle had normal notions about men, speculations, forbidden imaginings. There were times when she was of the opinion that David Phenwick, for instance, was the most handsome man in London. She could easily see how Elena might have been attracted to him. For that matter, there were moments when impish feelings of envy had come over and she had resented her twin's closeness to David.

Another who had momentarily attracted her interest was Derrick Molden, the man who had been hired by Gregory Phenwick to assist his family both with house chores and driving the carriage. Elena had been able to give the man looks that would cause him to redden, or to laugh salaciously. Like most people, Derrick could rarely tell the twins apart and once, mistaking Isabelle for her sister, had made curious, suggestive remarks. Isabelle was offended to think he might dare say such things to Elena. Afterwards she wondered if Elena's flirtatious ways had led the man on—and, if so, to what extreme. Both his facial expression and the tone of his remarks bore implications of familiarity. Ironically, despite her prudent reaction to Derrick's remarks, she found that she had a fascination—albeit well disguised—about the man.

No, Isabelle was not without her quiet, reserved interest in men. Only her tremendous shyness had caused her to withdraw and stand on the sidelines while Elena had moved forward. A singular thought occurred to her. Had she had her wits about her at the time of the accident, she might have been able to assume her sister's role, change places. Of course, at that time there was not a clue of evidence that Elena had been drowned. Besides, she rationalized, she would have never been able to pull off such a deception, even if she had really wanted to. Conversely, she was certain that Elena could have done such a thing with no compunction whatsoever.

Elena . . . Elena . . . Elena!

Why couldn't she erase her sister's name from her

mind? And why did she entertain such speculative thoughts about her? She thought again of Moorduke's theories about ghosts and immortality. She doubted that she could put much faith in his words. But, for that matter, how much faith could she put in his actual existence?

Gregory appeared at her cabin a short while later. After six months, he had discarded his black mourning attire and had begun to dress in the fashionable modern wear of Victorian aristocracy. As in his youth, he preferred light colors, soft blues, grays, and beiges. Isabelle considered that the elimination of the black mourning clothing caused her father to appear to be at least ten—well, maybe five—years younger. The pained look of sorrow was slowly lifting from his face and the sea air seemed to well agree with him.

"My darling Isabelle," Gregory began, his eyes sparkling with enthusiasm as they had done in the past, "are you feeling better?"

"I suppose I am, Papa," she replied. "It's foolish of me not to, isn't it?"

"That is not true," Gregory assured her. "You certainly aren't accustomed to sea travel. Besides, after all you've been through these past months—what we've all been through—well, just know I understand." He kissed her.

"Sit on the bunk beside me, Papa," Isabelle begged. "I promise not to get sick."

Gregory chuckled as he sat beside his daughter. "You are feeling better, aren't you? I can tell by your color, and your eyes appear to have a brighter glow to them."

"I'm a poor traveler, aren't I?"

"Just inexperienced, I suspect." He put his hand over hers. "Dearest Isabelle, I had quite a talk with your mother before we left London. You upset her, you know?"

"Yes, I suppose I did." Isabelle avoided the intense

look that had come into her father's eyes. "I didn't mean to distress her."

"I'm certain you didn't. Fortunately I had a chat with Josh earlier about the same matter. I can't compare you with his eldest daughter, Ophelia; still, there is a similarity of situation. The eldest always finds it most difficult to leave the nest. Once he or she shows the way, it isn't near as difficult for the younger siblings. And Josh made me realize that you have reached an age of maturity, haven't you? Your mother and I would very much like to see our children remain in our home indefinitely. But that isn't practical, is it? No, not in the least."

"It wouldn't seem to be."

"Precisely." Gregory cleared his throat and squeezed Isabelle's hand. "Your mother spoke of your speculative interest in remaining in the United States for an extended period of time. Have you long entertained such thoughts?"

"Of course I am dearly fond of Cousin Stuart and his son, Danny," Isabelle remarked. "I've enjoyed their visits to London. And Cousin Thadius was ever so nice to me on his last visit."

"Thadius is married now, you know?"

"Yes, so I had heard." She looked down, then over toward the porthole as if she half expected to see Moorduke sitting there.

"I see you were duly impressed by Cousin Thadius."

"What girl in her right mind wouldn't be?" Isabelle replied.

"Not being of that gender, I can't form an adequate opinion," Gregory returned lightly. The lines of his face altered and he looked serious. "Your mother and I have somewhat adjusted to our loss—"

"Elena?"

"Yes, quite." He blinked as he gazed into her face. "God knows it was difficult enough for us to make the adjustment. I can't begin to imagine what it has been like for you. Still the living must go on. But I can easily see how you must desire to get away from the home—yes, the very room in which you grew up with your twin sister. Under such conditions, I must assure you that you have my full approval of going anywhere you choose—within reason, of course. Also, I would hope that it would be in an area where there were close relatives who would look after you."

"Oh, Papa, you understand!"

"Did you think I might not?"

"I didn't know." She sat forward and kissed him on the cheek.

"As you know I have to spend some time with Jim Phenwick in Savannah. Originally I had planned that you would travel into that southern city with me. Under your present state of mind, I would judge, it would be wiser for you to remain in Boston while I go south. I'm certain Cousin Stuart and Ruth will be delighted for you to stay with them at Edward House. Or—" A curious thought came to mind, and he smiled.

"Or—?" Isabelle cocked her head to one side.

Gregory wiped the smile from his lips. "Nancy has moved to Greenfield, Maine, but the house is still there in Boston. I shouldn't think it would be very pleasant for you. And with Thadius in Greenfield, too, and Paul in California, I don't really know the circumstances with her other two sons. Last I heard, Daniel Louis had become quite a playboy, and John—"

"John Phenwick?"

"The brother just younger than Thadius," Gregory explained. "He's become an attorney and is doing quite well for himself. I believe Stuart told me when last we met that both John and Daniel Louis no longer lived at the old homestead."

"Papa—" Isabelle said, again touching his hands.

"Yes? What is it?"

"I don't believe you were going to tell me about Cousin Nancy and her four sons. That wasn't what caused you to chuckle."

"You're most perceptive, my dear," Gregory returned. "To be perfectly frank, Isabelle, another thought had entered my mind. You recall me speaking of Cousin Stuart's brother, Gordon, who was drowned many years ago?"

"I vaguely recall mention of something like that."

"Gordon's widow is extremely wealthy and lives in a marvelous large house overlooking the ocean, a short distance above Boston Harbor," Gregory explained.

"Is that Milli-something-or-other?"

"Millijoy. Yes." Gregory cleared a huskiness from his throat. "Millijoy is quite a person. I've stayed at Triumph House with her on several occasions. She is a gracious hostess. I always got along capitally with her. Your Aunt Marcia had a particular affinity for Millijoy. Oh, she has been much maligned by the family, although most of our relatives have done the best they can to tolerate her. *Tolerate* can be a cruel word. But Millijoy has adjusted and has amassed a fortune. Of all the Phenwick women I know, I suspect Millijoy is truly the most proud of the title."

"Does she live alone at—did you say *Triumph House*?"

"She has a son. I believe Tommy is a year or two younger than you," Gregory related. "Your grandmother was extraordinarily pleased that young Tommy had aspirations of becoming a concert pianist, as she was. Perhaps he may win greater fame than the illustrious Susannah Phenwick achieved."

"Grandmother?" Isabelle smiled. "Are you suggesting that I might like to stay at Triumph House—for a while?"

"Should Millijoy extend an invitation," Gregory replied, "I think it might be a pleasant change for you."

"It might." Isabelle again looked toward the porthole. "Papa, do you believe in ghosts?"

"I beg your pardon!"

"England is reputed to be full of ghosts," Isabelle said, measuring her words. "I just wondered what your opinions on such things were."

Gregory thought a moment. "What brought this on?"

"Thoughts I had been entertaining before you arrived," Isabelle answered. "I, of course, have heard the legends of Augusta Phenwick and how she chooses the Phenwick women. I don't suppose you've ever seen her."

"I was aware, at least I thought I was aware, of some unearthly presence prior to the time I married your mother," Gregory commented. "Whether I believe in the spirit of Augusta or not is quite another matter, don't you know. As to the notions about any other ghosts—well, I think it's a lot of poppycock contrived from superstitious imaginations."

"Did you ever meet mother's leprechaun?" Isabelle asked.

Gregory's eyes widened. "Aha! So it is your mother that put you up to all of this, is it? Ilene almost had me convinced that such things as leprechanus did exist, prior to the time we left to return to England. Then when she told me he just disappeared, well, I began to see through the fabrication of her story."

Isabelle knew her father to be a very pragmatic, unsuperstitious man. It was evident that, even if he wanted to, he could not bring himself to accept the idea of such things. She would do well to drop the matter.

"I say, are you feeling up to supper?" Gregory asked, indicating that he felt uncomfortable discussing the supernatural. "The captain has assured me that a lovely meal has been prepared and that he would be honored if we would join him at his table."

"So far today the queasiness seems to be gone," Isabelle said, "as it was most of yesterday. Perhaps it would do me well to get away from the cabin, to fix myself up and get some fresh air."

"That's my girl," Gregory remarked as he rose from beside her. "I'll give you half an hour before I come back to fetch you."

A curious excitement came over Isabelle. Was it because she was looking forward to the meal with the captain and, she suspected, several of the crew? Or was her change of mood brought about because of her father's earlier positive reaction to her desire to remain for an extended time in Boston? Whatever it was, she sensed new energy come into her spirit, as well as into her body.

First Mate Curtis Tinkersly had glistening black hair, vivid blue eyes, a large, smiling mouth that revealed big, brightly sparkling teeth. His stare was so penetrating and his smile so inviting that he could exert his will over almost any person he encountered. Ladies especially were overwhelmed by his exuberance. When Isabelle first saw him, she felt her knees tremble. When he spoke to her, calling her by name, the timbre of his voice seemed to vibrate through her.

Captain Lemuel Keswick, while a few years older than Tinkersly, was equally as charming. His hair had bleached a milky yellow from persistent hours in the sun at sea. Even his brows and sideburns were that light. His eyes were a disarming shade of green. He had a laconic way of speaking that underlined authority with a matter-of-fact, no-nonsense attitude. Like Tinkersly's, the captain's smile could readily be labeled suggestive, if not downright seductive. Isabelle felt incapable of controlling her reactions. She held to her father's hand and tried to keep from trembling.

"So this is the lovely Isabelle?" Captain Keswick commented as he bowed and kissed her hand. "I regret that you have been thus far indisposed on the trip. May I present the first mate, Mr. Tinkersly?"

When Curtis smiled, it was all Isabelle could do to keep from swooning dead away. She tried to remain nonchalant, verging on indifference—but she could control neither her trembling nor her nervous stammering.

After supper, Curtis Tinkersly offered to take her for a stroll around the deck. Once she gathered her courage, Isabelle accepted.

"This is your first crossing, I understand," Curtis remarked.

"Yes, it is." Isabelle looked to the starry sky. "You don't sound British."

"I'm an American," Curtis replied, his voice seemingly penetrating into her spinal column. "My home is in Pittsburgh, but I've not been there in several years. My family and I do not see eye to eye on certain matters."

"Do you often go to Boston?"

"Once or twice a year," Curtis answered. He wanted to stop by the rail and point out different constellations of stars.

Isabelle felt unsure of herself—and her reactions. "I think it best if I return to my cabin now. I fear I'm still a bit weak."

"Certainly, Miss Phenwick." Curtis strolled with her to the cabin. He lingered outside the door as if awaiting an invitation. Instead, Isabelle said good night and tried not to close the door directly in his face.

Curtis Tinkersly knew many women and was known to have had several shipboard romances during his years of sailing. So that night, when he was on watch, he reminded himself that no two women were the same, and each reacted differently to him. Because Isabelle was a Phenwick, he would pursue friendship only with her. When he was ready to settle down, he might discover a Phenwick girl who was both susceptible to his charms and eager for a liaison with the likes of him. He could wait.

At nearly midnight, while taking watch, Curtis Tinkersly was surprised to glance over to the deck and see a familiar figure standing in the soft radiance of moonlight.

"Miss Phenwick?" he asked, as he approached her.

"Yes." Eyes stared with burning penetration up at his.

"I was certain you would be sound asleep this hour of the night."

"Your eyes—your smile—they made me restless. I couldn't sleep for thinking about you."

"About me?" Curtis chuckled. "Why me?"

She reached to touch his hand and glanced cautiously from side to side. "I've no doubt you know full well why women think of you, Mr. Tinkersly. And you realize, of course, that I am a woman."

"That impression never escaped me, Miss Phenwick." His arms went to her shoulders. A moment later she fell into his embrace. Moonlight illuminated them. Then they hid from the moon's glow in the shadows where they would not be observed.

CHAPTER EIGHT

Shortly after the marriage of Thadius Phenwick to Nellie Collier and their settling into the remodeled O'Plaggerty house in Greenfield, Maine, Thad's mother, Nancy, made arrangements to sell the family home in Boston. Although she was now married to John Collier, Nancy was still considered to be the Phenwick matriarch in the United States. Because of her deep love for John and the nearness of her eldest son, Thadius, she was determined to live out her years in the congenial community of Greenfield at the elegantly elaborate new Phenwick House, which she herself had had a major hand in building.

Nancy's third son, Paul, was married and was devoted to establishing his own business in San Francisco. Her fourth and youngest son, Daniel Louis, had established himself as quite a dashing man-about-Boston. He had become an investment broker and took extensive trips to New York, Washington, D.C., Philadelphia, and other lesser populated cities. He was rarely in Boston and hardly ever even visited the old family home. He preferred staying in his own apartment.

Nancy's second son, John, had been in law practice for

several years and had purchased his own home a short distance out on the Lexington road. He, like Daniel Louis, was a bachelor. But unlike his youngest brother, John was a stable, solid citizen, not a playboy, nor one whose name often appeared in social columns.

John Phenwick had attended a dinner party at Edward House on the same day that word came announcing that Gregory and Isabelle were on their way to Boston. John's nephew Stuart and Stuart's lovely wife Ruth were gracious hosts. Prominent among the guests was the charming and beautiful Miss Maribelle Wilson. The raven-haired beauty was the daughter of influential Horatio Wilson, a textile industrialist, who owned mills in various parts of Massachusetts. Extremely wealthy, the Wilsons had two daughters whom they wished to marry into socially prominent Bostonian families. Naturally the Phenwicks were considered one of the choicest families, both in wealth and position. Furthermore, it was firmly believed that with rare exception, the Phenwick men were extraordinarily handsome. Maribelle had only to gaze at Stuart and John Phenwick each to realize it was a fact.

"So your mother finally has a buyer for her home in Boston," Stuart commented during a lull in conversation at the dinner table. He directed his remark to John Phenwick.

Masculinely handsome, John Phenwick glanced up at Maribelle with a brief smile before turning his attention to Stuart. "Yes. Not only is she getting a good price for the old place, but she is receiving it all in cash. Certainly she doesn't need the money, goodness knows, but it does save a lot of bother with drawn-out payments. The house is being purchased by a family who are presently living in Worcester."

"Where does your mother reside at the present time, Mr. Phenwick?" Maribelle asked in a liquid, melodic voice. There was no mistaking her obvious interest in John.

"Greenfield, Maine," John replied, his eyes flashing as they darted over her face. "My father passed away many years ago. She waited until my three brothers and I were grown before she remarried. And have you always lived in Boston, Miss Wilson?"

"We moved here from Canton, Ohio, when I was a small girl," Maribelle replied. "I confess I prefer Boston to what I remember of Ohio. I certainly *consider* myself a Bostonian."

Pauline Quigly, who was seated to Stuart's right, next to John, cast her husband a singular glance before speaking. "How ever does your mother abide the wilderness of Maine?" She was a long-faced lady with prominent teeth and a convivial disposition. Considered one of the important members of Bostonian society, Pauline was acquainted with many people, and she made it her business to get to know persons of wealth and position who had relocated in Boston.

"Greenfield has become quite a flourishing community since it has recovered from the epidemic of 1869," John announced. "Mother has seen to that. But then, Mother wouldn't be happy if she didn't have her little projects. That's her way."

Wilfred Quigly glanced up at the speaker and smoothed his moustache clear to the mutton chops. "Nancy Phenwick was always a—" He glanced toward his wife. "—quite a lady. Greenfield's gain is Boston's loss."

Seated between Maribelle Wilson and Pauline Quigly was Brewster Martin, a friend and business associate of John Phenwick. "I confess I am quite fond of Mrs. Nancy Phenwick—that is, Collier. Such a lovely person."

The lady to Brewster's left lightly cleared her throat. An eyebrow arched as she delicately reached for a fork. Her complexion was light olive and her eyes a mysterious shade of brown. Brewster Martin had been her escort to the dinner party. She gazed over at him. "If this a testimonial for Nancy Phenwick Collier, shouldn't someone propose a toast?"

Stuart gave his sister-in-law an amused look. "Do I detect sarcasm in your voice?"

"Sarcastic? Me?" she purred. "I dearly love Nancy. She was one of the first to accept me as a Phenwick woman—even when the others maintained reservations."

Stuart said, "I always accepted you as my brother's wife, Millijoy."

Millijoy skeptically eyed him. "I suppose you did, Stuart." She smiled. "Well, then, I'll drink to Miss Nancy."

"That is very kind of you, Millijoy," Ruth commented. The lovely Mrs. Stuart Phenwick was a perfect hostess. She baited conversation, then sat back to listen.

John greatly admired Stuart's wife. There was no doubt in his mind why his brother Thadius had once had such a tremendous emotional feeling for her. That was not the case with John, but he had become a good friend to Ruth. "Yes, Millijoy, mother will be pleased to know you think so highly of her."

Millijoy worded the tribute with flowery phrases. They all drank.

"What's this I hear about Gregory coming over from England?" Millijoy inquired a short while later.

"Quite true," Stuart returned. "He's coming first to Boston, then going to Savannah to appraise the situation with Jim. He's traveling with the surviving twin."

"What is a *surviving* twin?" asked Maribelle.

Stuart quickly related the details of the Carrickfergus tragedy.

"The poor thing," Pauline Quigly exclaimed. "The child must be beside herself with grief and peculiar reactions."

"I understand it has been a difficult period for her," Ruth inserted. "Olivia has written that Isabelle has had a difficult time in adjusting to her loss."

"My word!" stated Wilfred Quigly, "it's bad enough to lose one's brother or sister, I mean in a normal situation, but to lose a twin—when they were both so young. Oh, dear, dear, that even saddens me."

"Gregory and Isabelle will stay here at Edward House for awhile," Ruth commented. "We will be a bit crowded now that each of the children has a room of his own."

"We can make arrangements, my dear," Stuart interjected. "And Gregory will be going south shortly after he arrives."

Millijoy sat forward and made a soft noise to gain attention. "Edward House appears to be such a big mansion from the outside. I can see where, with all the children, you would be crowded. And there I am up on the hill with big, spacious Triumph House, and only Tommy and I to rattle around in it—with the servants, of course."

John said, "I don't think—" A foot touched his, and he glanced up into Brewster's reprimanding expression.

"Do you object to me opening the hospitality of my house to visiting members of the family, John?" Millijoy questioned. She turned to the others. "Young John is my late father-in-law's half brother. I suppose as an uncle-figure he feels he should hold some authority over me."

"No such a thing, Millijoy," John replied. "Of course, I feel you have every right to entertain whomever you please—family or otherwise. I was just thinking, under the circumstances—"

"Under the circumstances?" Millijoy asked.

"That is, of Isabelle's emotional state," John continued. "I simply wonder if Triumph House would be the appropriate place for her."

"If your mother still lived in Boston," Millijoy returned, "naturally she would expect to be hostess; but

Miss Nancy is no longer here. Do you distrust me, John?"

"Millijoy!" Stuart exclaimed. "I think it advisable that we discuss this matter in the privacy of the family and not distress our guests with such trite family bickering."

Millijoy raised an eyebrow. "Were we bickering?" She laughed heartily and a bit more raucously than was acceptable in polite society.

"Miss Wilson," John said, unruffled by the exchange of words, "would you do me the honor of going for a stroll about the garden? It is well lit with lanterns and, I should think you will be pleasantly comfortable with a light wrap."

"Why, yes, thank you, Mr. Phenwick," Maribelle replied. "I would be pleased."

"Stuart, Ruth, will you excuse us?" John said as he rose.

"We'll take coffee, tea, and liqueur in the parlor when you return," Ruth advised.

There was more of a chill in the night air than John had anticipated. He went back to fetch Maribelle's cape.

"Mrs. Millijoy Phenwick is quite a person," Maribelle observed as the young couple strolled out into the moonlit night.

"She has made her own way sufficiently," John commented. "Let's not speak of her. I confess she periodically annoys me."

"I have been hoping that we would have the occasion to be together again, Mr. Phenwick," Maribelle remarked with suggestion in her voice. "I find you a most interesting person to be with."

"Thank you, Miss Wilson." John led her toward the wisteria arbor.

"You strike me as being a powerful man," Maribelle continued.

"Powerful? I'm not excessively muscular, if that's what you mean," John returned with an amused chuckle.

"Oh, but you're tremendously handsome," Maribelle mentioned, "and that alone implies power. A man who is not attractive-looking has to work so hard to become powerful; while a man who has your attractiveness, just *naturally* is powerful. I trust you know what I mean."

"I'm beginning to get an inkling," John remarked. "However, I fear you have me confused with my brother Daniel Louis. He is the man-about-town, the *bon vivant*."

"I am acquainted with Daniel Louis," Maribelle said. "He is handsome; but, I confess, I find him a bit *too* powerful. He has a way of forcing himself on a young lady, insistent upon having his way. Why shouldn't he? After all, he is notorious for being a ladies' man. I'll confess another thing to you, too, Mr. Phenwick. I was untouched before I met your brother. He pursuaded me with champagne. I should have known I was dealing with the wrong Phenwick."

"Dealing with?" John paused and held his position. "Ah, I see."

"You do?"

"My dear Miss Wilson," John said firmly, "do you have any notion how many young ladies in Boston have aspirations of becoming Phenwick women?"

"Why, I—"

"Well, I won't venture to guess the precise number," John added, "but I'll tell you this, there are very many. Were I like my brother, I could unscrupulously take whatever I desired from any number of young ladies—and older ones, too. Unfortunately, with me, I have moral values. I can't simply just have my way, play upon a lady's emotions and passions, and—well, I could not be that way. I try to be tolerant of Daniel Louis and his ways because he is my brother. However, I find myself less tolerant of young ladies who have given in to his charming ways. If a woman has no moral respect for herself, how can a man respect her?"

"Oh, Mr. Phenwick, you make me feel so terrible," Maribelle whimpered. "Your brother—"

"My brother is entirely different than I am. Shall we go back into the house?" John continuously strode a pace ahead of the young lady. It was all she could do to keep up with him.

Ruth had planned a concert for the evening's entertainment. The guest pianist was none other than Tom Phenwick, Millijoy's son. The guests gathered in the music room at an aesthetic distance from the piano and gave their undivided attention to the handsome young man who had become a master technician of the keyboard.

Tom's skin was lighter than his mother's. His eyes were a steely gray-blue. While his black hair was curly, it was not kinky. He wore it shoulder length. Long fingers coaxed magnificent tones from the piano, and they moved with such agile swiftness that their dancing movement alone captured the fascination of those in his presence. The sounds he created enthralled.

Of all the Phenwicks, other than Millijoy, John was the one who had encouraged Tom's talent. Furthermore he fully accepted him despite the fact that his features indicated that he possessed Negro blood. John made a point of attending whenever his grandnephew gave a concert. And he was there with praise and admiration.

CHAPTER NINE

Isabelle's behavior aboard the *Twin Dolphins* had confused Curtis Tinkersly. On the one hand she had been extremely friendly and outgoing, even intimate. On the other hand, she appeared indifferent, distant, and annoyed by his persistent interest and attention.

"Miss Phenwick," Tinkersly called as Isabelle was about to disembark with her father at Boston, "may I have a word with you?"

Isabelle sighed with annoyance. "What is it, Mr. Tinkersly?"

"I've known of changeable women in my life," he commented, "but I believe you are by far the most severe case of—well, whatever you are."

"I don't comprehend your meaning, Mr. Tinkersly," Isabelle stated. "Now I am in a hurry, don't you know? My father is waiting."

"I mean nothing to you, then?" Tinkersly commented, his jaw stiff and tense.

"Nothing whatsoever," Isabelle replied. "Why should you? You're the first mate and I'm a passenger. You work for my family. If you persist in annoying me, I shall see that your term of employment is terminated."

"You led me to believe——"

"I led you to believe that I was not in the least bit interested in you, Mr. Tinkersly. Now will you excuse me, or shall I call the captain, who is standing just over there?"

Curtis Tinkersly closed his eyes and sighed. He motioned for her to go her way. From the beginning he had known who she was. Twice he had sailed under Captain Henry Ashton, who had married Ophelia Phenwick. After several lengthly conversations with Captain Ashton, Tinkersly had decided that he would like to try his hand at wooing and winning a Phenwick woman. He had ambition. Besides, after first seeing Isabelle, he was convinced that he would have to go a long way around the world to find a more attractive beauty.

As Tinkersly watched Isabelle leave down the gangplank, he shook his head and hurried to do his chores. His immediate desire was to go to a nearby seaman's tavern and drink himself into a stupor. He could not recall when ever before a woman had affected him as Isabelle had.

A short man with large hips passed Tinkersly. Bearded and wearing glasses, the passenger hesitated only briefly a few feet from the first mate before going directly to the gangplank. Tinkersly hardly noticed the person, and would have dropped the incident from his mind except that that was the first time he had observed the individual during the entire trip. Peculiar.

The entire Stuart Phenwick clan were at the dock to greet the new arrivals from England. Twenty-year-old, remarkably good-looking Danny Phenwick stood beside his pretty, eighteen-year-old sister. They were Stuart's children by his first wife, Marcia. Next to Danny was Alexander, Stuart's son by Barbara Phenwick. Alex had a round appearance and he was stockily built; still, he was pleasant-appearing, with good features. Standing with Ruth, their mother, were thirteen-year-old Richard, eleven-year-old Polly, and nine-year-old Donald. While the younger three bore resemblance to Stuart, the contour of their beauty was directly inherited from Ruth.

As her eyes met Danny's, Isabelle felt herself grow a bright crimson color. She was impressed. However, Danny could not help the seductive expression that perpetually enhanced his beauty. He was doubtlessly a Phenwick, but far more sensually appearing than his father, Stuart. Had anyone been alive at that time who had known the first Daniel Phenwick, they would have instantly seen an amazing likeness in young Danny to his predecessor.

Greetings were exchanged and introductions made. Gregory and Stuart immediately fell into conversation, while the Phenwick children and Ruth surrounded Isabelle with enthusiastic cheerfulness.

Still, as Gregory and Stuart separated themselves from the others, Gregory observed Isabelle and her obvious reactions to Danny. A jolt of apprehension went through him.

"Young Danny has become quite a man," Gregory observed, again looking to where the others were preparing to get into two carriages.

"I'm quite proud of him," Stuart commented, "as I'm certain your sister would have been."

"I trust Danny realizes that he and Isabelle are first cousins," Gregory said.

Stuart laughed. "What a curious statement! Of course Danny knows you are his mother's brother; therefore, Isabelle is—" He laughed again. "And don't you notice how much Ann Marie resembles Marcia? Her similarity to her mother is almost haunting."

"Yes, I can see that," Gregory returned, but could not

96

help noticing his nephew and his daughter's reaction to him.

As Stuart rode alone with Gregory in a separate landau, he observed his brother-in-law. "You *are* concerned about Isabelle, aren't you, Gregory?"

"I am. Oh, I'm just the concerned father of a pretty young daughter, as far as Danny is concerned," Gregory commented. "I'm certain, once they realize they're first cousins, my apprehension as far as that is concerned will be groundless. But, I confess, Stuart, I am deeply distressed—no, that isn't the right word—"

"Distressed?"

"It's Isabelle," Gregory replied. "She has been through hell with the death of Elena. Not that the rest of us haven't had our share of grief and suffering—we have. But doubtless you can see how Isabelle would have been affected."

"Yes, I do."

"Being under such emotional stress," Gregory continued, "I often fear how she might react to ordinary situations. Or should I say *overreact?* I confess, old boy, that I've not been as close to Isabelle in the growing-up years as I might have been. I suppose I felt a bit intimidated about the twins, don't you know? Hence, when Alexandria came along—well, it's difficult to admit one's weaknesses, isn't it?—I freely admit I was able to relate more completely to her. During the trip across, I found myself almost a stranger to Isabelle at times. I was quite inadequate."

"So that is why you *overreact?*"

"I overreact because I truly don't know how to deal with Isabelle's needs," Gregory stated. "I wish Ilene had come along. I will immediately wish to contact Ilene's older sister, Sheila."

"Between Sheila and Joseph," Stuart commented, "I think you will have your problem solved. Sheila is a lovely person—and childless. She'll take Isabelle under her wing as if she were her own."

"And Dr. Joseph Ornby?"

"My cousin has become one of the leading psychologists in this part of the country," Stuart boasted. "He and his brother, Cousin Augustus, have built a reputation. If anyone can assist Isabelle, it will be Joseph."

Gregory thought in silence for a few minutes. Things worried him. "Stuart," he said after some cogitation, "would you be frightfully upset if Isabelle didn't stay at Edward House?"

"Not stay at Edward House?" Stuart questioned. "Are you planning to take her with you to Savannah?"

"No. It's just that—well, Danny—"

Stuart laughed and placed his hand on Gregory's knee. "You will worry about that, won't you? Very well, we'll make other arrangements. My sister-in-law has extended an invitation for both you and Isabelle to stay with her at Triumph House."

"Millijoy?"

"The same. Despite her rather basic nature, Millijoy is very well-meaning. She has a big heart and her generosity cannot be denied," Stuart related. "Oh, I know she has a bit of a reputation around Boston as being a hard woman. But I've seen her stop her carriage to have her driver care for an injured animal. And every Christmas she goes down into the shanty sections and distributes gifts and baskets of food. She doesn't know I know that. Furthermore, she's set up four different scholarships in my late brother's name at different institutions. I would say Millijoy is one of the most compassionate ladies I know."

"Compassionate? Well, that is one thing, isn't it?"

"Ah, I can tell by the sound of your voice that you've heard of her reputation with men," Stuart mentioned.

"Well, yes, there is that," Gregory commented. "I am a

one-woman man, as you well know. Hence, I fear I have an intolerance for persons who—well—you know."

Stuart laughed loudly. "Yes, dear Gregory, I do know. But, human nature being what it is, well, certain things do happen, Millijoy has been widowed a good many years. And she is still a most attractive woman. She certainly has a continuing desire for men. She is never unkind to such individuals; if anything, she treats them far better than they desire, if you ask me."

"But Isabelle—"

"I'm certain Millijoy would do nothing to wrongly influence Isabelle in any way. Far from it. I suspect she's a bit paradoxical when it comes to such things. She's certainly overly protective of Tommy."

"Ah, Tommy!" exclaimed Gregory. "That's another thing."

"Tommy still has a room at Triumph House," Stuart informed him, "but he lives at the conservatory in an adjoining bungalow. The lad, too, needs his independence. Why don't you permit Isabelle to spend time with Millijoy? It might be the best thing in the world for both of them. I'll keep a close watch over Isabelle—and if I detect that Millijoy is influencing her in a negative way, well, I'll step in and make the necessary alterations in arrangements."

Gregory was not certain what to do. He would think the matter over for a while.

As the landau pulled up the circular drive in front of spacious Edward House, Stuart counted three carriages ahead of them. He recognized the two that belonged to the house and the third was a hired vehicle.

"It appears we have more company," Stuart commented.

"More company? Oh, I say," Gregory interjected. "Who do you suppose?"

"I might suspect it was either Millijoy or Joseph and

Sheila," Stuart speculated, "except they wouldn't come in a hired carriage."

As Stuart and Gregory alighted, the hired vehicle pulled away. They could see that it carried no passengers. Gregory led the way up the steps and Stuart held the door for him.

"What do you say to a glass of brandy in the library before we join the others?" Stuart suggested. "They'll be all in a commotion for several minutes."

"Good idea," Gregory agreed.

Stuart opened the first door to the right of the entranceway. The library was oak-paneled with a high ceiling and maroon leather-covered high-back wing chairs. The large table and desk were both of solid oak. Several portraits hung majestically from wires suspended from the molding. While the atmosphere was thick and somewhat somber, it was a place where men enjoyed to gather for drinks and conversation away from the ladies.

Brandy was poured from a crystal decanter. Stuart was about to raise his glass in a welcome toast to Gregory, when he became aware that there was another occupant of the room.

"We're not alone, Gregory. Who is it?" Stuart asked.

A moment later, the tallish, lean, handsome figure of Adam Truff rose from a large chair before the fireplace. Although a faint touch of gray streaked his temple and certain markings of maturity were in his face, Adam looked quite as he always had, youthful and radiant. He stepped with a slight limp, but refused to hobble once he had worked up momentum.

"Stuart!" Adam exclaimed, his arms open.

Stuart quickly went to him and hugged a warm embrace. "My dear Adam! We weren't expecting you."

"That is always when I show up, don't you know," Adam replied. "I like it best that way—to appear unexpectedly. I don't like people to fuss in preparation for my arrival. Besides, I'm one of the family, aren't I?"

"You most certainly are—a very dear and beloved member of the family," Stuart exclaimed. "I couldn't love you more if you were my own brother."

Adam laughed. "And knowing of your brother Gordon's reputation, I don't know whether I should take that as a compliment or not."

Stuart joined the laughter as he clasped him firmly on the shoulder. "You know Gregory Phenwick, of course."

"Gregory," Adam said as he went toward him with an extended hand. "It has been a year or two, hasn't it?"

"Longer than that," Gregory corrected, "if memory serves me."

"Gregory and his daughter Isabelle have just arrived from London for a holiday," Stuart mentioned.

"*Isabelle* is on holiday," Gregory returned. "I'm over here on business. And, come to think of it, Adam, you may be just the person I need for assistance."

"Assistance? In what way?" the extraordinarily handsome gentleman asked.

"I'll be on my way to Savannah next week," Gregory announced, "all going well. Josh has sent me to look in on Jim Phenwick and the floundering Medallion business in the south."

"I can read your mind," Adam interrupted. "That being the case, I must instantly advise you that I have at least a month's work ahead of me."

"For Collier Furniture?" Stuart questioned, passing glasses of brandy to each of the men. He motioned for them to take seats.

"On the contrary," Adam said. "I have trained others in the furniture business. I'm not really a salesman anyway."

"You're an adventurer," Stuart stated.

"I'll not deny that," Adam replied. He turned to Gregory. "I suppose you know of my escapades as a spy during the war."

"Yes, I had heard." Gregory tasted the brandy.

"Seemingly a double spy," Stuart added.

"Well, be that as it may," Adam continued, "not only did I work directly with Stuart Phenwick, but also with some very important government men." He laughed merrily. "I have a reputation." He wagged a finger. "And *not* what you're thinking, Stuart. No, I have a reputation for being a kind of a sleuth."

"A *sleuth?*"

"An undercover person, one who is able to wheedle information," Adam said. "Hence, I'm working—only part-time, of course—as a government agent."

"What in the world—?"

"There appears to be a great amount of illegal smuggling going on into this country from Europe and possibly Asia," Adam informed them. "I'm investigating the situation. And that is all I can tell you at the moment."

"Speaking of investigating," Gregory inserted, "we could use a good man like you over in London. We were badly embezzled last year and the authorities have been able to do nothing to solve the situation. Nothing but dead ends and false leads."

"I can't say that embezzlement is my cup of tea, Gregory," Adam commented, "but—and I might say this with reservations—if I do have the time, I might take a trip to London and have a look about. I suppose Joshua will have all the details."

"Yes, quite." Gregory emptied the glass.

"How long will you be in Boston?" Stuart inquired.

Adam shrugged. "That's impossible to answer at this time."

"You will stay here, of course."

Adam glanced up at Gregory. "It would seem you have a full house as it is."

"We can always make room for you, Adam, you know that," Stuart insisted.

"I have a hotel room for a week," Adam assured him. "You know me and my privacy. After that, well, we'll just have to see how things begin to work out. In the meantime, I came especially to see young Alexander."

"And not me?" Stuart questioned.

"Of course, I came to see you, Stuart. But I must confess that your son and I have become very good friends, and I have a particular desire to see the boy."

"I have four sons," Stuart said.

Gregory looked at Stuart. What was the strange tone he heard in his voice? "*Four* sons?"

Stuart ducked his head. "At the time Uncle Prentise was married to Barbara Callahan—an arrangement insisted upon by Barbara's father—Uncle Prentise became a hopeless invalid. Callahan used his daughter as a spy—supposedly—for the south. That was shortly after Marcia's death—and I was very emotional and very much at loose ends. Well, Barbara and I—we—Barbara was most attractive and extremely feminine and—well, I found it difficult to resist her charms. Milton Callahan was led to believe that Alexander Augustus was sired by Uncle Prentise. That would have been quite an impossibility under the circumstances."

"He's illegitimate?" questioned Gregory.

"He is my son and he is a human being," Stuart stated. "I can love him no less than other of my children. It was Adam who went to Savannah to find the boy."

Gregory glanced from one man to the other. "I think we should get on to settle in, shouldn't we? Isabelle will be wondering where I am. She frets so in her present state of mind."

"Frets?" Adam arched an eyebrow. He exchanged only a fleeting glance with Stuart.

There was a vague family resemblance among the six

of Stuart's children. Danny, the eldest, and Alexander looked enough alike to be full brothers, as did Richard and Donald, who were actually born of the same two parents. Alexander seemed to be a relatively happy boy, somewhat withdrawn at times, but cheerful and very much all boy. The boy had grown to know Stuart and Ruth. He basically accepted them as his parents. But Adam was the one person in the world whom he truly loved. Once aware that Adam was at Edward House, Alexander dropped what he was doing and went in search of the man.

"Why can't *you* be my daddy, Adam?" the boy asked, as he had done before.

"Because I'm not a Phenwick," Adam replied as he squatted before the child and gripped him by the shoulders. "My name is Truff."

"Then couldn't I become a Truff?" Alexander asked.

"I'm afraid not, dear Alex." Adam rose. "Now if you'll go downstairs to the library, you'll find a package with your name on it. It's by the fireplace."

"May I open it down there?"

"I would prefer you brought it up here to your room."

"Whatever you say, Adam." The boy ran from the room.

Adam chuckled to himself. He knew that in the great scheme of things he was never destined to sire a child of his own. Even if he could, he knew he would never be able to feel any closer to a child than he did to Alexander.

A door closed in an adjoining room. Adam glanced to the wall. Did he hear the sound of sobbing? Going to the wall, he listened. The distinct sound of sobbing came through the wall.

Leaving the room, Adam went next door and tapped lightly before entering. He stood in the open doorway. "Is there anything I can do for you?"

Isabelle looked up. Tears were streaking down her

face. Now a look of alarm and uncertainty. "Who—who are you?"

"My name is Adam Truff, and I'm *practically* a Phenwick," he replied with a large smile. "Who are you?"

"My name is Isabelle, and I *am* a Phenwick," she returned.

"And why is such a pretty young lady like yourself crying?" he asked.

"I—I don't know. I suppose I've become homesick—or something like that."

"Homesick? But you just arrived in Boston."

"I know." She put a handkerchief to her eyes. "I'm not really homesick, you know. I just said that. Fact is, I don't ever wish to go to my home in London again. But I confess I don't feel quite at home here at Edward House."

"Not at home here?"

"I just don't feel I belong here," Isabelle said.

"I know how that can be, Miss Isabelle," Adam remarked. "Some places immediately feel like home, and others—well, I suspect there are those in which I could never even relax a minute. Although I don't like to hurt Stuart's feelings, frankly, I feel more at home at Triumph House than I do here."

"Triumph House?"

"I'll take you there one day, if you'll permit me." Adam beamed such an intriguing smile that he knew he had won Isabelle in that moment.

"Adam! Ad-am!" called Alexander from the next room.

"It seems I'm being paged," Adam said with a broad grin. "Will you excuse me, Miss Isabelle?"

"Certainly, Mr. Truff." She curtsied and walked to the door after he left the room. She was standing in the open doorway, leaning her head against the frame when she sighed deeply.

"Don't tell me you've already put foolish thoughts in your head about Adam Truff," Ann Marie said as she came up behind her cousin.

"Oh, Ann Marie, you startled me!" Isabelle turned around to face the pretty dark-eyed beauty.

"Were Adam Truff the marrying kind," Ann Marie added, "he would have chosen a wife long ago. Miss Ruth once had a terrible crush on him. He nearly broke her heart before Daddy came along."

"Miss Ruth? I thought she was—"

"My own mother died a long time ago," Ann Marie started. "I tolerate Miss Ruth because she is married to my father. But I believe she only married Daddy because Adam didn't want her."

"What a terrible thing to say, Ann Marie," exclaimed Isabelle. "I'm certain Miss Ruth dearly loves your father."

"Does she?" Ann Marie raised an eyebrow. "You are very naïve, aren't you, Isabelle? I don't much care for other girls,—certainly not my half-sister, Polly. I pray that someday I will meet a wildly sensual man who will ask me to run away with him—and I'll do it, too. Then Polly can be the Phenwick woman, if *that* is what she wants so badly!"

"Ann Marie!"

Ann Marie quickly lifted her skirts and scurried down the hallway toward her own room. A moment later the door slammed.

Isabelle stared in the direction her cousin had gone. She was certain that she did not wish to remain in that house any longer than it was absolutely necessary. Turning again toward Alexander's room, she stared at the closed door. What was the singular feeling that had come over her upon meeting Adam Truff? No man had ever caused her to react quite like that before.

CHAPTER TEN

Hurt and bewildered by Ann Marie's attitude toward her, Isabelle decided that she did not wish to remain at Edward House any longer than was absolutely necessary. On the second day they were in Boston, Gregory took her to the home of Joseph and Sheila Ornby, her maternal aunt and uncle. Sheila embraced the girl and welcomed her into her home. Large and graying, Joseph was hospitable and pleasant, but a little reserved. He studied Isabelle, then cast a peculiar glance in Gregory's direction.

While the Ornbys' home was well built and in a good neighborhood, it lacked the opulent splendor of Edward House. Sheila was a good housekeeper, and the place was spotless. Since she had so much time on her hands, Ilene's eldest sister preferred not having others cleaning about her house. She was quite capable of doing it herself. The house had four bedrooms upstairs, two of which were used for other things than sleeping, but they doubled as guest rooms. It was a comfortable home, neat and well scrubbed, yet not in the least bit ostentatious.

While Sheila showed her niece around and out into the garden where she had planted spring vegetables, Gregory went into the study with **Dr. Joseph Ornby**. The Ornbys had been informed of the Carrickfergus tragedy from emotional reports sent shortly after it happened. Gregory filled Joseph in on the details. He especially dwelled on the state of mind Isabelle appeared to be in and how difficult it was for her to adjust to life without her twin sister.

"Perhaps she will consider coming to stay with us for awhile," Joseph commented at last. "Maybe I can help her in some way."

"You cannot bring Elena back," Gregory said. "I fear that nothing else will revert Isabelle to her old ways."

"Were her old ways so enviable?" Joseph asked.

"I beg your pardon?"

"Quite so." Joseph smiled and rubbed a hand over his broad face. "We have a curious way of thinking that the 'old ways' were the best, when they were actually pretty dismal. I wonder if Isabelle was truly happy in her life as an identical twin."

"She loved Elena deeply."

"I've no doubt of that—*but* was she happy?" Joseph asked.

"I'm afraid the question confuses me," Gregory admitted.

"Think back to your childhood, Gregory," Joseph suggested, his hands folded beneath his chin as he sat back and scrutinized his wife's brother-in-law. "You were deeply attached to your sister, Marcia, were you not?"

"Of course I was."

"Precisely. But weren't you just a bit envious of the fact that she was older than you? When Susannah first found and became acquainted with the two of you, there was a large amount of rivalry. And, I suspect, there was a time when you feared that you wouldn't be adopted along with Marcia. Conversely, I suspect Marcia was not altogether pleased that Susannah and Lex decided to adopt the *two* of you. Sibling rivalry is quite common."

"Marcia and I weren't twins," Gregory objected.

"True. But that is exactly the point I'm trying to make," Joseph commented as he recrossed his legs. "If sibling rivalry is so apparent among two children of different ages, can you begin to imagine what it must be like between twins? Funnily enough, I suspect such competition is less on the surface in the case of twins than it is with other children. The fact of the matter is, Isabelle has been miraculously freed from a binding situation, a condition almost impossible to escape from under normal circumstances. I suspect a complete transformation is taking place within her. It is a subtle thing, nothing that pops out overnight with blatant indications. I rather suspect it is a bit like having a leg amputated: It takes time to readjust to getting on without it."

"I confess you have me befuddled, Joseph," Gregory said. "What is it *precisely* that you're driving at?"

"Isabelle is simply going through a period of change and adjustment," Joseph explained. "If we can help her through this difficult time, it may make her burden a bit easier. In the time following the loss of a close relative, one's thoughts are often directed to their memory—or perhaps speculation about what they may be enduring since making that transition. It is at such moments that those who are very close to the one who has passed often feel as if they are haunted by the memory of the deceased. And there are those who have insisted that the departed have put in ghostly appearances. I have met several remarkable spiritualists in the recent past who have absolutely amazed me with their ability to contact the spirits of the dead. It's an eerie adventure at best."

"I shouldn't think it would be in the least bit pleasant," Gregory inserted, a tremble reacting through him.

"On the contrary," Joseph assured him, "there are those who take great delight in knowing that their dear ones are safely on *the other side*. The remarkable thing

109

that I have noted during such sessions is that the departed appear to be spendidly happy in their new estate. That reassurance is helpful to many of those left in earthly form."

"You're not suggesting——?"

"Suggesting?" Joseph blinked as a smile moved his lips. "My dear Gregory, I'm suggesting nothing. But with your permission, I would like to introduce this information to Isabelle and see how she reacts to it."

"I don't feel she is ready for such an experience."

"Isn't she? I wonder." Joseph laughed. "Well, then, I take that as a refusal of permission."

"Not ncessarily," Gregory replied. "I confess, Joseph, I don't know what more to do for Isabelle. You have dealt with such matters far more than I. I will leave Isabelle in your capable hands. I cannot tolerate the thought of her being unhappy, or frantic with apprehension about life. After all, she is the one left living. There *must* be a reason for that."

Joseph cleared his throat as he stretched his legs out before him. "Then you *are* giving me permission to work with Isabelle?"

"Yes." Gregory looked away. "I'll be leaving for Savannah next Monday. I have no idea how long I will be away. I realize that Isabelle needs help."

Gregory and Isabelle spent three days at the Ornby home. During that time Isabelle became fairly well acquainted with her aunt Sheila, who she found to be quite different from her mother. Sheila still spoke with a slight Irish brogue, while Ilene had completely eliminated it from her speech. Sheila was a simple, honest woman with no great ambition but to be a good wife and keep a good house; Ilene, while an honest person, had become a little more complex in her attitudes toward life. She was a Phenwick woman and the mistress of an elegant house in

110

London. To compare the two sisters, one would have to realize that both Sheila and Ilene had grown a considerable distance apart from their humble childhood as daughters of a poor Irish immigrant family.

"I believe I would really rather stay here," Isabelle said on the day she was scheduled to leave the Ornbys', "than to return to Edward House."

"Sure now, what's got into ye, lass?" Sheila asked. " 'Tis a lovely place, th' Edward House. I've nay bin in it much, but I've passed it often. Dr. Ornby an' meself have bin guests there a time or two."

"Does that mean I would not be welcome to stay here?" Isabelle asked.

"O' course ye would be welcome t' come an' stay here for th' rest o' yer days, if'n ye were a mind, lass. Ye should know that without askin'." Sheila hugged her. "I've niver had a child o' me own. Th' good Lord deprived me o' that."

Something in Sheila's manner startled Isabelle, and she felt herself pushing away from her. Her aunt got an expression on her face that reminded her of Elena.

"I'll come to visit you often," Isabelle promised.

"When ye come, bring yer thin's so ye kin stay a few days," Sheila suggested. A ring in her laughter was also similar to one which Isabelle had heard in her twin's voice. Wasn't it natural that certain traits would pass from aunts to nieces?

The Sea Lantern Tavern was a few doors from Long Wharf in an area that was largely populated by seamen and their friends. The atmosphere of the tavern was far from elegant. The smelly, rowdy ambience was hardly the place for gentlemen of position to be found. Because of the clientele and the unsavory activity that went on there, Adam Truff disguised himself in seaman's attire and contrived a swagger and a general attitude that he hoped would make him appear to be quite at home in the place. He had even omitted shaving for two days in hopes of giving himself a scruffy, unkempt look. A wool knit cap on his head, a heavy black jacket, worn and somewhat tattered trousers, and scuffed boots comprised his costume. The horizontal blue and black stripes of a soiled skin-tight shirt barely appeared until after he removed the heavy jacket. He had stood at the bar for nearly fifteen minutes before a table was vacated on the side of the room near the front window. He ordered a second drink and took it to the table.

A fight developed from a discussion about a certain young lady of dubious character. The beefy tavern-keeper quickly put a stop to the fracas with powerful persuasive muscular force. He commanded respect.

Adam watched and listened. When he was on such missions, he usually waited until he saw a seaman on the brink of inebriation; then, pretending to be in a similar situation, he would strike up a conversation, buy a drink or two, and begin probing for information. He was clever at that, since he had made an art of it during the Civil War.

Adam's attention went to a tall, nice looking youngish man, who was dressed in a tight dark sweater and trousers. His boots clicked with determination in his walk. Bareheaded and without a jacket, the particular seaman stood above the other men. There was no mistaking the fact of his occupation, especially when he ordered three drinks and downed them one after another.

Adam finished his drink and wedged his way through the crowd to order another at the bar. He stood directly beside the newly arrived man, who was one or two inches taller than Adam. A well-calculated jab of his arm hit against the sailor's and caused his drink to slosh. Adam immediately apologized and offered to buy him another.

"Yeah. Okay, it was an accident," the sailor acknowledged. "But you can buy me a drink, if you like."

"I owe it to you."

"What ship are you on?"

"I'm looking to find one," Adam replied.

"What do you do?"

"I'm just an ordinary seaman."

"I'm first mate on the *Twin Dolphins*," the man said as he downed the contents of the glass. "Tinkersly's my name. Curtis Tinkersly."

"I'm Jack Adams," Adam introduced. He had papers indentifying himself with that name. "I have a table over there. Why don't I buy a bottle and we go over there and drink? I've been trudging around town all day trying to find a ship to get outa this hole."

"Why not?" Tinkersly commented. He carried the glasses while Adam bought and handled the bottle. A pitcher of water was on the unsteady table.

"If you don't care what you do," Tinkersly said some time later, "I might could get you on the *Twin Dolphins*."

"What line is she?"

"Medallion. I reckon you've heard of the Phenwicks of Boston, haven't you?"

"Can't say that I have," Adam lied.

Tinkersly got sullen. "I wish I hadn't. God, will I ever be glad to get back to sea!"

"What's the problem?" Adam curiously asked as he filled his new acquaintance's glass.

Tinkersly's eyes had become red and glistening. "A woman! Lord, I thought I was too old to fall for a damn woman again."

"You're not *that* old."

"Don't get me wrong," Tinkersly boasted. "I've had my share of women from here to China and back. I never get attachments—not long-term ones, anyway. But I always leave the door open in case I go back to the same port and can't find anyone else."

"What happened here this time?"

"It didn't happen *here*," Tinkersly explained. "It happened aboard the *Twin Dolphins*. She was a Phenwick woman. I had met different ones of the Phenwick ladies before. But there was something different about this one. At first she was remote and indifferent. Then, that night while I was standing watch and the sea was calm and the moon was nearly full, she came up on deck and stared at me for the longest time. When I dared, I went down to speak with her. I called her Miss Phenwick, but she insisted I use her given name: *Isabelle*."

"Isabelle?" Adam sat forward. That was not the information he was searching for, but it whetted his curiosity. "Isabelle?"

"All the dreams I had had about her were suddenly in my arms," Tinkersly said, slurring his words. "I mean, from the minute I laid eyes on her, I began getting excited interest." He went into explicit detail. "It's a wonder we didn't go clear off course and land in Bar Harbor, or New York, or goodness knows where else." He laughed drunkenly.

"Are you certain you were with *Isabelle* Phenwick?" Adam asked when Tinkersly paused to drink.

"I know it was her." Tinkersly wiped his hand across his mouth. "The next day, she hardly acknowledged my presence—and then she was so indifferent to me that at first I thought she was putting on an act. But that night again, about the same time, she came up to where I was on watch. I questioned her about her attitude of that day, and she said she simply had to be careful because she was traveling with her father. That night was more frantic than the night before. The next day I understood her indifference—or at least I *thought* I did."

"How many nights did you meet like that?" Adam questioned.

"Six in all," Tinkersly related. "The last night before we came into Boston Harbor was the most—well—use your imagination. I asked her if I could see her while the ship was docked. She told me that I could not—and that I would probably not ever be with her again. Furthermore, she said that if I were to encounter her on the street or anywhere in Boston, she would undoubtedly ignore me, and she asked me not to draw attention to the fact that we had known each other."

"You complied?"

"I had no other choice." Tinkersly emptied the glass. "But, do you know, I believe I have come as close to falling in love as I ever will in this lifetime? Could I ache so badly inside if I weren't— Oh, hell, what's the use of going on about it?"

Adam put his hand to Tinkersly's shoulder and patted.

A large, burly man stomped his way into the tavern. He grunted and puffed as he scanned the crowd. Spying the object of his scrutiny, he pushed his way through the drunken men, tossing and shoving them aside as he reached the man he was after. A moment later, his beefy fist connected with the man's face and a brawl was under way.

Tinkersly was about to join in the festivities when a man's body came hurling toward the table where he and Adam were seated. The impact of the man knocked Tinkersly back into a sitting position, and the intruder fell across the table, spilling drinks as he did.

"Well, I'll be cussed!" Tinkersly stated as he lifted the man from the table and was about to punch him back in the direction from which he had come. "Derrick!"

"Do you know this man?" Adam asked.

"He sailed with me, didn't ya, Derrick?" Tinkersly said.

115

"Yeah." Derrick shook his head as if trying to get free of the stars that were twinkling inside it. "Curtis?"

"Have a drink, Derr—" Tinkersly belched.

Adam went to the bar to purchase another bottle of whiskey. The fight was beginning to die down, but still a major amount of commotion was taking place. Twice he got bumped on his way to where the assistant barman was waiting.

"Who's th' guy?" Derrick asked.

"A sailor," Tinkersly replied. "I'm gonna try t' git him on th' *Twin Whatchmacallits*. He's a good ol' boy."

Derrick squinted through the crowd to get another look at Adam.

"This is—what's your name again?" Tinkersly said when Adam returned.

"Jack Adams."

"This is—ah—" Tinkersly shook his head.

"Molden. Derrick Molden."

Adam offered his hand, but Derrick viewed it contemptuously and reached to pour himself a drink. Molden's attitude caused Adam to become suspicious. He would cleverly get to know him better and attempt to win his confidence. He would be patient and calculating. Some innate perception told him that he should be wary with Derrick Molden.

Isabelle had not felt up to partying that night. The Phenwicks had been invited to the home of Mr. and Mrs. Wilfred Quigly. The invitation included both Danny and Ann Marie. The Quiglys had a daughter whom they were hoping might interest Stuart's eldest son. Pauline Quigly had been so impressed with John Phenwick that he was invited along, too. Her reasoning was that if their Diane didn't impress Danny, she might well intrigue his—oh, dear, it was so complicated! How could a handsome young man like John Phenwick be the great-uncle of

Danny Phenwick, who was no more than ten years his junior? Still, both young men were Phenwicks, and that was what inspired Pauline.

What Pauline Quigly did not realize was that Ann Marie Phenwick had long had a curious interest in her great-uncle. Such an avid interest, in fact, that twice she had blatantly thrown herself at him. John was understanding, and dutifully treated her as an uncle should. Ann Marie secretly accepted the challenge.

Gregory also attended the Quigly party. He appeared ill at ease, and even more so when he discovered that Pauline had partnered him with Millijoy Phenwick for the evening.

Initially the idea of staying away from the Quigly party had struck Isabelle as being desirable. After all, most of the people present would be complete strangers to her. Nor was she in the mood to socialize. Yet when she found herself virtually alone in the rambling, monstrous old Edward House, she began to have second thoughts. Many of the servants were off that night, and the few that remained at the house were older and retired early.

Isabelle had found a book to read and had donned her dressing robe over her stylish nightgown. Fifty strokes of the brush made her hair glisten. Three lamps were lit in the room on the second floor at the back of the house. She extinguished one, but decided it was more comforting to have it lit.

Propped in bed with two pillows and a bolster, a lightweight comforter over her, Isabelle prepared to read. She soon found her thoughts were scattering as her eyes ran over words. Going back, she would reread certain passages. Try as she might, she could not get into the story.

An owl hooted outside the slightly open window. Isabelle thought to get up and have a look, but quickly reconsidered.

"Is-a-belle! Is-a-belle!"

"Moorduke?" Isabelle questioned as she sat up. "Is that you?" She peered curiously about the room. The leprechaun had not put in an appearance for several days, and she had thought that he had remained aboard the ship. In a way she hoped that he had. Yet there was something about him—*if he actually existed at all*—that fascinated her. She got on the floor on all fours and peered under the bed. No sign of him. Of course, he could still be invisible and might be playing a prank on her by calling that way.

"Is-a-belle! Oh, Is-a-belle!"

The voice was coming from outside. If this was Moorduke's idea of a game, she did not think it very enjoyable.

"What is it you want of me, you silly imp?" she questioned, rising and sitting back on the bed. "I'll not play any of your foolish games tonight. Do you hear me?"

"Is-a-belle! Come with me, Is-a-belle!"

A shudder of fear climbed up her spine. That was not Moorduke's voice. Yet it was so very familiar.

From the window, Isabelle could see the wisteria arbor silhouetted in moonlight. The moon was positioned on the opposite side of the house, but its glow filled the back yard. She saw no one.

A short while later, after she had gotten back into bed and had turned out two of the lamps, Isabelle heard her name being called again. Once more she went to the window, gazed out, then closed it tightly and drew the curtains. Unless the voice was in her imagination, she would shut it out. Or would she?

CHAPTER ELEVEN

A pillow over her head and buried under as many covers as she could find, Isabelle lay trembling in the bed. A frantic feeling of fear was rushing through her. If only she could contact one of the servants. An old person would be comfort even if they were not protection. But protection from what? What had she to fear? Someone was calling her name. Or was that merely her imagination? Doubtless the thing she feared most was the fact that the voice was very much like her own—a voice she had known from childhood—a voice that was silenced as a result of an accident in Carrickfergus, North Ireland.

"Is-a-belle!"

The voice was no longer coming from outside the house. It now seemed as if it were coming from the hallway outside her room. She cowered in the bed, curling herself into a tiny ball as chills went through her.

"Is-a-belle!"

"No!" she whispered and bit her finger to keep from making further vocal sounds. "No, oh, no!" she all but sobbed.

A faint tapping came at the door. *"Is-a-belle. It's me. Let me in."*

"No," she gasped, now fully aware of who belonged to the voice.

"Do you hear me, Isabelle? Let me in."

"No!" Isabelle cried. "Go away! Leave me alone!"

Another tap on the door. The doorknob turned. *"Is-a-belle, come join me. Do you hear me, Is-a-belle?"*

"Leave me be! Leave me be!" Isabelle shouted.

"We belong together, Is-a-belle. We were born together. It is wrong for us to be separated now."

Deathlike silence followed.

Isabelle remained under the pillow and covers for nearly fifteen minutes. Her ears were tuned to the tiniest sound. Her nerves had become raw with frantic fear.

Then she began to feel extraordinarily warm. She pushed off covers and the pillow over her head. Within a few minutes she was gasping as if she were suffocating. Tearing open the ribbon that held her dressing gown about her throat, she panted for air. The room was unbearably stuffy.

With effort Isabelle lunged to the window and raised it enough to permit a refreshing inflow of air. Beads of perspiration had come to her brow, and a sick feeling was in the pit of her stomach. Opening the window wider, she stuck her head out into the night air. Once she had filled her lungs, she went back to the ewer on the dresser and poured herself some water. She drank as if her throat were parched. Then she braced herself against the dresser as she endeavored to calm her nerves.

"Is-a-belle! Isabelle!"

The voice was coming from outside the window, down below in the yard. She pivoted about and hurried to where she had been, fruitlessly attempting to hide behind the curtains that were blowing into the room.

"Is-a-belle!"

"Elena, leave me alone!" Isabelle screamed as she clutched to the curtains, pushing herself tightly against the wall.

"Come with me, Isabelle. Come . . . Is-a-belle."

Isabelle wanted to slam the window closed. Her hands froze on the edge of it. She was standing fully exposed in the window.

"Is-a-belle!"

Isabelle put her forehead against the cold window pane, her eyes closed. Why couldn't she move the window? Then she opened her eyes and stared down into the yard below. Was the phantomlike figure she saw below in a grayish dressing robe the ghost of her dead sister? Or was she experiencing a kind of hallucination? What was a ghost but a hallucination, anyway?

"Is-a-belle—you're being foolish. Come down and speak with me. You wouldn't let me into your room. The least you can do is come down to me."

"Elena?"

"Why do you doubt your senses?"

"Elena, don't do this to me. Go back to your grave and leave me in peace."

"There is another grave beside mine, waiting for you, Isabelle. Papa was very considerate about that. He felt that if we were together in life, we should be together— after life."

"Go away, Elena, go away!"

"Come and see me up close so you will be certain that it is me."

"I know it is you. I know you've come to haunt me. But why? It wasn't my fault that the accident occurred in Carrickfergus. You can't blame me for that, Elena—you can't!"

The spectrelike figure beckoned with a hypnotic gesture.

Isabelle slammed the window closed and hurriedly

made her way to the bed, where she fell across it into a torrent of sobbing. "Oh, God, help me! Help me! Am I going mad?"

"Isabelle! Isabelle! Isabelle!" The voice was muffled, but it penetrated her eardrums.

Isabelle could still see the hand beckoning to her. Even with her eyes closed, it was there in her mind!

Slowly she picked herself up from the bed. Her brow felt feverish. In a daze and listless, she moved to the door. Turning the key, she pulled the door wide and went into the hallway. Drifting spectrelike herself, she wandered to the railing and to the top of the stairs. She leaned heavily on the banister as she aimlessly took the steps one at a time.

Lamps were burning in the downstairs hallway. Isabelle hesitated at the foot of the stairs. To her left was the library, to her right, the ballroom. Behind her was the hallway leading back to the parlor, the dining room, the kitchen, and the servants' quarters. She reasoned that her initial thought in descending the stairs was to go find one of the servants. Yet she had only a vague notion that their rooms were somewhere beyond the kitchen. Where? Before her was the door leading outside. The night. The street. Where would she go? She did not know her way around Boston.

A moment of courage possessed her. She eyed the door to the ballroom. A lamp was kept burning in there at night, in the window. It would not be dark.

What compulsion drew her to the ballroom? The grand piano with a silk scarf over it was in the far corner of the immense room. The lamp was near it. Isabelle could see her reflection in the many mirrors that lined the walls. Her eyes barely brushed over the huge portrait at the end of the room. She started for the piano. Why? Then her attention went to the French doors toward the rear of the room on the side wall. She had been in that room before, and knew that the doors opened onto a terrace and ultimately led to the back yard.

As Isabelle started for the French doors, the giant crystal chandelier over the center of the room began to make a tinkling sound. She glanced up, but turned her attention back to the doors. The crystal baubles seemed to ring louder and the entire fixture began to rock back and forth. She spun around as she stared up at it. What was that peculiarly sweet fragrance? Where was it coming from?

Again Isabelle headed toward the doors.

"Don't go out there!" The woman's voice was a thundering command.

Isabelle swept her eyes over the old painting on the wall. Reason told her that sound could not have come from it. Then she looked back at the French doors. There was a brightness beyond them. And in the brightness she saw her reflection. Yet, how could the reflection in the panes of a window be clearer than her reflection had been in the mirrors? Two feet from the door she hesitated and came to a full stop. By then the chandelier was clanging as if it were sounding an alarm.

Isabelle's reflected image glanced to the chandelier. Then, taking a posture entirely different from the one Isabelle had taken, her likeness beckoned to her.

"Don't go out there, I said. And I mean it!"

Isabelle pivoted about in the opposite direction to stare at the stoic likeness of Augusta Phenwick captured on the canvas. She glanced back at the French doors to observe her likeness observing the painting, too, with a curious, confused expression.

The scent of violets became so pungent that it was nearly overwhelming. Isabelle tore at the gown about her throat. The ribbons were still untied, but she felt as if she were being strangled.

"I have chosen you, Isabelle Phenwick. Listen to me!"

Frantic, confused and terrified, Isabelle looked once more at the noisy chandelier, then at the likeness of Augusta, and finally back at the doors before she lost consciousness. Limply she fell into a sprawled position on the floor.

"Why don't they listen to me anymore? Have they forgotten who I am? Or have I simply lost my power? At least I can still manage the violets. And that chandelier has never let me down. I'm so glad Patricia moved it from the old house when she built this new one." The chandelier baubles jingled again. *"I know she heard me. How else could I have kept her from going outside without scaring her into a faint? Tsk, tsk. Pity."*

The Quiglys' mansion was large and spacious. Their ballroom was not near the size of the one at Edward House, but it was sufficiently grand and accommodating. A small musical ensemble, a sextet of strings and piano, played lilting waltzes and lively polkas. Gregory danced three dances with Pauline Quigly, who found him fascinating. Ruth joined Gregory for two, and she waltzed four times with Stuart.

Diane Quigly and Danny Phenwick made a handsome couple as they danced most of the dances together. Dreamy-eyed and blushing with innocence, Diane appeared quite infatuated with the young scion of the Phenwick family. Danny did not quite share her enthusiasm. And, when the opportunity arose, he accepted the chance to dance with other young ladies. He even condescended to a spritely polka with Ann Marie.

Ann Marie had saucily persuaded John Phenwick to dance with her. But the handsome young attorney insisted that he was not a dancer and felt as if his feet were wrapped in burlap stuffed with goose feathers.

"You know, my dear," Wilfred Quigly observed to his wife, "with all due respects to Daniel Phenwick—and he is a gregarious, sparkling lad—it would seem to me that John Phenwick would be a far better prospect for our Diane's hand."

"John Phenwick? The lawyer?" Pauline questioned. She raised a silver lorgnette to examine him from a distance. "My dear, John Phenwick is all of thirty, and our Diane is just eighteen."

"Twelve years is a good space between husband and wife," Wilfred returned. "How do you expect a woman to respect a man who is practically her age?"

"Daniel is gay and flamboyant," Pauline argued. "Every woman in the place has eyed him conspicuously all evening. He's a prize."

"Women have eyed John Phenwick, too," Wilfred countered. "I noticed you gave him the once-over more than once."

"True, but look at the difference in Diane's age and mine."

"I'm well aware of that difference, Pauline."

"For that matter—would you think it—well—unladylike for me to suggest a dance with John Phenwick."

"I suppose it depends on with whom you suggest it."

"Myself, of course."

"With John Phenwick?" A worried expression came to Wilfred's face. He wrinkled his nose and blinked. Well aware of his wife's sometimes indiscreet nature, he finally shrugged and told her to do as she pleased.

John Phenwick had stepped onto the veranda for a breath of fresh air after an accelerated polka with Ann Marie.

"*Did* you come out for fresh air," Pauline Quigly asked as she came up behind him, "or to escape your niece's persistant attention?"

"I beg your pardon? Oh, Mrs. Quigly," John said as he blotted his brow with his handkerchief. "Ann Marie is quite a dancer. And she is my *great*-niece, not my niece."

"Whatever she is, she *is* lovely," Pauline commented. "Are you enjoying yourself?"

"I know it is proper to tell the hostess that I am," John remarked, "but if you want to know the truth—"

"Spare me the truth! It's never flattering."

"Do you wish to be flattered, Mrs. Quigly?"

"I would be better flattered if you would stop calling me Mrs. Quigly. My name is Pauline." She stepped closer to him as he stood at the railing.

"I have a brother named Paul. Same root: Paul—Pauline." He laughed. "Named for a saint. Paul's in California—San Francisco. He writes that he would like me to come out and join him."

"Is your brother Paul married?" Her hand lightly brushed against his arm.

"Both my brothers, Thad and Paul, are married now," John replied casually. He was aware of the lady's tactics, but he could play games, too.

"You and Daniel Louis are the playboys, then?" she questioned, suggestion in her voice.

"We're both still bachelors," John returned. "I can only speak for myself, and I don't consider myself a playboy. Hardly." He chuckled amusedly.

"I read Daniel Louis's name in the paper all the time," Pauline stated. "And I've heard the gossip. Naturally, I thought that quality—or should I say *tendency* ran in the Phenwick family."

"*What* tendency?"

"Don't be coy, John. We're both adults. It seems funny that you've gone so long without marrying," Pauline said, insinuation in her voice.

"Well, as a matter of fact, I have been waiting for my distant cousin to grow up," John contrived. "We're not really related biologically, you know. Her father was adopted by another distant cousin, who was really daughter of my great-grandmother's adopted son."

"I beg your pardon? I didn't follow all of that."

"I don't believe I could repeat it, Mrs. Quigly." John smiled broadly. "If you don't mind, I'll excuse myself and get something to drink. The dancing raised quite a thirst."

Before Pauline could object, he was gone. "The daughter of a father who was adopted by his distant cousin? Was that the way he put it? Goodness, how confusing!"

"My dear," Wilfred Quigly announced, emerging from the shadows, "I suspect he was referring to that young girl whose twin was killed in the accident."

"Wilfred!" exclaimed Pauline. "Were you spying on me?"

"If I was, my dear, it was a pretty dull show," he returned. "Come, dearest, they're playing a slow waltz, and we really should dance at least one dance together."

An uneasy sensation had come over John Phenwick almost immediately after leaving the presence of Pauline Quigly. He could not explain the sense of urgency, nor his sudden desire to leave the party. He went directly to encounter Stuart.

"I don't want to say a lot of farewells and that sort of thing," John explained. "I just want to leave. Will you thank the Quiglys for me and relate to Ann Marie that I was a bit under the weather?"

"Are you not feeling well," Stuart asked.

"It's just a—well—I suppose you could call it a restless feeling that's come over me," John said. "I guess there are servants at Edward House, aren't there? I left a package I need to pick up for tomorrow."

"You know how to get through the side door through the ballroom if you can't rouse anyone," Stuart replied. "Chances are, since only the older help is at the house, you won't be able to get their attention." He put his hand to John's shoulder. "Very well, uncle, I'll give your apologies to everyone."

"We must have lunch one of these days, nephew," John returned. "I've things I wish to discuss with you."

John hurriedly left the house on Beacon Hill. It was only a short walk to Edward House in the next street, two blocks down. Since he had come with Stuart and Ruth, he would walk.

A lovely night, starry and spring warm. John sprinted his long legs over the slab walks. Persons on bicycles were riding about, and walkers were out for strolls. Birds rustled in trees and the green scent of grass was in the air. Despite the pleasantness of the night, John was ill at ease. At one point he thought he was being followed, but when he glanced back, the street behind him was empty. What a strange foreboding.

Upon reaching Edward House, he went immediately to the left side of it and to the terrace onto which the ballroom opened. A key was kept in a crockery pot underneath a potted fern. While he was putting the plant back into place, he sensed that he was being observed. He strode to the corners of the terrace and gazed in all directions into the yard. Nobody.

Not completely satisfied that he was alone, but convinced that if someone was there they were well hidden, John applied the key to the lock. The door swung open with a faint whine. Upon entering, he automatically glanced at the portrait of Augusta. As a boy, he had been told that his face resembled that of the lady in the portrait. He could not detect even the slightest likeness.

At first he thought the figure on the floor was merely a pile of clothing or draperies that had been left by the cleaning people. Then he recognized the outline of a person. Seconds later he was on his knees examining her.

Isabelle responded to the smooth touch of his hand upon her brow. She gazed weakly up into his shadowed face. "John? John Phenwick?"

John smiled as he held her. "What ever are you doing in the ballroom—and unconscious?"

"I don't really know, John. I seem to have—that is—oh, yes, I recall." Isabelle seemed confused. "I don't think you would understand if I told you."

"What makes you think I wouldn't?"

"Because I don't understand myself," Isabelle replied.

"Can you stand up?"

"I think I can."

John helped her to her feet.

"I feel a bit peculiar—dizzy."

"Would you care for a glass of brandy?"

"I don't usually take spirits, but—yes, I think that might help."

John took her arm. "We only have to go across the hallway to the library. Stuart keeps very good brandy. I generally don't imbibe, but an occasional brandy, or a port offers me a bit of relaxation after a tedious day."

In the library, John poured two glasses of brandy and took them to Isabelle, who had taken a seat in a wooden library chair.

"Now would you mind explaining what you were doing passed out in the library?" John asked.

"I really would mind; you know. It's too embarrassing," she said softly, avoiding his eyes. "You see, I fear I am losing my mind."

"I beg your pardon."

"It's quite true, you know," she sighed. "It's been progressively getting this way ever since the accident in Carrickfergus."

"When your sister—?"

"I don't like to think about it, but the scene keeps playing over and over again in my mind," Isabelle explained.

"Of course, such a tragedy would persist in memory," John argued, "but that doesn't mean you're losing your mind."

"Doesn't it?" Isabelle spoke softly. Then she related precisely what she had experienced that night.

"I suspect you *were* dreaming, including the part of thinking you heard old Augusta speak," John said with a touch of amusement.

"Then how did I get downstairs and on the floor of the library if it was all a dream?" she questioned.

"I believe there is a logical answer to that," John replied. "I just don't seem to know what it is at the moment. Oh, I know the Phenwicks are allegedly haunted by their ghosts, superstitions and all that rot—but I don't put much stock in it. Only a fool would."

"Do you think me a fool, John?"

"No, of course not."

"And you don't think I'm verging on insanity?"

He laughed. "Not in the least," John stated. "Our minds do have ways of playing tricks on us at times. You were tired, perhaps exhausted, and all by yourself in an old house. That alone would set anyone's imagination to working. I suspect the memory of your sister is still very much in your mind. Her voice, which you say was identical to yours, is very familiar—so familiar that your own thoughts could reflect it. As to your experience in the library, I suspect you had worked yourself into such an emotional state that—"

"That I imagined all of it?" she fired.

"That is the opinion I am left to reach."

"But I did *not* imagine it!" she all but screeched. "I did *not!*"

"Whether you did or you didn't," John added, "I suggest that you don't tell anyone else about what happened. They are liable to get some funny ideas about you, if you continue passing around such tales."

Isabelle rose and firmly put the glass on the table. "I'll go to my room now."

"I'll accompany you."

"That won't be necessary, John," she stated defiantly.

"But I insist."

"And I insist you don't."

"Why?"

"Because I—" She began to tremble. "I've got to go before I begin crying."

John caught her in his arms and held her as steady as he could. "Now just breathe deeply several times and think yourself calm."

The emotions she had been experiencing were suddenly changed as new feelings were superimposed over her former ones. Men had touched her before, always in a gentlemanly, respectful way. Never had they held quite as he was holding her. Her eyes went from his hands, up his arm to his face. She remembered their first meeting and the feelings she had had then. She smiled helplessly and fell against him.

John held her, rocking gently from side to side. As she sighed and he felt her giving in more to him, ridding herself of her cares and permitting herself just to be held, a sudden realization came to him. He liked the feel of Isabelle in his arms. For that matter, he liked her very much as a person. He could not explain how or when it happened, he simply knew that it had—and it felt very good to him.

CHAPTER TWELVE

"I'm frightened, John," Isabelle moaned, after he had carried her upstairs and gently put her on the bed. "I can't remain in this house."

"Would you feel less apprehensive if I were to remain here with you?" John asked.

"Can you protect me from a ghost?" Her voice trembled as chills of emotional reaction quivered in every part of her body. "I thought if I left London I could escape Elena."

"Do you believe you actually saw your sister?"

"I saw what I saw! Oh, John, please understand!" Her voice was shrill. She stared with eyes that seemed to focus on nothing. "I spent most of my life with Elena. Of course I know her. And her voice—she knows I'm here! She's calling to me from beyond the grave." She cried hysterically, wild fingers tearing at her hair. Rising from the bed, she went frantically toward the window. "Elena is out there—somewhere in the night. She wants me to join her!"

John stood as much as he could. Finally stepping to her, his hand slapped crisply across her cheek. The hysterical sobbing ceased, to be replaced by childlike whimpering. Then she put the side of her hand to her mouth and bit it.

As John put his hands to her shoulders, her gown fell over her upper arms. His fingers gripped into the smooth, soft flesh. "Isabelle, I didn't mean to hurt you. You must understand." Quickly his lips went to her cheek where he had slapped. Slowly he kissed from her cheek, down her neck and over onto her shoulder.

Isabelle stared down at him. "I've no freckles on my shoulder. Elena says her freckles are her beauty marks."

John rolled his eyes upward but kept his lips at her shoulder. "Freckles?"

"My shoulders are clear." She laughed as tears streaked down her cheeks. "Mama says Elena claims that about her freckles because she is rationalizing. If I had had the freckles and she hadn't, she would have taken quite the opposite attitude towards them."

Lifting his head, John again kissed her on the cheek. His attention was on her mouth, and soon his lips were there.

"Oh, John! Hold me! Please hold me with all your might. I know the only hope of maintaining my sanity will come from the love you give."

"*Love*?" John raised his head and gazed into her eyes. "Yes, I believe I do love you, Isabelle. Something strangely remarkable seems to be happening within me. I've always been coldly calculating and logical—at least since reaching adulthood. Now I seem to be reacting emotionally and quite unlike myself."

"Love me, please love me, John."

"I do." He kissed her again.

"And if you do love me," she whispered a short while later, "you'll take me away from this place."

"Take you? Where?"

"Don't you have a house? Even if you only have an apartment . . ."

"My dearest Isabelle, this is Boston, and Bostonians are very concerned with propriety," John said. "A man's reputation can become bad enough if he lives unwed with a woman; but a woman's reputation becomes far more tarnished."

"I didn't mean—"

"What would the rest of the Phenwicks say? Or your father?"

"Are you really *that* concerned?"

"If I do truly love you, dear Isabelle, I must be." He kissed her softly on the cheek.

"Then take me away from here. Please, take me away!"

"I'll drive you to the Ornbys'. Dr. Joseph and Sheila will be pleased to have you stay with them," John suggested.

"Yes, to Aunt Sheila and Uncle Joseph's," Isabelle stated. She broke from his hold and quickly went to throw things into a small satchel.

John found an old carriage in the stable, and a horse that looked more suited to pulling a plow than a vehicle. Isabelle was with him. She did not want to be alone for a minute at Edward House. They both sat on the driver's seat as they rode.

The Ornbys were not at home. Since they had no servants, there was no one to let the young couple in.

"There is another possibility," John mentioned after returning from the door, where he was unable to rouse anyone. "Triumph House."

"Triumph House?"

"You've met Millijoy and Tommy, haven't you?"

"Yes, of course. And Millijoy did invite me to come and stay with her," Isabelle said enthusiastically.

"I have a fondness for Tommy," John admitted. "I believe he has tremendous talent as a pianist. I encourage him at every opportunity. Neither Millijoy nor her son have been popular with the Phenwicks. But I feel that, since Tommy is my grandnephew, that I must extend a certain amount of affection and concern. After all, neither he nor his mother can help the fact that they have Negro blood."

"They have?"

"Didn't you know?"

"No."

"Will that make a difference about going to Triumph House?"

"Not in the least. Let's go!" Isabelle clasped his hand and put her head to his shoulder.

Victor Samson was a firmly built, muscular man, who looked slightly out of place in a white butler's uniform. All other butlers in Boston wore gray and black attire—but not at Triumph House. Millijoy had gone through a catalogue of butlers, all of whom were good-looking and had a similar physical appearance. The mistress of Triumph House required special duties over and above butling from her servants. Samson had lasted longer than most, and that was because he was very accommodating.

Despite his condescending arrangements with Millijoy, Samson was known to have a prudish and exacting disposition. When he first eyed John and Isabelle at the front door, the outwardly reprehensible butler arched an eyebrow. He immediately recognized John, of course, but he was not that familiar with Isabelle. John quickly explained what brought them to Triumph House.

Being introduced as Isabelle Phenwick, Samson received the wrong impression and instantly congratulated John. When he learned that Isabelle was not John's wife, but a distant cousin, Samson again took a stoic expression and coolly looked down his Bostonian nose.

"Miss Phenwick has had a very trying evening," John

135

explained to the butler after seeing Isabelle to the guest room on the ground floor of the spacious mansion. He tried to clarify the situation to Samson, who remained dubious. "The fact of the matter is, I know Mrs. Phenwick takes sedatives and sleeping draughts. I think it would be well if Miss Phenwick were to be given a little of each."

"I shall see if I can find such things, Mr. Phenwick," Samson said with an austere expression. "Please excuse me. I'll take them directly to Miss Phenwick."

John waited outside the guest room, where he believed Isabelle was preparing for bed. Samson was pleased to see the young Phenwick on the outside. The servant rapped on the door, and Isabelle asked them both to enter.

"Stay a few minutes with me," Isabelle begged of John after she had taken the drugs.

Samson pursed his lips at one side and lowered his eyelids. He would wait just outside the door.

"When you kiss me like that," Isabelle said a short while later, "I feel as if it is the only reality in my life— and everything else is like frantically wading through a nightmare. I'm certain, if I'm ever to escape the ghostly hauntings of Elena, that it will happen from the strength I receive from—well, from *your* love."

"Why did you hesitate?"

"I was simply going to say *love*," Isabelle explained. "But I realized that just any love was not enough—I want *yours*."

John kissed her again.

Everything was happening too fast, John thought as he left the room, leaving a faint glow of lamplight behind. He realized he had very sincere feelings for Isabelle. But what if she were actually losing her mind? Could he or his love be strong enough to save her from mental destruction?

Samson stretched in his tightly fitting uniform and stifled a yawn. "I believe Master Thomas has arrived."

"Tommy?" John glanced up from his thoughts. "Oh, yes, to be sure. Did he go to his room?"

"Unless he has drastically altered his habits," Samson informed him, "I suspect he has gone directly to the kitchen to find a bite or two to eat."

"Thank you, Samson," John stated. "I'll see if I can't find him. However, if you should spot him wandering about, tell him I'm here and looking for him."

"Yes, Mr. Phenwick. Will that be all?" Samson asked.

"Yes, thank you."

Samson moved with the agility of a runner as he disappeared into the shadows of the hallway.

Tommy had removed his blouse, boots, and stockings. A satin cummerbund was still about his waist above the form-tailored formal trousers. The skin over his upper torso was a rich tan, smooth and well proportioned. His strangely interesting, if not altogether handsome face brightened as he beheld his uncle. Dropping what he was doing, he ran to John's open arms. Although he was seventeen, in many ways Tommy was still very much a little boy.

"Uncle John!" Tommy exclaimed as he wrapped his arms around the man. "What are *you* doing here?"

John explained about Isabelle. "But right now, I'm here to visit with you. Did you play a concert tonight?"

"No, just a recital. They're not the same, you know. A concert is for strangers. One hopes a recital is for friends. I had hoped you could have come. But I knew you were invited to the Quiglys, as mother was. I didn't bother to ask you."

"I would have preferred a concert, Tommy, believe me."

Tommy had removed cold roast beef, cheese, and bread from the cooler. He shared with his uncle.

Before actually indulging, John excused himself to look in on Isabelle. He discovered she was soundly sleeping.

"I had hoped Ann Marie would be at the concert," Tommy related a while later. "But I knew she was invited to the Quiglys, too. Mother is often invited to social gatherings these days, too. I suspect all the Phenwicks are—but me."

"Why do you say that, Tommy?" John asked. "The only reason I can see is that you're not yet eighteen."

"That's not the only reason, Uncle John." He lowered his eyes and picked at his long fingers. "They say you can tell by the cuticles of my fingernails. I suppose they can see it in my features, my larger-than-most-people's lips, my curly hair."

"See what, dear Tom?"

"The traces of Negro blood," Tommy replied. "I was named for Tom Clegghorn, the black man who sired my mother. I know all about that. Why should all of those lily-white bluebloods of Boston want to invite a mulatto to their social affairs where he might meet one of their precious daughters? How silly people are! Don't they realize that their daughters fall all over me when I play a concert? And do you know why? Because when I play, it is an expression of my soul that comes out. And my soul is neither black nor white, yellow, or brown. And those precious daughters see the beauty of my soul, that which seems to be attuned to the Universe."

"You're not bitter, are you, Tommy?"

"Bitter?" He laughed. "No. On the contrary, I'm proud," the young man stated. "But I'm in a quandary."

"A quandary?"

"Mother is determined that I marry a Phenwick woman," Tommy related. "But she's as silly as the rest of them. Any woman I choose to marry will become a Phenwick woman. Mother wants me to marry a girl who is already a Phenwick so it will be assured that she is accepted as a Phenwick woman. Isn't that ridiculous?"

"Knowing Millijoy," John commented, "I can follow

her reasoning. She has had a difficult time making herself be accepted for what she is."

Tommy poured himself a second cup of tea and added milk to it. "I'll confess one thing to you, Uncle John. I have a very strong feeling for Ann Marie."

"Ann Marie?" John widened his eyes.

"I know what you're thinking—Ann Marie is my first cousin and that's too close for people to marry," Tommy commented. "I'm too young to consider marriage anyway. However, I do believe I could fall in love with Ann Marie. And I think she likes me, too."

"I think Ann Marie has a fondness for most men," John observed. "Oh, I don't mean in an intimate way—but then again—"

"Are you saying that to upset me?"

"Not in the least, Tommy. You know I love you dearly, as I do Danny and Ann Marie and the rest of Stuart's children—even Alexander," John said. "I have a strong family feeling and I'm proud of being a Phenwick." He rose and clasped Tommy by the shoulders. "Now I must get back to Edward House. Surely Gregory will have returned by now. I must let him know where Isabelle is before he worries himself sick."

"I thought you would have spent the night," Tommy returned.

"Under other circumstances, dear nephew, I would have."

Bare to the waist and shoeless, Tommy saw his uncle to the front door. He went out into the night with him, where they embraced before John climbed up on the carriage, waved, and cracked the reins.

Tommy returned to the house. The marble floor was cold to his feet, but he liked the feeling. Stealthily he made his way to the guest room and opened the door. For nearly five minutes he stood staring at his cousin.

As the youth emerged from the room, he glanced into

the suspicious eyes of Samson. Not all that impressed with the servant's moral values, Tommy simply smiled contemptuously and took a nonchalant attitude as he returned in the direction of the kitchen.

Gregory had arrived back at Edward House with Stuart and Ruth only minutes before John appeared. Because of concern over Isabelle, Gregory went immediately to her room. He returned frantically down the stairs to announce that she was missing.

John was there. He explained what had happened and that she was peacefully sleeping at Triumph House. After a brandy with Stuart and Gregory, John excused himself and went to his own home.

"I'm worried, Stuart, I swear I am," Gregory commented as he took a second glass of brandy. "I fear it was a mistake bringing Isabelle with me—certainly a mistake not to have brought Ilene, for she seems to be the only one who can handle her."

"I suspect my Uncle John is learning how," Stuart remarked curiously. "John is so different from any of his three brothers. I suspect that, of the four, he is the kindest, most intelligent—and the deepest. A girl could choose far worse than Uncle John."

CHAPTER THIRTEEN

"Sometimes it amazes me how well things work out according to the way I want them to," Millijoy stated two days later. "I really should attend more of Mrs. Eddy's lectures."

Samson was standing at the window of the second-floor sitting room. "Mrs. Eddy? Not Mary Baker Eddy?"

"The same." Millijoy lounged. "You don't approve of Isabelle Phenwick staying here, do you?"

"It is none of my business," Samson replied. "However, I do fear that a young woman of her age and beauty could well have a strange influence on Master Thomas."

"Do you think so? Oh, I do pray that is the case," Millijoy exclaimed.

"Madam?"

"Oh, put on your trousers and stop looking so indignantly at me," Millijoy scolded. "Your prudish attitude while out of costume is nothing but paradoxical, if not ludicrous. Even in costume, as my butler, I feel your opinions are a bit outspoken."

"I'm sorry, madam."

"Don't become so contrite, it doesn't become you,"

Millijoy said. "I knew I should have quizzed you about your moral convictions before I hired you. You're the first butler I've ever had, out of a great stream of them, who has been so—well, so paradoxical."

Millijoy ruminated about the man as Samson left the room. She found him amusing and efficient. A rare combination, she thought. Still, she realized she was beginning to get just a little tired of him and his puritanical ways. She wondered how he could rationalize his relationship with her with the rest of his disposition.

She was laughing to herself when Samson reappeared to announce that Millijoy had a visitor.

"A visitor?"

"Miss Phenwick. She didn't have a card," Samson said stiffly.

"Isabelle?"

"No, madam, Miss Ann Marie Phenwick. Shall I show her in?"

"Have her wait three minutes, while I slip into something more appropriate."

Millijoy wore a wine-colored satin dress that was styled in the latest fashion when she appeared to greet Ann Marie. She extended her hand as she went to greet the girl. "My dearest Ann Marie, what a pleasure this is."

"I hope it is, Aunt Millijoy," Ann Marie replied.

Millijoy offered tea and Ann Marie accepted.

"I'll get to the point," Ann Marie said after the usual chitchat of greeting was over. "I was—until recently—concerned that you were thinking of me and your Tommy in romantic terms. I'll readily admit I've given the subject some thought. Yet, while putting many things together, I realize that I would prefer an older man. As inexperienced as I am, I believe I will require a man of experience."

Millijoy cocked her head. She had not yet heard enough to analyze where the girl's words and thoughts were leading. "I assume, from what you say, dear Ann Marie, that you have discovered an interest in someone else."

"That is most perceptive of you, Millijoy," Ann Marie sipped from the teacup. "Fact is, I've come to the conclusion that my Uncle John is most attractive and is desperately in need of a wife, now that he has become a successful attorney."

"I see. And what does your father think of such an arrangement?"

"We haven't discussed the matter."

"Oh? Well, then, what is John's feeling about it?" Millijoy questioned.

"John is evasive. As a matter of fact, I've not broached the subject to him, nor he to me. Still, I sense his love."

"John Phenwick is a very loving man. I might add, he is a very loving uncle—at least he is to Tommy. I suspect he is equally loving to you, Danny, Richard, Polly, and Donald." Millijoy spoke with a soft lilt to her voice. "Oh, yes, and to Alexander as well. He is very much like his brother Thadius in that way—and Paul. Are you certain you're not mistaking an uncle-niece relationship for something more?"

"I know how I feel," Ann Marie said firmly.

"And do you know that he comes regularly to Triumph House to visit your cousin Isabelle?" Millijoy asked.

"I've suspected as much," Ann Marie snapped. Anger flared in her face. "If you ask me, Isabelle was responsible for her twin sister's death—that's why her father brought her to Boston. If the truth were known—"

"Where have you gotten such allegations, Ann Marie?"

"They're thoughts I've had."

"Because you dislike Isabelle?"

"I had them when I first met her. She claims she doesn't recall much that happened from the time she got into the carriage with Elena on that tragic day. I suspect that is merely to underline her alleged innocence," Ann Marie stated.

"Did you honestly feel this way prior to the time you realized your Uncle John had taken an interest in Isabelle?" Millijoy inquired, a faint whimsical smile on her lips.

Ann Marie sputtered.

"I see." Millijoy lifted herself languidly and moved to Ann Marie. She cupped the girl's chin in her long fingers. "My dear Ann Marie, I am aware of precisely what you're doing. Furthermore, I suspect I know what your ultimate plan is. Very well, I'll make a confession to you." She stepped away as if she were speaking to the vast view of the ocean from her large window. "I know you have given speculative thought to Tommy, and perhaps you have an honest romantic feeling for him. However, Tommy is a year younger than you are—and he is a first cousin—"

"Dr. Joseph said—"

"Never mind that," Millijoy interrupted. "I believe you are far more suitable for John than—well—"

"Than Isabelle?"

"That may well be the case," Millijoy returned. "I have become fairly well acquainted with Isabelle, despite her present condition, and I feel—well, I think she might be destined to other arrangements."

Ann Marie stared. She rose. A smile came to her pretty lips. "Aunt Millijoy, I suspect we are alike in many ways. I know precisely what you're thinking. You want Isabelle for Tommy, don't you?"

Millijoy did not reply. She smiled broadly.

"Then you help me get Uncle John and I'll—"

"Help you? How?"

"Simple. Persuade Isabelle against him and in favor of Tommy. You're clever, Aunt Millijoy, you'll find the way," Ann said triumphantly.

"How kind of you to observe, Ann Marie." Millijoy laughed. "You're quite right, you know. I suspect we are very much alike, dear Ann Marie. Far too much alike to become in-laws."

A jab of apprehension moved through Ann Marie, but she refused to recognize it as anything more than a passing feeling.

"I feel much more at peace," Isabelle said that evening as she and John Phenwick strolled along the shore below Triumph House. "There is something about Edward House that makes me very uncomfortable."

"Is there someone there who disturbs you?" John questioned, his fingers entwined about hers as they walked into a secluded place.

"I can't think of anyone."

"Not even Ann Marie?" John asked as he stopped to face her.

Isabelle smiled awkwardly. "I don't know. Now that you mention it—"

"Ann Marie is a strange girl," John explained. "She was so very young when her mother died. Then there was the war, and Stuart was so very busy all the time. Danny and Ann Marie came often to stay with us. By the time Stuart married Ruth, Ann Marie had grown enough to feel jealous of any other female who usurped her father's affections. It was different with Danny. He was older, and when Ruth came along, he immediately took to her. Perhaps Ruth was responsible for part of that. I suspect she found she could relate better to little boys than to—"

"Ann Marie?" Isabelle filled in.

They spent nearly an hour together on the beach. Their conversation was light, a means of getting to know each other better. They were in harmony, meshing together as if they had been destined to share adult years of life.

As the afternoon sun began to set, John walked Isabelle back to Triumph House. They lingered at the side entrance for a while, where they stood in a secluded spot and exchanged expressions of affection. Then Isabelle went into the house.

John thought a moment of his reaction to the pretty young lady. He had to admit to himself that he had become enchanted with her. When she was troubled, she was entirely different, sweet and loving. He could tell she had not had the kind of physical show of love she had needed during her growing years. There was still confusion and an inability to cope with sensitive emotions; still, she was doing an admirable job of adjusting, he thought. As he walked to the front of the house, where he had left the buggy waiting, it occurred to him that he should call on Joseph Ornby and discuss the matter with his cousin, the psychologist. He was certain Joseph would be understanding.

Tommy was waiting at John's buggy. He took a casual stance and tried to look nonchalant. "May I have a word or two with you, Uncle John?"

"What is it?"

"I think it would be best if we were to drive down the hill and onto the road," Tommy replied. "I can walk back."

"Hop on the seat with me," John ordered. The buggy soon pulled around the circular drive that went up to the entrance of Triumph House.

"Mother and Ann Marie are scheming," Tommy related.

"Scheming?" John briefly glanced at his nephew. "About what?"

"About you—and me, Cousin Isabelle, and Cousin Ann Marie." Tommy explained the details of the conversation he had overheard between Millijoy and Ann Marie.

"Are you certain of this?"

"Positive," Tommy replied. "But let me assure you, I

146

have no romantic interest in either Isabelle or Ann Marie. For that matter, I may have a normal curiosity, but I'm not romantically interested in any girl at this time."

"You will in time," John said with a chuckle.

"My present love is my music," Tommy explained. "Now that I have two organ positions, I am kept busy and am bringing in some money. I got to thinking about our conversation the other night, and I realized that my music was very important to me."

"Can you devote your life to it?"

"I intend to."

"With that attitude, I would say you were correct in your devotion to it," John returned. "I don't want to take you too far away from home. Thank you for the information. I'll keep it in mind."

"I'll get out here," Tommy stated. "Incidentally, I'll be giving a concert in October at the conservatory. I want you to promise that you will attend."

"You know I will," John commented as he pulled up long enough to let Tommy off. Then he shook the reins and coaxed the horse into a good gallop.

Tommy watched until the buggy was out of sight before he turned and climbed back up the hill to Triumph House.

John Phenwick had purchased a small seven-room cottage on a bend of the Charles River, near to the bridge that crossed over to Cambridge. He was still attending Harvard when he acquired the property, which coincided with the time his mother married John Collier in Greenfield, Maine. The cottage was comfortable to his needs. Nicely furnished and decorated to fit a bachelor's disposition, the place was kept in good condition by a hired man, who came once a week to tend the exterior chores, and a cleaning woman and general housekeeper who worked weekdays. If he intended eating in, he would leave word for the housekeeper to prepare something before she left at four. That particular evening, he had arranged to have supper with his good friend and associate, Brewster Martin. He would go home, freshen up and change clothing, then go back into town and meet Brewster at his club.

Having removed all of his clothing, John washed himself from a basin of warm water. He leisurely took his time, enjoying the sensation of stroking himself with the wet washcloth. With the house to himself, he was not overly cautious about his attire when he knew he was alone. Although he would never admit it to anyone, not even to Brewster, he often lounged about in privacy without the benefit of any clothing whatsoever.

Startled by a light rapping at the front door, John wrapped a towel about himself, stepped into a pair of slippers and went to answer it. Only his head appeared around the door, and that wore a startled expression.

"Isabelle?"

"I had to come see you, John. May I come in?"

"Please, you must wait out there a few minutes."

She laughed. "Very well, John."

John scurried back into the house and recklessly pulled on the clothing he had laid out. Less than five minutes later he was back at the door, presentable and not as haphazardly appearing as he feared he might be. "Dearest Isabelle!"

"May I come in *now,* John?" she asked.

"By all means. I confess you caught me in the altogether," he confided.

"Had I known that—" She laughed suggestively. "But our time will come, won't it, dearest John?"

"What brings you here this evening?" John questioned.

"Don't you think I deserve a kiss first?"

John smiled as he tilted his head to the side. "I must say you're in a different mood."

"Different? How do you mean?"

"Why, I might almost say 'aggressive,'" John replied "Aggressiveness seems a bit out of character for you."

"Would you prefer I always remain timid and shy?" she asked.

"No, I think not." He showed her into the parlor. "I was about to prepare myself a drink."

"I would like a glass of sherry, if you have it."

John stared at her curiously. "Yes, of course." What a marvelous transformation had come over her, he thought as he poured the wine and brandy.

"To us, John!"

John joined in the toast. "To us, dearest Isabelle."

"Shall I tell you why I came tonight?"

"If it will ease your conscience," John returned lightly.

"What a singular thing to say!" she exclaimed. "If I were a conscience-stricken person, I wouldn't be here in the first place."

"Meaning?"

"I should think that obvious."

John cleared his throat and reached for the brandy decanter. "You amaze me, Isabelle."

"I sometimes amaze myself, my dearest." She was staring intently at him until the clothes he was wearing felt inadequate to cover his modesty. "The fact is, I'm of the impression two people should get to know each other *well* before they entertain the notion of getting married."

"Oh? *Well?*" John's throat was dry.

"*Very* well," she answered.

"Isabelle—?"

"Surely you're experienced in such things," she taunted. "Or is it that I have caught you off guard and you suddenly feel unqualified for the situation?"

"I do have an appointment in just a short while."

She pulled a handkerchief from her sleeve and put it to her eyes. "You don't love me, then."

"But, dearest Isabelle, I do love you," John replied.

"And it is because of my love and respect for you that I must control my passion."

"It won't be that way after we're wed, I trust."

"Quite the opposite." John drank, sighing with pleasure as he downed the brandy. "I thought I had made it plain to you that I am basically a moral man. I believe in the church and the laws it has set up."

"What does the church have to do with it?"

"You told me you had spent long hours in the church, Isabelle."

"Longer hours than I care to remember."

John reached again for the brandy decanter. Before he could connect with it, he felt a gloved hand about his wrist. The gloved hand had greater strength than he imagined it to have. He felt his position altered as he was suddenly facing her, her lips very close to his. She pressed against him as her mouth went for his.

John had kissed Isabelle several times before, each time with an increasing ease as one becomes aware of what the other prefers. Passion had arisen in both of them, but it had never reached the heights that it did at this time. She had backed him to the table and was pressing forward with such force that it was all he could do to keep from falling onto it. Her hands had never been as aggressive before, and if anything, they had only lightly caressed his sleeves or the front of his blouse.

"My Lord, Isabelle! I've never wanted anyone as I want you at this moment," exclaimed John. "Do you realize what is happening?"

"Full well," was the reply. "Do you?"

John closed his eyes. She pushed herself so far forward that she lost her balance. As she fell to the side, he caught her, positioned her back on her feet, and reached for the brandy decanter.

"Do you need that to fortify yourself, John?"

John swallowed hard. He was ruffled and confused,

anxious and wary. Things were not as they should be. The brandy seemed to have less fire as it touched his tongue; yet when it went into his stomach, he feared he would not be able to keep it down. He braced himself.

"John—"

"No more, Isabelle," he said defiantly. "We are not married yet. It is sinful for us to carry on in such a manner before our union has been blessed before God. We have been caught up in the passion of the moment, but we must control ourselves. It is truly unfair of me to rouse you in such a way."

"Unfair of *you?*" She rolled her head back and laughed. "My dearest John, you *are* naïve, aren't you?"

"Isabelle, I'll drive you back to Triumph House," John stated. "Then I must get to the club. Brew is expecting me."

"I borrowed one of the buggies," she commented. "I can drive myself back."

"A frail woman can't handle a buggy and horse."

"Perhaps I'm not as frail as you may think, John." Before he could object, she kissed him again. This time she was reserved and ladylike. "I wondered what it would be like to do this. Now I know. I see I was mistaken. From now on, I will allow you to become the aggressor and I will acquiesce to your desires. Now I know, beyond the question of doubt, that I do love you very much, John. You needn't see me to the buggy. I can well manage."

"I insist."

"Very well, but don't make yourself late for your appointment."

John helped her into the buggy and stood in amazement as he watched her drive away. Her skill with the horses fascinated him.

Later that evening over dinner at the club, John gave Brewster a modified version of what had transpired between Isabelle and him that evening.

"I say, she's a young lady who seems to know what she's doing," Brewster observed.

"I beg your pardon, Brew?"

"That is to say," Brewster corrected himself, "she appears to know what man she wants. There's no doubt in my mind that you're a goner. She's got her cap set for you all right."

"But suppose I hadn't resisted her advances?" John suggested.

"In that case, you might be a wiser man at this point—however, I fear, a bit disillusioned. Besides, it has been my experience, by proxy of course, to note that many a woman is able to compromise a man into marrying her. Men are really such clumsy boobs at times, don't you know?" Brewster prepared to drink his coffee.

"I don't feel myself a boob!" John stated. "I feel myself a righteous individual. And I wasn't compromised. Yet I wonder——"

"Ah, second thoughts," Brewster said, shaking his finger. "Had you had second thoughts then, dear John, I fear you would have lived to regret it."

"No doubt."

"But I suspect that Miss Phenwick is such a clever woman," Brewster continued, "that she led you into such a situation, just to see *how* you *would* react. No doubt she was checking your strength and will power. In that case, you undoubtedly pleased her immeasurably."

"Yes," John thought. But he had not quite convinced himself. There was something queerly disturbing about the entire situation of the evening and Isabelle's visit to his cottage.

Later, after John left Brewster to go his way, he ruminated again over the situation with Isabelle. Had she indeed tested him? Why? And what had brought about the amazing transformation in her attitude as well as in the state of her mind? She had been loving that afternoon, and had not seemed as near as confused as she had been in the last few days. Still, for her to be so totally different would require a better explanation than he was capable of giving. He would make it a point to call on his cousin, Dr. Joseph Ornby in the next day or two and discuss the matter with him.

John knew that he loved Isabelle. Yet the question came to his mind regarding her sanity. He had heard of dual personalities. And, from somewhere, he had gotten the idea that Isabelle might attempt to take on the characteristics and personality of her dead twin sister. Or—and he shuddered at the thought—suppose Elena had begun to possess Isabelle's body in an attempt to get back into earthly form. He had read the account of Rachel Phenwick, who was possessed by two alien spirits, years before. The very thought of it had given him nightmares. He had to speak with Joseph as soon as possible. But even if what he suspected might be true, what could Joseph do to stop Elena's invasion, if that was happening?

CHAPTER FOURTEEN

The *Twin Dolphins* had been at sea for nine days. The crossing thus far had been relatively pleasant. There had been only two nights of severely choppy waters. During that time Adam Truff had worked as a deckhand, and did his best to appear to be just another seaman, taking the attitude that prevailed among such men of doing as little work as required of them and perpetuating a feeling of general apathy. Such men were not strongly motivated, and rarely was a long-distance goal found among them. Life at sea was basically easy, with food and lodging provided, hours of physical work balanced with leisure time in which to dream.

Life at sea was contrary to Adam's basic makeup. He was both ambitious and adventuresome. He quickly learned that the life of rowdy sailors was not as romantically adventuresome as one might be led to believe. Such persons were known to drink heavily and brawl when they were in port, a means of making up for lost time while at sea. Still, what they did on land was pretty basic and devoid of anything constructive or truly exhilarating. Most of the seamen, Adam discovered, were illiterate, without education, and crudely animalistic as they went about satisfying their essential requirements as best they could.

For all of the above reasons, Adam had to lower himself to the level of the seamen just to establish a rapport with them. He spoke slovenly with an affected mixture of accents. Still, try as he might, the men realized he was different. However, during that period at sea, Adam had discovered that one of the galley cooks and two of the general hands that helped with the victuals were involved in what appeared to be a smuggling plot. He made concerted efforts to get to know them better and to gain their confidence.

Initially one of the men let slip the name of Cherbourg, France, in context with a "pickup." The assistant cook, Ryder, tried to cover the error by relating to Adam that they would "pick up" a supply of French bread while in Cherbourg. That struck Adam as being peculiar since the French port was only a short distance across the channel from Southampton; and generally, to Adam's knowledge, such items as bread were made by the cooks aboard ship.

When Adam mentioned that fact to Crisp, one of the hands involved, the crusty sailor let slip that there was more than dough in the loaves of bread. It was finally Boxer, the third man involved, who told Adam that this was his last sea voyage as a seaman, and that if he traveled again, it would be as a first-class passenger.

"I suspect your share of the diamonds will make you a rich man," Adam speculated.

"My share o' th'—?" Boxer blinked. "Now see here, Jack, 'oo tol' ya about th' diamonds?"

"I know," Adam returned. "And I want in on the deal."

"Do Crisp and Ryder know this?" Boxer asked.

"Not yet, but they will know soon," Adam said. "Now you can either tell them that I am going to join you in

Cherbourg, or I'll tell Ryder that I know about the escapade because you told me."

"When did I tell ya?"

"Just now. I previously had suspicions, but you just now confirmed them," Adam said.

"Oh, don't tell 'em I tol' ya," Boxer exclaimed. "I've bin sworn t' secrecy, I 'ave."

"Good. From now on there will be four smugglers, right?"

"Neither Crisp nor Ryder is gonna be too 'appy about this," Boxer moaned.

The conspirators indeed were not in the least pleased that they had been forced to include Adam in their venture. They considered doing away with him. But none of the three were murderers at heart. At length they agreed that the only thing they could possibly do was to include the man they knew as Jack Adams in their plans.

Because Curtis Tinkersly had the late watch, from ten at night to six the following morning, his was often a lonely vigil. Still, many a mishap was avoided by his watchful alertness. Most of the crew were down below asleep during those hours. Adam noted after a few days at sea that most of the men slept when they were not on duty. He presumed it was motivated by extreme boredom. What else was there to do?

Adam got so he would arrange his time so that he would have gotten sufficient rest prior to midnight. Then he would rise and stealthily creep away from the sleeping men to go above and engage Tinkersly in conversation. Curtis got so he looked forward to Adam's nightly appearances. Because he had aspirations and ambition, Tinkersly was of a far different ilk than the other seamen.

"Curtis, I've a confession to make," Adam admitted.

"A confession?" the first mate questioned.

"I deliberately arranged to be hired aboard the *Twin Dolphins*."

156

"Deliberately? Do you mean with a purpose?"

"Yes," Adam replied. Assured of the excellence of Tinkersly's character and his trustworthiness, Adam explained what his mission was and how he had detected the three men involved in the smuggling.

"What do you intend to do?" Tinkersly asked, feeling honored that Adam had confided in him.

"I consider you my good friend, Curtis," Adam replied. "Therefore, I wish to enlist your assistance in this matter. And to demonstrate the confidence I have in you, I will inform you that my name is not Jack Adams, but Adam Truff. I am a long-time friend of the Phenwick family—meaning I carry influence with them—if you grasp the significant meaning of my words."

"You mean—?"

"A word to the right person would assure you of an early captaincy," Adam said slyly.

"Jack—I mean, Adam—I—" Tinkersly had become choked with emotion. His greatest desire in life was to become a sea captain and, moreover, to be the commander of a Medallion ship. "How can I help you?"

They formulated a plot.

The *Twin Dolphins* docked at Cherbourg at four o'clock in the afternoon. Although the ship carried some cargo, it was basically a passenger vessel. Her schedule called for her to be tied up at that French port until the following morning when, with passengers who wished to cross the channel aboard, she would head for Southampton.

Adam joined Crisp and Boxer at a rendezvous on shore. Ryder would remain isolated from the others in a cheap room he had rented for the night.

The three sailors, appearing to be in a happy-go-lucky mood, jauntily made their way through the village of Cherbourg and up the hill to a farmhouse with a thatched roof and animals informally milling about. Adam thought it a most peculiar place to make such an exotic pickup; but he realized such deeds required extreme precautions.

Adam was scrutinized with a keen eye by the farmer. Boxer had to persuade him that Adam was one of them. Shortly after, the farmer's plump wife, a round, flat-faced creature with scarlet cheeks, arrived with an armload of long loaves of French bread. The loaves were thin and probably measured waist-high from the ground. The emotionless woman dutifully bound the loaves into two bundles, stared momentarily at her husband, and crept away.

Crisp exchanged two hefty bags of what Adam guessed to be gold for the bundles of bread. Adam carried one while Boxer carried the other. Few words were exchanged. Adam reasoned that was because the sailors spoke little or no French and the French peasants were equally as ill-equipped with English.

The farmer stood at the door and tossed a handful of grain to the chickens that gathered around him. His attention was on the men as they trudged down the hill.

The loaves of bread were taken to the hotel room where Ryder was waiting. After counting them, he instructed Boxer and Adam to take them aboard the *Twin Dolphins* and down to the galley.

As the two men reached the top of the gangplank with the loaves, Tinkersly suddenly appeared. Boxer became terribly nervous and trembled so that he dropped his bundle.

"I'll take one of those," Tinkersly ordered.

Boxer turned brilliant red.

"All I want is the end of it to tide me over until mealtime," the first mate assured the man. "Come on then, haven't all day."

Boxer removed one of the loaves from his bundle. He

158

immediately motioned for Adam to accompany him below.

"On second thought," Tinkersly called as the men were about to go down the steep stairs, "I don't think I want this bread after all. Here, take it below."

Boxer sighed with relief as he scurried to retrieve the loaf of bread, not realizing that Tinkersly had cleverly replaced it with one he had only a short time before purchased from a bakery near the dock.

Shortly after the bread was deposited in the galley under the sharp eye of the cook, Adam was summoned to the captain's quarters.

The loaf had been sliced down the middle, where a row of priceless diamonds were revealed. They had been baked into the bread.

"There's a fortune in this one loaf alone," the captain observed as he glanced from Adam to Tinkersly. "What do you propose be done about it?"

Adam thought a moment. "The moment we dock in Southampton, I want you to send your second mate to the authorities. I will compose a note he is to take to them. Then I wish for the entire crew to be detained aboard ship until the authorities arrive. I will arrange for the loaves to be confiscated and those involved with this matter to be arrested. For the sake of appearances, I will be arrested along with them. One never knows when subterfuge will be required again. It's well to have Jack Adams known as an unscrupulous character among the seamen. Since the *Twin Dolphins* will be in port for an extended period of time for repairs etcetera, I would appreciate Curtis Tinkersly being given a leave for at least two weeks. He will then meet me in London—with your permission, Captain Keswick."

"Certainly, certainly, by all means," the captain replied. "I must say you are a deucedly clever man, Adams."

"The name is Truff. Adam Truff. My stage name, as it were, was Jack Adams," he said, laughing.

The plan went smoothly, with the three men and Adam arrested on smuggling charges. The loaves of bread were taken in a separate carriage, directed to Scotland Yard. Adam rode in manacles with Boxer, Ryder, and Crisp. Only Ryder was in the least bit suspicious of Adam. Still, if he were going to be prosecuted with the rest of them, Ryder soon would change his mind.

The prisoners spent one night in Southampton behind bars. The next day they were transferred to London. Prior to leaving, however, each man had been separately interrogated. At that time Adam was able to tell the police representatives from London where the Cherbourg farmhouse was located. English or French agents would have to take it from there, since he, as an American, had no jurisdiction in the European countries.

A quick trial was set up in a London court. Adam stood trial with the others. Both Captain Keswick and Curtis Tinkersly were called as witnesses. All the men involved were found guilty as charged.

As a precautionary measure, the prisoners were separated and taken to different places of incarceration. At least Boxer, Ryder, and Crisp were. Adam was immediately freed; but as far as the others were concerned, Jack Adams was as notoriously guilty as they were.

That evening Adam had supper with both Captain Keswick and Curtis Tinkersly in an elegant restaurant in the Strand. There they were joined by Joshua, David, and Albert Phenwick. Special bonuses were arranged for Captain Keswick and First Mate Tinkersly.

"At Adam's recommendation, Mr. Tinkersly," Joshua announced as he lifted a glass of wine, "once you've completed your holiday, you're not to return to the *Twin Dolphins*."

"Not return?" Curtis questioned.

"You will come to the Medallion office," Joshua continued, "where you will be commissioned as captain of a cargo vessel by the name of the *Valliant*. The *Valliant* is in New York, so perforce you must return to America on the *Twin Dolphins*. Once you get your sea legs as captain, and sufficient experience behind you, no doubt you will be given one of our better vessels."

"Thank you very much, Mr. Phenwick," exclaimed Tinkersly. "I don't know how to thank you enough."

"Don't thank me, young man," Joshua replied. "Adam Truff is your benefactor in this. Without his recommendations, I shouldn't have known you from the next first mate who is employed by the Medallion Enterprises."

"Adam—?"

"Let's drink to Curtis's success as captain of the *Valliant*," Adam stated. "For that matter, let's have several drinks and get terribly lightheaded. Even Albert. Why not? The boy is old enough to taste the effect of spirits."

Albert grinned. "My mother might not approve, but I do."

As the men indulged in the main course of the meal, the subject of conversation moved to the matter of the money embezzled from Medallion nearly nine months before.

"No," Joshua admitted, "it has never been solved. I presume Inspector Alister Crook considered the issue dead with the murder of Melvin Ferrett, the man who actually embezzled the money."

"And was the money ever recovered?" Captain Keswick asked.

"Never." Joshua shook his head. "I fear it will never be found. We've written it off as a capital loss, and that's that."

"Did Adam happen to mention," Tinkersly inserted, directing his comment to Albert, "that an old friend of yours had been a member of the crew of the *Twin Dolphins*?"

"A friend of mine?" the sixteen-year-old son of Gregory Phenwick asked. "Who is that?"

"His name is Derrick Molden?"

"Molden?" Joshua questioned.

"Ah, then you know him, too," Adam said.

"I should hope we do know him," David Phenwick interjected, glancing to his father. "Molden once worked for us."

"David, your cousin Albert is still a boy," Joshua warned his son.

"Bertie is old enough to understand this," David returned. "We didn't learn until recently, but Molden sufficiently terrorized my youngest sister, Elizabeth, with his improprieties. Had she not had a long, sturdy hatpin with her at the time, goodness knows what the villain might have done. Elizabeth, of course, didn't confess this to any of us, not even to my sister Carrie, until after the accident in Carrickfergus. It was only by accident that my eldest sister, Ophelia, extracted the information out of her."

"How do you happen to mention the accident in Carrickfergus?" Adam questioned, leaning forward to the handsome scion of Joshua Phenwick's family.

Albert said, "Derrick Molden was the driver of the carriage in which my twin sisters were riding."

A curious thought came to Adam, but he did not voice it. However, of one thing he was certain; he intended to investigate the matter of Derrick Molden.

The dinner party adjourned at 10:30 with all six men amply stuffed and lightheaded with the effects of spirits.

Adam had taken a room at the Savoy with two beds in it. He had invited Curtis Tinkersly to join him, as the two planned to take a short holiday.

"I think I should like to go over to Bath," Curtis commented as he lay upon the soft sheet. It was summer and the humidity was high. Only a faint touch of a breeze came through the window. The man was as comfortable as he could be under the circumstance.

"Bath? That sounds charming," Adam returned, sitting with a towel draped about him on the edge of his bed. "I've always wanted to go to Brighton. I understand it is quite a lovely seaport."

"So it is," Curtis returned. "I suppose we could spend a few days in both places."

"True." Adam extinguished the lamp. Street light filtered into the room and glistened in shadows over their bodies. "But I have been thinking, Curtis."

"About what?"

"A place called Carrickfergus, in Northern Ireland," Adam replied. "It might prove interesting to make a trip up there."

Curtis gave no opinion.

Adam glanced over to the other bed. "We'll discuss it later."

CHAPTER FIFTEEN

To look at Dr. Joseph Ornby, one would get the initial impression that he was a gentle, middle-aged, simple man, who lived a rather mundane existence. He rarely created the impression of being a scholar, much less a person with deep thoughts. Many an individual who came to him as a patient, upon first sight, thought they had come to the wrong place. Even when he had engaged basically in the activities of a physician before he got into the psychological approach to treating illnesses, he was judged by appearance; therefore, because he was not the prototype of how a doctor was presumed to look, he had to demonstrate his knowledge and ability before he was accepted.

But Dr. Ornby, like his brother Augustus, had established himself as one of the foremost practitioners of his profession in Boston. Still, Joseph and Augustus and others of their profession had made giant steps and had accomplished much. Joseph and his brother agreed that most physical illnesses were psychosomatic in origin; and such cases were relatively easy for them to diagnose and deal with. It was the abnormalities of the mind and related conditions that deeply concerned them. Augustus spent many years in Europe, specifically in Vienna, studying and doing research. He had written several important papers and had studied with noted professors in the field. Joseph had read his brother's papers, and tried to apply his theories in working with patients in Boston. He was the first to agree that he understood very little and that he had a great need to learn more.

"Dear John," Dr. Joseph Ornby said as he leaned back in the chair and rested his feet on an opened bottom drawer of his desk, "I can see—or at least, from what I hear, I must deduce—that you indeed are very much in love with your distant cousin Isabelle. Oh, I have long observed the look Phenwick men get when they fall in love. I should imagine it is very like the expression that old Augusta must have got. Or perhaps it comes from that British soldier she married because she liked his name." He chuckled and caught his lower lip between the index fingers of his clasped hands. "But I can also see you have concern."

"I told you of the incident that happened a week or so ago," John said, "when, after I had visited Isabelle in the afternoon, she later came to my house in a provocative, and I must add, seductive attitude. There have been other times when her paradoxical behavior has been most unusual. I am of the impression that she contradicts herself."

"Quite so." Joseph studied the young man's face. "Do these changes of—shall we say, moods—alter your opinion of your emotions toward the young lady?"

"They certainly don't vary my feeling of love for Isabelle," John explained. "If anything, the confusion I see in her actually increases my desire to want to help her."

"Confusion?"

"I suspect the confusion is in me, Joseph. At one point she is sweetly innocent, and at another, she is—well, the opposite."

"Ah! Upon first observation," Joseph said, "I would

suspect a case of dual personality, one that goes to two different extremes. From what I have learned of my wife's niece, in younger days she was a somewhat timid girl, shy and standoffish; at least that was the basic impression she created as a child. The reason for this, however, is that her twin sister was quite the contrary. Where Isabelle was timid, Elena was bold; where Isabelle was shy, Elena was compulsively outgoing; and where Isabelle was standoffish, Elena was aggressive."

"That is my understanding, too," John commented.

"My first thought is that Isabelle may be attempting to take her dead sister's place and become the extrovert that Elena was," Joseph stated. "That has been known to happen in cases of normal siblings, not necessarily with twins. And I believe it would be reasonable to assess this as being the situation here."

"How so?"

"If Isabelle's timid characteristics were actually caused by Elena's dominant attitudes," Joseph continued, "now that her sister is no longer in the flesh to intimidate her, Isabelle is slowly beginning to assert herself. Her personality is beginning to emerge after being overshadowed by Elena's all these years."

"That would seem logical."

"On the other hand," Joseph remarked, "—and I confess this *does* worry me—it may be possible that Elena's spirit is trying to take possession of her sister's body."

"Trying to do *what*?" John incredulously asked as he sat forward.

Joseph altered his position. "We have found evidence of several such cases of spirit possession. They are very rare, of course, and, in deference to the established precepts of *the* church, such information is kept quite confidential. But the theory is that when a soul or spirit of a person finds itself suddenly without a body due to an accidental or sudden death, and they can't accept the reality of the change, they desperately try to get back into human form. Allegedly such spirits prey on weak personalities who seemingly do not have the resistance to withstand an alien invasion. I'm not saying this is the case with Isabelle, but there is a vague chance that it might be."

"Impossible!"

"Don't be too quick to make judgment, John." The doctor leaned back again. "Suppose such a thing was possible—hypothetically—and such *was* the case between Isabelle and Elena. The dead sister, who had always been the stronger personality, wants back in the body; and she has an identical twin, who is weak. What more logical place to invade? Somehow Elena might have been able to manifest first in ghostly form to even more terrify and weaken the already frantic Isabelle. Ultimately the dominant spirit, albeit disincarnated, finds the weakened spirit in the flesh more and more vulnerable to attack. Soon it is able to take over for short periods of time. Gradually it gains more and more control until ultimately—"

"No!" John exclaimed as he rose. "I can't believe any of this."

"Can't you?" Joseph stared directly into the young man's eyes. "For that matter, I'm not certain I can believe it either. Still, I am reciting a theory, which might apply in this case."

"How could it possibly?" He rose, his muscles flexing with nervous annoyance.

"Think back, John, to the evening the lovely lady came to your house," Joseph persisted. "You saw the Isabelle you knew, the Isabelle with whom you were falling in love, the physical person you know. But was it Isabelle's personality? Did she react as you have known Isabelle to react? I think not."

John shook his head.

"It would be curious if this sort of encounter were to happen to Gregory," Joseph went on. "He, of course, knew both of his daughters from the past. I am certain he would be able to discern their personality differences. Had he been in your place that night, I believe he might have recognized Elena's personality, and not Isabelle's. Since you never knew Elena, you have no way of knowing."

"This is all preposterous, Joseph! I don't wish to discuss it any further," John said, going to the door.

"Not even if we can help Isabelle by pursuing such a theory?"

"I don't see how that could possibly be," John returned. "In any case, I wish to think about it, to debate the theory with my own logical mind. I don't wish to discuss it any further now."

Joseph watched John Phenwick retreat from his office. He wondered if there were a more subtle way of approaching such an indelicate subject. John was usually very understanding with an open mind. Still, Joseph realized that the young man was emotionally involved in the situation and conceivably could not be objective about Isabelle at that point.

John, too, pondered the circumstances. He did not want to even entertain the notion of such a theory as far as Isabelle was concerned. Yet he had to. The thought had occurred to him any number of times that Isabelle was somehow being influenced by her dead sister.

Adam Truff and Curtis Tinkersly went to call on Ilene Phenwick in Hyde Park, where they took tea with her. The lovely lady related every detail that she could remember about the fatal holiday she and her children had spent at Carrickfergus.

"Isabelle was deeply distressed over the loss of her sister?" Adam questioned.

"We all were," Ilene returned. "It was a terrible

tragedy that I fear will be indelible in all of our minds. Yet the thing that caused me to worry most about Isabelle was when she told me about encountering Moorduke."

"Moorduke?"

Ilene related details about the leprechaun, both from the time she was a young girl and first encountered him, and that which Isabelle had told her of the wee creature.

"In other words," Adam concluded, "Isabelle has slipped into a kind of world of fantasy."

"Fantasy?" Ilene bristled. "Oh, what's the use? How can I expect a person who has never seen a leprechaun to understand?"

She permitted Adam to take a small oil miniature of Elena with him.

From the house in Hyde Park, Adam and Curtis went to the Medallion offices, where they had a short meeting with Joshua Phenwick. He knew few of the details about the accident at Carrickfergus; and, as to the embezzlement at Medallion, he could give no further details.

"How long did Melvin Ferrett work for you?" Adam asked.

"I believe it was something like eight or nine years," Joshua replied. "David could give you the precise time."

"We won't bother him," Adam said. "An approximation is all that's necessary. Had there ever been any incident that had caused you to be suspicious of Ferrett prior to that time?"

"None whatsoever. He was basically a trusted workman," Joshua returned.

"How well were you acquainted with the Phenwick twins?" Adam continued.

"Isabelle and Elena?" Joshua paled slightly. "Of course I have worked side by side with their father all these years, don't you know. The twins just always seemed to be around."

Adam asked a few more questions, but, getting little

satisfaction, he thanked Joshua for his time and excused himself.

"What are you getting at, Adam?" Curtis questioned.

"I don't know," Adam replied with a broad smile.

"You don't suspect there's some connection between the embezzling incident and the accident at Carrickfergus, do you?" Curtis asked.

Adam grinned strangely. "Why, dear Curtis, what a question to ask! *How* could there *possibly* be?" He controlled an ironic smile.

"Yes, how?" Tinkersly scratched his head.

The next interview Adam had he preferred to conduct without Curtis present. By then it was evening and Curtis was sent off to have supper on his own while Adam entertained Alexandria Phenwick.

Since most women found Adam extraordinarily handsome, it was to be expected that the impressionable Alexandria would be abundantly impressed with the man. She kept staring at him and periodically got dreamy expressions on her face.

"I wish to know about your sisters," Adam said after purposefully leading her on.

"My sisters?" Alexandria blinked and shook her head. "You do know about Elena, don't you?"

"I'm aware of the accident and the consequences of it," Adam replied. "But I'm curious to know about your sisters and how they were prior to that time."

"We were occasionally mistaken for triplets," she said brightly. "But isn't it strange, I don't think I look remarkably like either of them."

"Other than in looks."

"Well, you see, I'm known as being the talkative member of the Phenwick family," Alexandria continued. "I can't deny that. Aunt Joanna says I'm a compulsive talker, and she suspects I would continue talking even if

170

everyone left the room and I was alone. I don't know how she ever guessed that."

Adam laughed. "Then maybe you would talk to me about Elena."

"Elena?" Alexandria breathed deeply. "Aunt Olivia said I should always show an indication of grief whenever my dead sister is mentioned. That sigh was my expression of grief. Well, what would you like to know, Adam?"

"What was your impression of Elena?"

"Elena could have been an actress. I've been thinking about becoming an actress. Aunt Joanna *almost* encourages me. She thinks I have a wonderful imagination," Alexandria expressed. "Oh, you want to hear about Elena, and *not* about me, don't you?"

"That would be preferable. I'll hear about you later, dear Alexandria." Adam smiled in such a way that the girl trembled.

"I always thought Elena was foolish to treat David as she did."

"David?"

"David Phenwick, our cousin," Alexandria explained. "Oh, they often went places together."

"Elena and David?"

"Elena didn't like to remain at home," Alexandria related, "not the way Isabelle did." She giggled. "Mama always said that, although Elena and Isabelle were identical in appearance, Elena and I were more alike in disposition. I love to go out to parties and to the theatre. And I'll tell you the truth, I take an active interest in handsome young men, too."

"Too?" Adam questioned as he poured wine into his glass.

"You see, that is what was funny about my twin sisters," Alexandria went on. "Elena loved men. Oh, she did, I'm not exaggerating. Aunt Joanna said she was nothing but a flirt all of the time. But, on the other hand, Isabelle

171

habitually seemed to be terribly shy and backwards around men. She used to blush so easily. And she could have had a very good chance with David, but she didn't take it. Frankly, I think she's abnormal."

"Did Isabelle not go out with young men?"

"Only when she had to," Alexandria said. "Mama tried to make her become socially aware. Poor Mama, I think she began to despair on that score in time. She doesn't have to encourage me, though."

"I'm certain she doesn't, Alexandria." Adam ordered coffee. "Was David the only young man with whom Elena went out?"

Alexandria laughed, then covered her mouth with the back of her hand. "Mama says it isn't ladylike to laugh out loud in public. Elena used to sneak out. I don't think Mama or my father knew about it. I did. I used to watch her. When I asked her about it once, she said she enjoyed adventure and there wasn't much of it in our house. That was very true."

"What men did Elena know?"

Alexandria shrugged. "I know she was caught once with the groom out in the stable. And, although I don't know the details, there was some kind of rumor about a headmaster at Mossweed. There's no headmaster at Mossweed any longer—not since Elena was there. And we had a butler once—"

"Alexandria," Adam said firmly, "are you making all of this up?"

Alexandria blinked innocently and widened her eyes. "I may be embellishing somewhat, but I'm *not* making it up."

"How did you discover all this about Elena?"

"She told me. Oh, she and Isabelle were the twins and always seemed to be close, but there were certain things Elena could not confide in Isabelle, but she could in me."

"I see." Adam thanked her and called for the check.

The next day Adam and Curtis Tinkersly went to Scotland Yard to call on Inspector Alister Crook.

The somewhat crotchety police inspector eyed Adam curiously, then glanced at his friend. "What business is this of yours?"

"I happen to be a good friend of the Phenwicks," Adam returned.

"American?"

"Yes. I reside in Greenfield, Maine, on the Phenwick property," Adam said as he produced credentials to show the inspector. "Actually, it was Mr. Gregory Phenwick, who is presently in America, who asked me to look into the situation here at Medallion—I refer to the embezzlement problem."

"You're wasting your time with that, Truff," Alister Crook stated. "We've run into nothing but dead ends there. Our man was Melvin Ferrett—and I refer to him in the past tense, because he is no longer among us. We found no clues to his murderer. And, for the sake of the family, we assume that he came by Elena Phenwick's fan by chance. Perhaps she had visited the Medallion office and left it there . . . and he picked it up."

"If you don't mind me saying so, sir," Curtis commented, "that seems pretty weak."

"Oh, it does, does it?" Crook fumed. He did not like private investigations into police matters. "Well, even if there was something more between Ferrett and the Phenwick girl, it won't appear anywhere in the records, in deference to the family."

"I see," Adam remarked. "And what information do you have on Melvin Ferrett—I mean personal information?"

Grudgingly Alister Crook got a file of papers. "He was a bachelor, in his late thirties, plain of appearance, but mathematically shrewd."

"That's brief and to the point," Adam mentioned,

amused at the inspector's annoyance. "What of his family?"

"He was born in poverty," Crook recited. "His father left the mother with six children. They were raised on the streets of London. Later Sadie Ferrett remarried and had four other children."

"Four more?"

"Three of which ended up in the poor farm," Crook stated.

"Do you know where Sadie Ferrett is now?"

"Her second husband died, and she married a third—a man by the name of George Carne. Sadie used to hang out down in Soho, where she peddled flowers to get enough money to buy drink. As near as I know she's still in that area. That's all I can tell you."

"Thank you, Inspector," Adam said, "you have been very helpful."

"How was he helpful?" Curtis asked as they got out on the street.

"I'm not certain," Adam replied, "but I think he must have been."

"You are a strange one," Curtis commented.

"If I weren't uniquely singular," Adam boasted, "I wouldn't be the eccentric and popular Adam Truff that I am." Laughing merrily, he clasped Curtis on the shoulder.

"Now, dear boy, I think it time we proceed to Northern Ireland."

"Northern Ireland?"

"To a place called Carrickfergus, as a matter of fact."

Mrs. Cleo Duffy had taken over the management of the small inn in Carrickfergus while her husband was away on holiday in Belfast to visit his aged mother. Since the place was rarely fully occupied, Mrs. Duffy had rooms for the two men who came by boat across the North Channel from Portpatrick, Scotland. A casual but somewhat suspicious person by nature, Mrs. Duffy scrutinized Adam and Curtis with great curiosity.

"We're Americans," Adam explained, giving her his most alluring and persuasive smile. "And, to come to the point, we're seeking information."

"Ay, that much I figured about ye," Mrs. Duffy returned after assigning them rooms. "We in Carrickfergus are nay talkative, especially t' strangers." She was a large, pink-faced woman with bulging blue-gray eyes. Swollen thighs and ankles caused her to walk peculiarly and with obvious effort. She thought a moment. "Ay, th' inn ain't prosperin' too greatly now. Sure now, we've hardly had enough guests t' keep th' place open. An' times have bin hard." She turned him a sad, pathetic expression.

Interpreting her words and projected emotions, Adam reached into his pocket and produced an impressive amount of money. The lady's blue-gray eyes widened even more and her lips pursed as if she were preparing to whistle. He smiled condescendingly.

"What is it ye want t' know?" Mrs. Duffy asked.

Adam took the oil miniature of Elena Phenwick from a case he had been carrying. "Do you happen to recognize the likeness in this portrait?"

"Sure now, it's Kathleen O'Dwyer," she gasped.

"Kathleen O'Dwyer?" Adam glanced back at Curtis.

"Who would be doin' a picture o' Kathleen? Glory be! An' her a-runnin' off th' way she did," Mrs. Duffy commented.

"Look again, Mrs. Duffy," Adam said. "I'm certain this is not Kathleen O'Dwyer."

As Mrs. Duffy studied the image in oil, Curtis interjected, "What happened to Kathleen O'Dwyer, Mrs. Duffy?"

Cleo Duffy stared into the seaman's eyes. She shrugged. "Th' O'Dwyers have a farm between here an' Larne, maybe fourteen miles north o' Carrickfergus. I nay recollect how many wee ones they do have. Kathleen was one o' th' middle ones. What happened t' her is what happens t' many o' th' lasses that live around places where vagrant sailors come an' go. She up an' run off wif one, an' ain't bin heard from since."

"How long ago was that, Mrs. Duffy?" Curtis questioned.

"Six or eight months ago, I reckon." Mrs. Duffy scratched herself.

"Take another look at the picture, Mrs. Duffy," Adam encouraged.

The woman reached into a drawer for a cracked magnifying glass. She held it at several angles as she examined the painting. "I kin see now it's nay Kathleen." She looked up as her eyes blinked wider. "O' course! There was two o' them."

"Two?" Curtis asked.

"Ay, th' twins, one o' what got killed." Mrs. Duffy told the story of the accident as she had heard it. Adam let her go into full details without indicating his deep interest.

Adam did, however, encourage Mrs. Duffy to relate any rumors she might have heard concerning the event. Then, when the lady had exhausted her supply of information, he inquired where the accident had taken place.

Hiring a cart, Adam and Curtis were driven to the bridge where the tragedy occurred. The cart driver remained disinterested, lounging back on the cool grass while the men went to look around.

The narrow bridge was wide enough for a full-size carriage to pass over it. The structure was sturdy; it did not even sway when both men jumped up and down on it.

"You know, Curtis," Adam said as he stood staring down at the bridge and the bubbling water flowing beneath it, "the thing that strikes me strangely in the whole report was that the carriage driver allegedly hit a boulder that had been placed on the bridge. Why would anyone place a boulder on this bridge?"

"To make a contrived incident appear to be an accident?" Curtis asked.

"Precisely."

"And, while I'm upon that point, doesn't it seem peculiar to you that the driver, in the state of nerves he must have been in," Adam added, "would climb back on the bridge and roll the boulder off the bridge?"

"I have to disagree with you," Curtis commented. "Any decent citizen with respect for others certainly would have done what he could to keep another similar accident from happening."

"So be it." Adam thought a minute, puzzling other facts. "How do you suppose the horse got free of the coach? Every horse that I've ever hitched to the tongue of a wagon or a carriage has always been securely attached."

"Perhaps the carriage tongue broke."

"A possibility," Adam admitted. "Still, it leaves cause for speculation." He stretched. "It's a hot day, isn't it?"

Twice Curtis had mopped his brow. He had left his coat and cravat in the cart. "I didn't think it got so hot this far north."

"How about a dip in the creek?" Adam suggested.

"Good idea." Then Curtis realized what Adam was up to.

"Fall in off the bridge, don't dive," Adam ordered. "Check the depth of the creek here, along with the swiftness of the current. Then, if you feel you can do it, simply relax and float with the current, avoiding any resistance whatsoever."

Curtis stripped down to his underthings and jumped into the water. A moment later his head and shoulders appeared. "I'm standing on the bottom here. The current, while bubbly, isn't all that swift."

"What is the bottom like?"

"Sandy."

"Can you dive under and see if you can find a boulder?"

Curtis dipped his head under water, and then his feet appeared. He was down for several seconds. When he reappeared, he was about eight feet away from where he had been. "There's several small rocks on the bottom, most of them pretty much wedged into the sand. But there's one good-sized boulder right here under my foot. Shall I try to bring it up?"

"No. That won't be necessary," Adam replied. "Now just let yourself float and see where you drift to. I'll follow along on the shore."

Curtis floated downstream in a completely relaxed position. He had gone no more than twenty-five yards before he stood up, the water catching him below the knees. "I could possibly float further, but I'm dragging my rear end across rocks and things not far below the surface."

Adam instructed Curtis to wade as far downstream as he could, then asked him to go upstream until he could no longer swim. Finally, the seaman went under the bridge and beyond until he was again able to wade.

After drying himself, Curtis dressed and joined Adam at the cart, where the cart driver had acknowledged that he knew the O'Dwyer farm. Adam's generosity with money easily persuaded the man to drive them to the farm.

What they learned from the O'Dwyers was that Kathleen had run off the previous autumn at cider-making time. The earthy O'Dwyers showed little respect for their child, freely explaining that Kathleen had conceived when she was thirteen and again when she was fifteen. Neither time had she been married. Since she displayed such an uncontrolled interest in men, the O'Dwyers were basically pleased that she chose to run off with the tall, redheaded, freckled-faced sailor, who, in their humble opinion, was passably good-looking. They would gladly give Adam any further information he desired, for an additional fee. Adam was satisfied.

Adam was pensively quiet during the boat crossing of the North Channel and throughout most of the train trip back to London. He kept working at pieces of a puzzle. He wished Isabelle were in London where he could confer with her. Perhaps she might have been able to fill in the missing pieces.

"What missing pieces?" Curtis asked when they were back in the rooms at the Savoy.

"For one thing, I would like to know when was the last time the carriage had stopped before it reached the bridge," Adam explained. "Secondly, I would like to know how well she knew the driver of the vehicle, if she was acquainted with him at all."

"Couldn't Mrs. Phenwick tell you that?"

"Perhaps." Adam scratched his head. "And that's another thing, what happened to the carriage? I would like to examine it. Since the creek was shallow a short distance from the bridge in both directions, I shouldn't think the carriage would have floated away. Someone must have removed it. The driver? I wonder."

"Those may be questions you can never answer," Curtis speculated. "Frankly, I don't see what you learned by speaking with the O'Dwyers about their runaway daughter."

"I don't either, yet, Curtis," Adam replied. "But it's one of those things I have an intuitive feeling about."

Curtis laughed. "*Intuitive feeling?* You're more than singular, Adam, quite a bit more."

"You'll laugh out of the other side of your face," Adam stated, "when you see the results of my intuitive feelings after I get to the bottom of this thing."

"The bottom? I can't even discern what sort of a case

you're building," Curtis commented as he stretched out on the bed.

"Neither can I—at the moment," Adam said with a broad smile. He poured himself a glass of port and got comfortable. "But I will."

"You will *what*?"

"Discern the sort of case I'm building," Adam replied. "Because, you see, my intuitive feeling tells me that I very much am onto something."

"Then, my friend, can you tell me what possible connection you hope to find between the embezzlement case you're investigating," Curtis asked, "and that unusual accident that occurred in Carrickfergus?"

"At the moment," Adam stated, "only that the Phenwicks were in some way involved with each."

CHAPTER SIXTEEN

John Phenwick had had a busy day in court. He was a shrewd and effectual lawyer; but sometimes he realized he was put in the position of defending someone whose innocence he could not believe in. Brewster Martin worked along with him on the case, but it was John who actually had to address the court.

"It's the ethics of it," John told his friend during an afternoon recess.

"Would it be any more ethical to pull out of the case and leave your client stranded?" Brewster asked.

"Maybe I'm in the wrong profession," John returned.

"I doubt that," Brewster commented. "Look at it this way, you were hired to defend the man. Using all the evidence he has given you, the facts as you see them, you are doing your job. If he has misrepresented himself to you, that isn't your fault. And if he is convicted, it will be because the jury couldn't swallow the story your client gave—not because you lack ability as an attorney."

"But suppose they don't find him guilty and I win the case," John suggested, "I'll have my conscience to live with."

"Do you know for a fact that he's guilty?"

"No."

"Then on what do you base your feelings?"

"The man himself," John said. "He's dishonest to the core."

"You're not the judge, and the man's character isn't at stake, is it?"

"In essence it is—as is my own," John confessed. "You can see my predicament, can't you?"

Brewster laughed. "I know you too well, Johnny. If you don't want your client to win, you'll find a way to bring the truth about him to light."

John examined his watch. "Oh, dear, this thing will go on until six, I have no doubt."

"Have you an appointment?"

"I promised to see Isabelle tonight," John replied.

"She won't mind if you're a bit late."

"I'm certain she will be able to tolerate that," John said. "What might disturb her is the fact that I won't be able to pick up the locket. I was having the clasp repaired for her."

"I don't need to sit in court after the recess," Brewster related. "Can't I pick the locket up for you?"

"Would you? That would be most kind of you, Brew."

"What is so urgent about the locket?" Brewster asked after receiving instructions where to run the errand.

"Last Thursday Isabelle again came to my house in an unusual mood," John confided.

"Unusual?"

"The best way I can bluntly describe it is *seductive*."

Brewster laughed. "Oh, I say."

"It's that peculiar side of her nature that seems to contradict the sweet innocence she usually has," John stated. "Joseph is of the opinion she has a split personality. At least, I hope that's the conclusion he has reached."

"What do you mean by that?"

182

John explained Joseph Ornby's theory of possible spirit possession.

"Well, you'd better get to the bottom of that before you get too serious about the young lady and lose your heart to her," Brewster advised.

"It's too late for that. I've already fallen deeply in love with her."

"Which her?"

"I beg your pardon?"

"The innocent side, or——" He laughed suggestively. "Or the seductive side?"

"I won't even honor that question by attempting to answer it," John stated. "Now I'd better get back to court—and you had better hop over to the jeweler's."

John had a difficult time keeping his mind on what was going on in the courtroom. His thoughts continued returning to Isabelle and the previous Thursday night, when she had appeared at his house. He had been more than abundantly impressed by her seductive ways. Had he not exercised supreme control, he might have given in to her advances. Never before had he considered himself so sensually inclined. But he had responded to her, and the thought of that night had never escaped his mind. Still, he was determined not to violate the sacred marriage laws, nor allow himself to weaken his moral code.

Persistantly John had to shake himself back into the awareness of the moment and try to concentrate on what was being presented in court. Why was he unable to control his thoughts and master his emotions? Was that what love was truly all about? Still he found that the question of morality and ethics kept coming to mind.

It would be unsurprising if John lost the case he was representing. Why was he such a moral and ethical man? He thought of his mother, Nancy, aware of her years of guidance and training. He was convinced that Isabelle was destined to be his Phenwick woman, and Nancy Phenwick

Collier was the prototype of the ideal Phenwick woman in his mind.

That same evening, Thomas Phenwick was to play a concert at Braintree. Millijoy, her son's most avid supporter, would not miss the program. She attempted to persuade Isabelle to join her. They would have sandwiches with tea, then wait until after the concert to dine. Tommy did not like to eat a few hours prior to a performance. Millijoy respected his wishes.

Isabelle said she would prefer not making the carriage trip to Braintree and mentioned that she was expecting John Phenwick to call on her. Millijoy had raised an eyebrow at that, but made no further comment, except to tell her that Victor Samson would be accompanying her to Braintree.

When Millijoy and Tommy were gone, Isabelle found that Triumph House seemed to be remarkably quiet. She went looking about for the servants. Only old Clara Whiteside could be located. The elderly housekeeper had a small room in the basement, where she kept largely to herself when she was unoccupied. The woman was hard of hearing and verging on blindness.

"No," Clara said, "the others are all gone into town. They're like that. Once Mrs. Phenwick leaves, they scatter—if their work is done. And they had enough warning about tonight to have their chores all finished before teatime." She cleared her throat and spat.

"You're the only one here, then?" Isabelle questioned.

"How's that?"

Isabelle repeated the question four times louder.

"Yes, and I go to sleep shortly after sundown," Clara explained. "If you want anything, you'll have to get it yourself. Dynamite won't awaken me when I sleep. Just you remember that, so don't come around tapping on my door."

Isabelle left the kitchen, where she had had the conversation with the housekeeper. She wondered about Clara. With all of Millijoy's contemporary attitudes and progressive ideas, it seemed incongruous for a person such as Clara to be in the position of housekeeper.

The cold marble floors caused whispered echoes of Isabelle's footsteps. The austere marble and plaster in the round entrance hallway, augmented by the iciclelike crystal prisms of the great chandelier hanging high in the center of it, gave the area a stark feeling. Black marble statues that stood on pedestals at an equal distance from each other gave a foreboding ambiance. The statues were recent acquisitions of Millijoy's, contrived to enhance the entrance way with shocking beauty: mythical male gods in all their glory.

Isabelle had frequently cast fleeting glances at the depiction of masculine attributes, had appraised the statues for their artistic merit, and had concluded that they appropriately fit in with Millijoy's attitudes and uninhibited way of life. Of course, to nineteenth-century, Victorian, Bostonian standards, such unadorned works of art would have been unacceptable anywhere else. Because of her enormous wealth and influence, Millijoy's tastes were tolerated.

The large chandelier had not been lit in the main entranceway. That was not unusual, since it was rarely illuminated except for large gatherings. Two small lamps, one on either side of the room, glowed dimly. Samson had seen to lighting them before he left with Millijoy and Tommy. Only one lamp was lit in the second floor hallway, just outside the large sitting room, where Millijoy preferred spending most of her time.

Isabelle climbed the curved stairway to the second floor as a feeling of apprehension came over her. From the top railing, she stared down at the huge chandelier and the black statuary. The only sound she heard was that made by wind chimes on the terrace outside the sitting room. Curiously, she turned and went toward that sound.

Twilight on the ocean was Isabelle's favorite sight from Triumph House. There would be nearly an hour of that gray light before stars began to appear. An hour before Clara Whiteside would be soundly asleep, she thought. Gulls soared on the horizon, swooping occasionally down over the water. Although she could not see clearly, Isabelle was certain each downward swoop meant a catch of fish.

The summer evening was almost balmy, yet refreshingly cooled by the gentle sea breeze. Isabelle put her delicate fingers to the wind chime to momentarily stop its chatter; then she brushed it with force to make it ring all the louder. That bit of whimsy accomplished, she left the sitting room and passed through the curved hallway until she came to the suite of two rooms Millijoy had assigned to her. Finding a diaphanous cerulean blue gown, she took it to the full-length mirror and held it to herself. Was it too revealing? Sleeveless, designed after an ancient Grecian pattern, it had been one Millijoy had had made for herself. She had worn it twice and had garnered the effect she had wanted to get from it. When Isabelle had admired, it immediately became a gift. The girl had tried it on, but only wore it in her room.

Turning up the lamp, Isabelle again examined her reflection. Moments later she removed her dress and slid into the flimsy garment. A silken underslip kept it from being transparent. She felt daring and just a bit promiscuous wearing it. A tingle of excitement went through her. A slight breeze coming through the window blew the skirt to the side. She went toward the window, and her hair which had been styled with a braided crown and was loosely hanging in back, moved with the breeze. She liked the sensation. From the window she could see the stretch of beach below the house. Did she dare don a pair of slippers and run along the shore in that startling attire?

She returned to the mirror. At first she saw Elena's face. "No, it's *my* face . . . *only* my face now!" Then she giggled. Elena had hated the color blue. Since they always dressed identically, they never wore blue. Isabelle decided then that she would have at least three more dresses made of blue material. She liked blue. Furthermore, when she was dressed in that color she would not see Elena.

The whole notion of wearing blue so thrilled her, filled her with a jubilant excitement, that Isabelle resolved to run along the shore dressed as she was.

The path leading down to the beach was steep in places, but easy to navigate. What had come over her? She was not taking her usual precautionary measures. Why should she? The exhilaration within seemed to motivate her, and she dashed with her arms held out to the sides, the cerulean diaphanous material flying around her.

At the shore, she removed her slippers and, holding them in one hand along with the skirt of her dress, Isabelle ran barefoot through the fingers of foam and the shallow water that ebbed and flowed with the tide. She danced, twirled, and skipped. What a wonderful sense of freedom had come over her!

Thoughts of John Phenwick came to her. She was convinced that she was deeply in love with him; so much in love, in fact, that, were he to ask her to marry him, she was certain she would accept without even asking her parents' permission. Of course, she knew that both Ilene and Gregory would eagerly approve of John. After all, Ilene had been so certain from the day she was born that Isabelle was meant to be a Phenwick woman; and Gregory had nothing but tremendous respect for John. There would be no question—except—

"No!" she exclaimed loudly, and cringed slightly when

a dead echo came back at her. *"I'm not losing my mind.*
I'm not! I *will* marry John Phenwick! I *will!"*

Not until she spoke his name did Isabelle remember
that he had said he would call on her that night. A sudden urgency came over her to get back to the house. How
had she forgotten about it? She did not even wish to take
time to catch her breath before she headed back. What
would John say if he saw her dressed like that? He was
such a proper gentleman that he would doubtless be
shocked. That thought caused a frantic feeling of panic to
flush through her.

Not watching where she was going, Isabelle tripped and
fell. Before she could pull herself to her feet, a wave
rolled over the lower part of her body. The skirt of the
dress was wet and sandy. Now there was all the more reason to hurry back to Triumph House. As she crawled to
her feet, she was suddenly touched with the eerie sensation that she was being watched. Impossible! Who would
be there?

The frantic feeling increased and she ran as if her life
depended on it. She dropped one of her slippers. Her first
impulse was to leave it behind. But, upon remembering
the gravelly path leading back up the hill, she reasoned it
would be prudent to go back and look for it.

"Well, Isabelle, aren't you a sight?"

Isabelle froze in her tracks just inches from the slipper.
Fear pierced through her. She recognized the voice: it
was her own. Or—? Pivoting around as sea water lapped
over her feet, she held her hand over her mouth to hold
the sounds of terror in.

"You know I hate the color blue."

"Elena?" Isabelle managed to get to her second slipper
before she circled around again.

"Are you going mad, sister dear? Is that why you've
got yourself up in that silly way?"

"Elena? Where are you?"

188

A ghostly gray figure seemed to waft out from behind a rock. It moved steadily toward Isabelle until it was not more than ten feet away. "Did you think to elude me by moving to this notorious woman's house? Don't you know that in the spirit world we are quite capable of seeing through such schemes?"

"Don't come closer, Elena, I don't want you here," Isabelle said feebly. "I don't know what you want of me."

"I'll tell you then. I want to possess your body. You deprived me of mine—now I wish to have yours."

"No, Elena, no! *I* didn't deprive you of your body. You were killed when the carriage overturned," Isabelle stated.

"Yet had you let me sit on the left side as I usually do," the other uttered, "I would not have drowned. I would have been thrown clear of the carriage as you were."

"And I would have—"

"It is universally agreed that I was the most essential of the two of us. I had ambition and determination—not you. You were quite the opposite. Mama was wrong! *I* was destined to become *the* Phenwick woman—not you. And I *will* manage it! I swear I will!"

"How? By stealing my life and my happiness?" Isabelle asked defiantly.

"Is there any other way?"

"How would that be possible?"

"I've known about spirit possession, long before the accident. You, with your prudish ways, wouldn't go where I went or learn what I did. Now that I'm on this side, I've learned. And do you know who is assisting me? Augusta, herself."

"Augusta Phenwick?"

"You know the influence she has over Phenwick women."

Isabelle was trembling. "That's impossible! I know such things are impossible!"

"Shall I tell you how it will happen?"

"No!"

"The fact is, you're losing your sanity. Right now you're losing it. And the weaker you get, the stronger I will get. Then, one day, when I am certain of myself, I'll emerge fully in your body and you will be off into the spirit world, as I have been since the accident."

"No, Elena, no! Leave me alone! Please, leave me alone!" Isabelle turned and began to run. She had managed to go about twenty feet before she lost her balance again and fell. Frantic with unbelievable terror, it was all she could do to muster courage to glance back. The sky was beginning to darken, but there was still enough light to see that the beach was vacant.

"Elena!" she called. "Elena?"

There was no reply.

Why didn't she have the strength to get to her feet? She had to get up, had to climb the path and get to the house before John got there. Why had she ever decided to put on that dress or climb down to the shore? Had those thoughts been put into her mind by Elena's spirit? And if Elena had given those thoughts to her, how would she avoid other thought vibrations from her dead sister?

"Sure now, I do wish ye would watch where ye're fallin'. Drunk er not, yer behavior is most unbecomin'."

"Moorduke?" Isabelle questioned. "Is that you?"

"Ay, 'tis me. An' ye wouldn't believe th' size o' th' head I got on me. For a wee one, it feels like me head belongs on a giant."

"Where have you been all this time?" she asked.

"In the spirited land o' intoxication, lass, I am happy t' say," Moorduke replied "At least I was till I awakened wif this head. Glory be!"

"Can you help me?" Isabelle asked, trying not to whine.

"I do nay believe I kin help meself at th' moment, lass. But then, what seems t' be ailin' ye?"

"My sister!" exclaimed Isabelle. "I just saw my sister. Not only that, I spoke with her."

"Sure an' b'gorra, what's yer sister doin' over here? Ay, that Alexandria is quite a lass."

"Not Alexandria," Isabelle corrected. "Oh, I wish it were she. It was Elena. She was standing there as big as life—then she disappeared."

"If'n me head were clearer, lass, I'd take a wee look about an' see what I could see," Moorduke commented. "I see no evidence o' Elena on th' physical side. An' as fer gittin' into th' spiritual side o' thin's, that takes a clearer head than I got at this moment."

"Oh, you're no help at all, Moorduke," Isabelle complained. "I have to get to the house."

"I'll come along if'n ye'll let me ride on yer shoulder. Ye won't even know I'm there—I'll be light as air."

"Very well, but I must hurry." Isabelle sensed something the weight of a small feather on her shoulder. Were she not aware of a tiny voice, she might have thought she had left him behind. The first of the path was easy to climb because it was on a gradual incline. However, it soon became steeper.

Isabelle had climbed approximately three quarters of the way up when she had to stop for breath. Bracing herself against a boulder embedded in the side of the cliff, she rested her brow on the back of her hand. That frantic feeling still moved through her, and when she could work up the courage, she glanced back down the path and to the beach. Shadows of night had nearly engulfed the sand. Only the whitecaps and the line of foam at the edge of the flowing water stood out.

"Ye know, lass, I've bin doin' some thinkin', I have," Moorduke announced. "Combinin' thinkin' an' hangin' on

191

fer dear life is a major accomplishment, I want ye t' know. An' it occurs t' me that I owe ye a favor."

"I beg your pardon?" Isabelle had not been fully paying attention.

"Ay, 'tis true, I've bin shirkin' me responsibilities," Moorduke continued. "Ye see, ye're me human, an' I'm yer leprechaun. There's no changin' that fer th' present. Now then, such a relationship is a rare thin' in these days, let me assure ye o' that. D'ye have any notion what Elena wants o' ye?"

"She desires to possess my body," Isabelle answered. "I don't know how she intends doing such a thing. I do know Elena always had remarkable determination."

"Ye don't understand th' spirit world at all, do ye, lass?"

"I'm afraid I don't," Isabelle said.

"That's all right, most humans don't. It's natural. But there are them what do. Ye see, it's like I tol' ye before, ye're as immortal as ye'll ever be right now. But there will come a time when ye'll completely change outa this here earthly costume ye're a-wearin'. That immortal that ye are will go on bein'. It kin't stop. O' course, th' same thin' is true about Elena, only she's slipped outa her costume. Fact is, she is nay doubt confused, bein' in that free state, an' she feels cheated about nay bein' able t' live out a full life. So she sees ye wearin' th' identical costume she wore less than a year ago, an' she wants yer costume. Ay, 'tis possible fer her t' git it, too, if'n ye don't watch yerself."

"Watch myself? How?" Isabelle leaned her back against the boulder.

"If'n ye lose control o' yer mind an' yer reason," Moorduke advised, "she kin move right on in. That's why, I suspect, she keeps appearin' t' ye in ghostly form. She's nay only tryin' t' drive ye outa yer mind, but outa yer body as well. 'Tis a miserable trick, but there are them

192

what does it. I knew a lad oncet in Londonderry who'd lost control o' his mind an' his body. Ay, th' poor dear, he was set upon by nay one, but three alien entities who wanted his miserable body fer their own. An' by that time th' poor lad was nay more than skin an' bones. T' make a long story short, th' three entities fought so o'er th' severely weakened lad that he escaped th' body before any o' th' others could git into it. That could happen wif yer sister, too, ye know."

"You're not very consoling, Moorduke," Isabelle commented as she pushed herself into a walking position and began to climb the remainder of the path.

"Ay, lass, don't ye see what I'm tryin' it' tell ye? Ye've got t' hold on t' yer sanity, or she'll surely git t' ye."

Isabelle hurried, her thoughts on John Phenwick and the urgency of getting to the house before he arrived. Yet as she reached the gate leading onto the grounds around the mansion, she closed it firmly behind her and leaned against it.

"When you say to hold onto my sanity," Isabelle questioned, "do you mean to keep my mind functioning as a normal person's?"

"Ay, that is th' truth."

"And if it doesn't function like a normal person's, then that would be an indication that I was losing my sanity?" Isabelle continued.

"Ay, I do believe ye're beginin' t' see th' situation."

"I have known many allegedly sane, normal people all my life," Isabelle went on, "and I've never known of one—not a solitary one—who ever thought he or she spoke with a leprechaun."

"Ay, that is because ye are privileged."

"Or I started to lose my mind right after I first thought I saw you," Isabelle remarked, a cloud of confusion coming over her.

"Ho-ho! Hold on, lass!" Moorduke interrupted. "Ye're

forgittin' one thin'—I manifested meself t' yer mithe[r]
years ago."

"My mother?" Isabelle was trembling.

"An' yer mither is as sane as th' next lady, ain't she?"

"Yes. Oh, Moorduke, yes!" She brightened. "Oh, i[f]
only Mother had come to Boston with me. I need t[o]
speak with her."

"There, there, lass, 'twill be all right," Moorduke com[-]
forted. "Now I'll make ye a promise. I'm takin' a oat[h]
this very day that I'll nay imbibe o' liquid spirits until w[e]
sort this thin' out about ye an' th' spirit o' yer sister. M[e]
bright red nose itches, an' that means that there's some[-]
tin' mighty peculiar goin' on somewhere."

"Oh, thank you, thank you, Moorduke!" Isabelle ex[-]
claimed. "I wish I were small enough or you were ta[ll]
enough that we could dance—"

"Dance a fairy dance?" Moorduke questioned. "Ay[e]
but nay wif th' size o' me head t'night. Spin yerself a tim[e]
er two, an' I'll hang on fer dear life. 'Twill be th' neares[t]
thin' t' a fairy dance ye an' me'll ever be able t' do."

Impulsively Isabelle skipped and danced around th[e]
yard. She lifted the wet ends of her skirt and pranced a[s]
she imagined the wee ones moved in celebration. Her hai[r]
flew and she found herself laughing as she had no[t]
laughed in a long time. Then she fell to the ground an[d]
continued laughing merrily as she looked to her shoulde[r]
to see if Moorduke approved.

"Very pretty."

"Moorduke?" Isabelle blinked, then looked forward t[o]
see the shadowed outline of a man. She scooted backwar[d]
in that position until she pushed against a prickly shrub[-]
bery. "Who—who is it?"

"Don't you recognize my voice yet, dearest Isabelle?"

"John? Is it you, John?"

"Had you forgotten I was to come by this evening?"

194

John asked as he went to her. He reached his hand down to help her up. "Apparently you had."

"No," Isabelle returned, clinging tightly to his hand. "No, I didn't all the way forget. That is, it slipped my mind for a while—and I—I don't think I can explain."

"Explanations aren't necessary, dearest Isabelle." He kissed her lightly on the cheek. "Although I suspect you must have been expecting someone else."

"No, I wasn't."

"Not even Moorduke?" John asked, a tone of half-teasing in his voice.

"I wasn't expecting Moorduke at all," she related. "He just appeared. You know Moorduke is a leprechaun, don't you?"

John took her in his arms. "My funny little, precious Isabelle. You have the most amusing imagination in all the world."

"I'm not trying to be amusing," Isabelle explained. "Oh, I don't suppose I'll be able to explain Moorduke at all. How can I explain something I don't understand?"

After kissing her again, John led her into the house. They went directly to her room, where he left her just outside the door. He would give her no more than ten minutes.

Ten minutes later, John knocked on the door to Isabelle's room. Isabelle was standing before the mirror, clad in a periwinkle-blue gown, fresh and gay, elegantly styled to her lovely body.

"How beautiful you are, my dearest Isabelle," John said as he went to where she was standing. His fingers went to her shining hair before he caressed down to her shoulder. Then, directing her face to his, he put a kiss on her trembling lips. His mouth moved from her lips to her throat and down to the bare part of her upper chest.

"I have just the thing for you, my dearest," John announced, his fingers still lovingly caressing about her neck. "I had a late day in court, so I had to send Brew to the jeweler's to pick it up." He took the repaired locket from his pocket. "I had it fixed just like I promised I would."

Isabelle's expression changed to amazement, then to alarm. "John, I—"

"Your cameo locket, my darling. Shall I put it about your neck?"

She caught the carved coral set in gold lace in the palm of her hand and stared at it. "Where did you get this?"

"Don't you recall giving it to me the last time you came to my house?" John questioned lightly. "You told me the clasp had to be fixed." He cocked his head to attempt to comprehend her expression. "That is yours, isn't it?"

"Yes. It has my name on the back of it," Isabelle replied as she examined it. "It has my name. Papa gave Elena and me identical lockets for our sixteenth birthday."

"Then let me fasten it about your throat."

"No!" She threw the locket across the room. She stared wild-eyed. "I've—I've never been to your house, John. I swear I haven't! Or, if I have, I don't remember it at all. Furthermore, how could I have given you that locket to have repaired, when I made a definite point of leaving it in London?"

"But I swear you did give it to me to have fixed," John said, taking her in his arms. She turned her cheek to him as he bent forward to kiss her. "Forget the silly locket, Isabelle. I have something better for you to wear. I'm taking you to supper, you know, at one of the finest restaurants in all of Boston." He moved her face with his fingers so that their lips would touch.

"What else did you bring me? I'm almost afraid to ask," Isabelle murmured.

"A nosegay of violets. Fresh violets," John announced, producing the flowers.

Isabelle pinned them to the top of her dress. The blue

and lavender blended well, with the round dark green leaves to separate the violets from the dress. "They're so lovely, John."

"Lovely, because I love you." He embraced her again. "Now I have a carriage and driver waiting for us outside. I want us to both be very happy tonight."

"Is there a special reason?" she asked as they descended the curved stairway to the main entrance.

"Because I intend to propose marriage to you, my darling." She started to interrupt, but he put up his finger. "That is to come later, so I don't want to hear any answers now. Understand?"

The lovely young couple were laughing when they emerged from the house. The carriage man opened the door for them and offered a lap robe. Upon closing the door, he climbed to the driver's seat and they were off.

Isabelle sat as close to John as she could. He held her hand. She decided that she was going to put as much of that day from her mind as she could. She wanted only to share that time with the man beside her, the one with whom she was certain she was in love. When images of Elena, or the cameo locket, or even Moorduke came to mind, she would quickly force herself to think of something else. And with John so near, she filled her thoughts with him.

As they drove through the cobbled streets of Boston, gas lamps lit along the walks, Isabelle caught glimpses of people and places. She was surprised to see so much activity in the downtown area.

"Is Boston always like this at night?" Isabelle asked.

"Much of the time," John replied, and squeezed her hand.

A traffic snarl caused a brief delay, and the carriage remained idle for several minutes. When John got out to ask the driver the cause of the stop, he left the door open and Isabelle stared out at the passing people.

A tall, redheaded man with passably good-looking features came to the corner. His face was freckled and he had strange blue eyes. His attention was on John and the driver. Isabelle gasped as she saw him and pulled back into the shadow of the enclosed compartment.

Almost immediately John was back beside her and the vehicle had begun to move. He reached to take her hand.

"My dearest, why are you trembling?" John questioned after they had gone a block or two down the street.

"While we were stopped," Isabelle said evenly, "I saw a man—a man I know. A man from London. He used to work for my father."

"Do you recall his name?"

"Yes. It is Derrick Molden," Isabelle replied.

CHAPTER SEVENTEEN

Piccadilly Circus, Soho, London, was nightly a maze of hustling, hurrying humanity from all walks of life. It was where the wealthy came to hobnob with the poor; and the con artists, who kept themselves in perpetual poverty by living ruthlessly by their wits, came to take the wealthy for as much as they could get out of them. In a way it was a kind of a game. Ladies of the street lingered in darkened doorways. Children begged for pennies, but settled for whatever they were given. Pearlies danced and sang. Street vendors were busy with their wares. Carriages rumbled by to the accompaniment of cracking whips. Aromas, sights and sounds blended into a kaleidoscope of merriment and confusion. Pickpockets were everywhere. The taverns were brimming with patrons—singing, dancing, rowdiness everywhere.

The narrow streets in Soho seemed to have just appeared without any plan. Some, which were hardly more than alleys, lured with evil temptation; while others revealed a row of cafés and cabarets. There were also quiet streets which were occupied with day business and were only darkened lanes at night. The beggars and persons of low estate crept there at night, along with stray cats and mongrels.

Near the top of Wardour Street, near Oxford Street, was a small alley beside a crumbling building. The Gossip's Tongue tavern was hardly a place where aristocracy might be seen. Even the hordes of middle-class curiosity seekers stayed away. Thieves gathered in the cellar below, which had underground entrances from several different areas along the sewer system. Ale was cheap. Traveling musicians, if they dared, were the only strangers who entered in an attempt to coax a farthing or two with their dubious talent.

Adam Truff had advised Curtis Tinkersly that they should dress as seamen and augment their appearances with a few additional tatters and smears of grease. The information that Adam had received indicated that one Sadie Carne was known to frequent the Gossip's Tongue regularly each night. Curtis prepared himself with two sets of brass knuckles and still was not certain he wanted to tread into such an establishment.

Twice, en route, Adam had felt deft fingers slide into his empty hip pocket. He avoided the sad eyes of waifs who were obvious decoys for one sort of underhanded dealings or another. He pulled Curtis along.

Terrible, haunted eyes greeted the two Americans as they entered the sleazy tavern. Nowhere before had either man seen such a conglomeration of downright ugly people.

"It's a regular horror show, ain't it?" Curtis commented, ready to leave before Adam tugged him toward the bar.

Adam ordered ale and explained to the curious bartender that his mate had been drinking. They found a corner table. A boy of nine or ten, emaciated, with bulging eyes, had a tin cup tied at the string around his waist. Adam poured part of his ale into the lad's cup.

"What's your name, boy?" he asked.

"Cox."

"Well, Cox, how would you like to earn a crown?"

"Cor, blimy, go on wif ye," the boy returned. "Wot would I have t' do?"

"Tell me when a woman by the name of Sadie Carne comes in. You do know Sadie Carne, don't you?" Adam questioned.

"I do, but wot d'ye want wif 'er?" he returned.

"Just to speak with her. I mean to do her no harm," Adam assured Cox. "You can sit close by and I'll keep your cup filled."

"I 'ave me a friend, I 'ave."

"No friends. You point out Sadie Carne to me, and I'll reward you with enough to go out and treat your friend for the rest of the night," Adam said.

Nearly an hour later, Cox, so inebriated he could hardly keep his eyes open, observed the lady in question skulking in. Splay-footed, she shuffled as she walked, giving the appearance that her pelvic bone was out of place. Hair straggly and greasy, most of her teeth missing and all of four feet tall, she curiously eyed the clientele as she made a useless gesture of brushing off her skirt. Then, upon spying Cox, she moved to the table.

Tinkersly had to bite on his finger to keep from laughing out loud.

Cox shook his head and observed with glazed-over eyes. "That's 'er." He passed out.

" 'Ere now, wot 'ave ye gone an' done t' that lad?" Sadie asked, her voice crackling and most unpleasant.

"I suspect we've gotten him intoxicated."

"Done wot?" Sadie blurted.

"He's drunk," Curtis filled in.

"Ay, I kin see that, kin't I?" Sadie blinked and showed her two good teeth in front. "Wal, d'ye buy me a pint or do I report ye fer gittin' Cox drunk?"

"If you're Sadie Carne," Adam said, "I'll buy you a gallon. No, a whole keg."

"An' wot if'n I do be Sadie Carne? Wot's it t' ye?" She spat.

Adam produced a crown. "This money is for Cox here. If you tell us what we want to know, we'll give you six crowns."

"Six crowns?" Her gray eyes brightened. "Couldn't ye make it four? I'm a poor woman an' needs all I kin git."

"Six is more than four," Curtis inserted.

"Hit is?" Sadie questioned. "Wal, ye gi' me four an' six, buy me a tankard, an' I'll talk me bloody 'eart out."

Once the ale arrived and Sadie had taken several large gulps of it and perforce belched, she wiped her practically toothless mouth with the back of her hand and smiled idiotically at the two men. "Ye kin ast yer questions now."

"You were married to a man by the name of Carne, weren't you?" Adam began.

"Ay, I reckon I were. Yep, 'Arry Carne, hit was."

"Harry?" Curtis questioned.

"No, no, I take that back," Sadie said, then took another swig of ale. "Hit were George Carne, hit were. 'Arry was one o' t'other ones."

"How many husbands did you have, Sadie?" Adam persisted.

Sadie thought a moment then held up three fingers. "This many." She rolled her head back with laughter. "Them's wot was legal."

"Your first husband's name was Ferrett, was it?"

"Ferrett?" She brightened as she made an attempt to snap her fingers. "So that's wot hit were. I was tryin' t' remember jus' t'other day."

"How many children did you and Mr. Ferrett have?"

Sadie rolled her eyes and pushed up on her chin with her index finger as she thought. "Five er six, I reckon."

"Was one of them named Melvin?"

"Melvin?" Sadie stared with glassy eyes, then squinted. "Yep, I b'lieve one was called Melvin. That were a long time ago. I don't remember such fings so well. But now I remember. Melvin, he were one o' th' brighter ones. Some o' my kids were so dumb I woulda done them a favor t' take 'em t' th' Thames an' drown 'em. But I niver."

"When did you last see Melvin Ferrett?"

" 'Oo?"

"Your son Melvin."

Again Sadie thought. To assist her memory, she took another prolonged drink from the tankard. "Reckon 'e weren't much taller 'n Cox 'ere last time I seen 'im. Blimey! That was a long time ago."

"So you were married to Mr. Ferrett and to George Carne," Curtis commented. "Who else were you married to?"

"That's all," Sadie replied. "Or, no, I reckon—let me figger." She closed one eye. "George Carne an' Ferrett— Jim Ferrett, I reckon it was."

"Then who was Harry?" Adam asked, jumping in before she could catch her breath.

" 'Arry? 'E were me 'usband, too," Sadie returned. She belched loudly. "I only 'ad one kid by George Carne, an' 'im we put in th' work'ouse right arf. George tried t' sell 'im, but nobody wanted 'im."

"Harry must have been your second husband," Adam suggested, "between Jim Ferrett and George Carne."

"Ay, that's where 'Arry come in all right." She cackled merrily.

"How many children did you and Harry have?"

Eyes rolled as Sadie poked her index finger into her chin. "Reckon there was three. Lordy, I niver thunked o' them in a 'undret years." More laughter.

"Do you remember their names?" Adam asked.

"Ay, o' course, I do. They're me kids, ain't they?" Sadie rolled her eyes and grunted in attempt to get the

203

names to appear in her memory. "Ay, there were Mary, she was the first. Always called me first girl-brat Mary. Hit's a Christian name, ye know?"

"Mary who?"

"Mary Sue."

"Mary Sue *what?*"

"Wal, Molden, o' course," Sadie replied.

Both Adam and Curtis sat forward. "Molden?"

"Yep, 'Arry Molden, that were me 'usband's name," Sadie beamed. "Ay, I could tell ye tales 'bout 'Arry. 'E 'ad a good mind, 'e did."

"And your other children's names?" Adam pushed.

"Wal, there was Sam an'—an'—wot th' bloody devil were that other kid's name?" Sadie shook her head and stared blankly.

"Was it by any chance Derrick?" Curtis asked.

"Derrick? Derrick?" A vacant expression filled her face. She drank again. "Derrick? Yep, 'Arry woulda named a kid somefing like that. Ay, it were Derrick. I remember now. Ye know, now that I fink o' it, little Derrick an' that other boy ye mentioned—"

"Melvin?"

"Ay. Derrick an' Melvin were real close," Sadie added. "Ye see, I wanted t' see if'n 'Arry couldn't sell Derrick. 'E was a bright kid an' one wot deserved better than wot th' likes o' us could gi' 'im. But 'Arry 'ud 'ave non o' hit. An' 'e feared I'd up an' peddle th' kid whilst 'e was out; so 'Arry, 'e took Derrick t' stay wif Melvin—an'—an' I niver seen Derrick or Melvin—or 'Arry—much after that. I 'ope there's nuthin' more ye wants t' ast me. I'll take me crowns now an' pass out."

Adam put the ten pieces of gold in Sadie's hands and she deposited them somewhere in the interior of her garments. Almost immediately thereafter she lost consciousness. As the two men rose from the table, Adam reached over and put a crown in Cox's pocket. In the midst of curious stares, they left that terrible place.

"So we have a connection between Melvin Ferrett and Derrick Molden," Adam commented as they went back toward Piccadilly Circus.

"And Ferrett is dead, and we don't know what happened to Molden?" Curtis interjected.

"It is time we went to interview the most illustrious member of the Phenwick family," Adam stated.

"The most illustrious one? Who is that?"

"You'll see, my friend, you'll see."

CHAPTER EIGHTEEN

The ceiling was high, the bedroom overlooking the street and the park across the way was enormous. Adjoining the bedroom, through sliding doors, was another large room, which was a kind of upstairs parlor or sitting room. Irish lace curtains hung at the front windows with heavy golden and white satin draperies behind them. The woman in the long maroon velvet dressing gown steadied herself against the side of the window, trying not to cause the curtains to move. From this position she would sometimes watch the street below for hours. It was her enjoyment of people, she rationalized, that caused her to be so curious.

The tops of the dresser and the bureau were covered with framed tintypes and photographs, hand-painted miniatures, and a collection of other mementos. At the edge of the dresser was a wig stand with a freshly arranged piece upon it. Joanna had studied the wig for several minutes. She was not altogether convinced she was satisfied with the shade of color. After all, a strawberry-blond hairdo hardly would look natural on a woman who could pass for forty-eight in shadowed conditions, and who was actually in her sixties.

Joanna was about to go back to the dresser to try on the new wig when she saw a landau pull up to the curb before her house. She stood on tiptoe as she curiously watched Adam Truff and Curtis Tinkersly alight from the vehicle. Recognizing Adam, Joanna realized there was not time to debate the issue of the suitability of her wig. Her old one had gone for repairs, and the ones prior to that had been taken to the theatre to be used as stage props. She removed the scarf from about her head as she heard the doorbell tinkle in the distance. She had time to see that the wig fit properly to her head. After all, the butler would have to bring up Mr. Truff's card and she would have to detain him and his friend for a few minutes while she made herself presentable. In her opinion, an uninvited guest or guests was expected to wait. Even if she were perfectly prepared and waiting, the grand actress would insist upon leaving such a caller to meditate in the downstairs sitting room.

The butler took word to Adam and Curtis that Miss Phenwick would see them shortly. The young, remarkably handsome servant bowed and excused himself.

"What do you make of that?" Curtis asked.

Adam chuckled as he examined a magazine on the table. "The butler? I rarely have opinions about butlers."

"Now, Adam—"

"Well"—Adam flipped his hand—"as you know, Miss Joanna Phenwick is a leading actress on the London stage. Among other things, she has a distinct partiality to handsome young men. I believe she thinks the association makes her young in spirit. When, actually, I suspect that being seen in the company of such Adonises, the contrast of youth and the grand lady makes her appear—well, at least her age. I have visited Miss Joanna on several occasions over the years. I could not help but notice that there has been a whole parade of handsome young servants in her employ. The same is the case at the theatre. You instinctively know that she has hand-picked her supporting cast of male actors. I even understand that, when she commissions plays to be written for her, she stipulates that there be several parts for young men. I think I have clearly projected a comprehensive picture of the lady."

"And how long will a young man like this present butler remain in her employ?" Curtis questioned.

"I should think that would depend upon him," Adam replied, "and how exacting he is to her wishes. But let's not be vulgar and discuss such gossipy things."

"Gossipy? Vulgar?"

"Curtis," Adam said with a raised chest, "it wasn't accidental that I suggested you dress as you did for this visit, nor that I donned the costume I'm wearing. If Miss Joanna is sufficiently impressed with our outer appearance, she will be apt to be generous with her opinions and information."

"Now that you've told me that," Curtis commented, "I'll be so nervous and self-conscious that I'll doubtlessly commit one blunder after another."

"In that case," Adam said, "leave the talking to me and you just stand or sit and look attractive. I know she'll be impressed."

"*Impressed?* Impressed with what?" Joanna exclaimed as if she were making a well-timed stage entrance. "Ah, dearest Adam! What an unexpected pleasure to see you again. I had heard you were in London. I was certain you would turn up one night at the theatre and beg me to break an engagement so that we could dine afterwards in one of those private little places."

"I assume that means you haven't changed your opinion of me," Adam returned with a broad smile.

She closed her eyes, showing full eyelids and a look of disdain. "Unfortunately it does. Still, I forgive you for *not* being my ideal sort through and through, don't you know. One adapts." Joanna turned her pleasantly smiling face to

Curtis. Her eyes flickered back to Adam. "I received only one card."

"May I present Mr. Curtis Tinkersly?" Adam introduced. "He is the first mate on the Medallion's *Twin Dolphins*. The old gal is having her barnacles scraped and is temporarily out of commission."

"I trust you're speaking of the ship," Joanna remarked, a touch of whimsy in her voice.

"My dear Joanna," Adam teased, "how ever, with all of your activities, could you possibly collect barnacles?"

Joanna slapped him playfully with her fan. "Naughty boy, naughty boy!" She giggled girlishly and again turned her attention to Curtis. An insinuating smile lit her face as she glanced back at Adam. "I'll reserve my comment, Adam."

"Think what you will. You may be mistaken," Adam returned. "Are you offering brandy, or shall I help myself?"

"Take your choice," Joanna replied. She stepped nearer to Curtis and permitted her eyes to run the full length of him. Then she went back to reexamine one or two spots along the route before establishing eye contact with him. "So you're Curtis Tinkersly. That's an English name, isn't it?"

"Yes, ma'am," Curtis replied. "My grandfather was from Manchester, but he emigrated to New York and later moved to Philadelphia. I hired on with Medallion in New York when I was fourteen just going on fifteen."

"So very young," she commented.

"I hope to become a ship's captain before I'm thirty."

"Such marvelous ambition," Joanna remarked. "I've always enjoyed men of the sea. I think there is something basically romantic about adventure. And sailors do have such wonderfully naughty reputations." She chuckled, making a throaty sound.

"I suppose we should get down to our purpose for being here," Adam said after he emptied his brandy glass.

"It wasn't merely for a quiet Thursday afternoon visit?" Joanna asked as she turned her attention back to Adam.

"Alas, no, dear Joanna," Adam said. "The fact is, I am here in London doing a bit of investigation. Curiously enough, my trail of tidbits and clues has practically led me to your door."

"My door? Am I involved in some way with whatever you're going on about?" she asked.

Adam explained what his basic mission in London was, and part of the progress he had made thus far. "So you see, I enigmatically come again to the name of Derrick Molden."

"Derrick Molden?" Joanna arched a brow. "Sounds theatrical."

"Yes, doesn't it. I've been able to unearth little about one Harry Molden; but what I have discovered indicates that he was a kind of entertainer," Adam related. "One source said he was a pearly, another that he was a street clown. I suspect he was in a bad period of his life when he married Mary Ferrett. But there was still enough of the theatrical in him to give his son a dramatic name. Derrick Molden. It has a ring, hasn't it?"

"And *how* has the name Derrick Molden led you to my door?" Joanna questioned, settling herself into an armchair that gave her a very regal posture.

"Think back, dear Joanna, perhaps eight or ten years ago," Adam persuaded. "Derrick is a tall, redheaded young man with extraordinarily good features, considering his background. With that hue of hair and blue eyes, it is almost inevitable that he has a rash of freckles from one end to the other."

"Not completely," Joanna corrected. "Derrick only

freckled where the sun hit his body, which would imply his face and arms, except—"

"Except?"

"Except in the summer, when he would go bathing at the shore," Joanna said. "As I recall, he was quite fond of Brighton, although I never went there with him. We did, however, journey once to Bath when I was on holiday between plays. Yes, my memory is still strong. And now that I put the name with the—uh—face, images of Derrick Molden play back upon the screen of my mind. But what curious thing about him has caused his trail to detour to me?"

"We merely learned that he had been associated with you for a period of time," Adam remarked. "We thought you might be able to shed some light upon his character, that is all."

"Ah," Joanna sighed. "Let me think. If you don't mind, I'll ramble for a few moments as I get a clearer picture of the man. Oh, yes . . . yes, of course." She smiled dimly, then changed her expression. "For appearance' sake, Derrick Molden played the role of my *secretary*. I've had so many *secretaries* that surely the very word must have become synonymous with something else. Ta-ta, so what?" She sighed. "He was just in his very early twenties, I recall, although I often suspected he was still in his teens. I fear he grew bored with me and my way of life—I mean the theatre, of course. With such immaturity, he found it difficult to find *constructive* things to occupy his time while I was busy. One realizes, when dealing with such a youth, that he is to but occupy a brief interlude in one's life. There was nothing concrete in the situation—nothing lasting."

"I trust you reached that conclusion," Adam interjected, "after you had had sufficient time to investigate his potentials."

"Of course, dear boy, of course!" Joanna fluttered her

eyes in Curtis's direction. "Growing tired of men has become a habit with me. I don't mean with all men, of course; and I am enthusiastic while my interest is aroused. But, as with so many, I soon grew tired of Derrick Molden. Besides, there was somebody or other who had captured my curiosity by then. Such a scene that transpired when I told Derrick it was time to terminate the relationship. It was then I became aware of what an out-and-out liar he was. He actually had the audacity to confess sincere love for me. I may become emotionally involved with certain individuals, but I'm not naïve . . . far from it."

"You did let him go?"

"He was in the way," Joanna said. "One must cast out the old to make way for the new. But I confess, Derrick did play on my emotions. As a result, I arranged for him to get a position with my brother Joshua, at Falstaff Mews, you know, Lilac House. Well, Derrick was not an industrious sort when it came to actual labor. I know he intrigued Olivia Phenwick at first—she was always easily impressed; but she soon saw that Derrick was ogling her daughters, Ruth Carrie and Elizabeth. The fool should have known it would have done him no good to pursue the young girls. What influence did they have? I can't recall if Ophelia and Leo were still home at the time, or not."

"I assume that position quickly terminated," Adam expressed.

"By all means. Joshua refuses to put up with nonsense," Joanna explained, "especially if it involves his children. Well, Derrick returned to me—not to ask for a position, but to attempt a bit of extortion."

"Extortion?" Curtis questioned.

"Derrick claimed he had observed an indiscretion on my part," Joanna commented. "Whether he did or not is questionable. But since he knew of the incident in rather lurid detail, I was forced to—shall I say—'assist' him. I gave him certain funds and arranged for him to acquire a position with Gregory Phenwick. It was there he remained until shortly after the accident in Carrickfergus."

"You'll forgive me for mentioning it, dear Joanna," Adam said, "but timewise, there seems to be a discrepancy."

"I omitted saying there were times when Derrick disappeared, as it were, for periods without being heard from. You can't expect me to keep chronological data on everyone in my cluttered head."

"Quite understandable, Joanna," Adam commented. "Did you ever have the occasion to meet his brother Melvin?"

"Melvin?" Joanna squinted as she searched her memory. During that time the butler brought tea things and she poured. "Oh, yes, Melvin Molden—I do recall meeting with Derrick on one or two occasions." She passed teacups.

"Melvin *Molden?*"

"A rather plain-faced sort, don't you know. He lacked both beauty and charm. So unlike Derrick," Joanna related. "Where Derrick was at least interesting, Melvin was dull. Still, I couldn't help but believe there was some sort of conspiracy going on between Derrick and his brother."

"Conspiracy?" Adam questioned as he sat forward. "What sort of conspiracy?"

"It was just something in the manner that—they appeared so secretive," Joanna stated. "I noticed exchanges of glances and furtive movements. I tell you, I didn't much care for Melvin Molden at all."

"His name was Melvin Ferrett," Adam corrected.

"Melvin Ferrett? Was it the same man?" Joanna questioned.

"Melvin Ferrett and Derrick Molden were half-brothers," Adam explained. "They had the same mother, but different fathers."

"Aha! That explains why they were so different! I knew there must have been a reason," Joanna exclaimed. Her triumphant expression changed as a thought came to her. "*Melvin Ferrett*? Wasn't that the man who allegedly embezzled from my brother at the Medallion company?"

"The same, Joanna."

"Oh, dear, I fear I may have been instrumental in getting Melvin that position in the first place. I didn't associate the name." Joanna put her hand to her head. "Will Joshua ever forgive me?"

"I'm certain he will, Joanna. Of all the men in your life, dear lady, it is your brother who loves you the most," Adam said.

Joanna would have liked for the two young men to remain longer, but Adam assured her they had much to do in the next two days, before they returned to Southampton in preparation to sail on Monday. If he could arrange it, Adam would try to have supper with her before departing, but he could make no promises.

"Now what have you pieced together?" questioned Curtis Tinkersly as they left Scotland Yard a short while later.

"That we have found more information regarding this case than Alister Crook has done in the past several months," Adam replied. "I don't mean to denigrate Inspector Crook. After all, there are times when one simply chances upon information. I can tell you this, my dear friend. I find it most singular—and perhaps circumstantial—that Derrick Molden and Melvin Ferrett are related. But how there is a tie between the embezzlement of funds and that which is happening with Isabelle Phenwick would be two different matters. Yet I have an intuitive feeling that there is a direct connection."

The two men arrived at a three-story structure that had been constructed in such a way that there was a tavern on the street level and rooms to let on the second and third floors. The establishment below was called the Earl's Head. A side door led to the rooms above.

Mrs. Edna Stout, a short, thin lady with warts, appeared at the door marked "manager." She suspiciously eyed Adam and Curtis. "What is it?"

Adam explained that they wished to see the room where Melvin Ferrett had lived.

"It's all bin changed, it 'as," Mrs. Stout replied. "After th' blokes from Scotland Yard was satisfied, I took 'is other fings out an' burned 'em."

"Did Mr. Ferrett have any friends who came regularly to call?" Adam asked.

"Nay one I know," Mrs. Stout answered. " 'E was usually quiet an' kept t' 'is self. Ye kin imagine 'ow surprised I was t' 'ear 'e'd embezzled money, kin't ye? Lor', that were a shocker."

"Did you know his brother, Derrick Molden?"

"I often seed th' man called Derrick come around," Mrs. Stout mentioned. " 'E was a pincher. I took me broom t' 'im, I did. I know 'is kind wif th' ladies."

Adam controlled a smile. "Did Mr. Ferrett have any lady friends?"

"None t' speak o'. Oh, there's that Sprague woman on th' third floor back," Mrs. Stout said. "She carried on some'un terrible after 'e was dead. I reckon there mighta bin a bit o' 'anky-panky there. She's in three-F."

Mrs. Stout watched as Adam and Curtis climbed to the third floor. Neither spoke as they went to the designated room.

Bertha Sprague pulled her robe protectively about her throat with one hand while the other went to make a futile attempt to straighten a nest of flying hair. She was a sad-faced person who had never been a beauty; still, she possessed some charm. Her hair was brown and gray and her long face was a web of lines and dark places. She made the men wait while she pushed a few things out of sight. Even then the place was cluttered from one end to the other.

"What is it you want of me?" Bertha Sprague asked after showing the two men in and indicating chairs upon which they could sit. "You're not with the police, are you? Or with Scotland Yard? We've had enough of those around here."

"I happen to be an American," Adam explained, "but I am seeking information concerning the death of Melvin Ferrett."

Tears came to Bertha Sprague's eyes. "Finding out who did it isn't going to bring Mr. Ferrett back."

"You were fond of him, weren't you?" Adam questoned.

"I was," Bertha replied. "I'm no beauty, Mr. Truff. I have had very few close relationships with men. I'm not proud to admit that, but it is a fact. Consequently, when I discovered that Mr. Ferrett showed an interest in me—a personal interest—I did my best to encourage him. We became good friends."

"You'll excuse me for observing," Adam interrupted, "but you don't sound as if you come from a lower-class family."

"I come from a good family," Bertha said proudly. "But I was caught during an indiscreet situation when I was eighteen. When I defied my parents, they sent me away, never to darken their door again. I did what I could to survive. I could do certain things when I was younger and had the bloom of youth still in my cheeks. But hard spirits and hard living brought me to where I am today. I work hard to scratch a living. I had hoped that Mr. Ferrett would one day propose to me. That day never came."

"Were you acquainted with Mr. Ferrett's brother, Mr. Molden?"

Bertha spat as a disgusted expression came to her weary face. "Yes, I knew him. And if I weren't in the presence of gentlemen, I would tell you precisely what I thought of him."

"Why did you dislike Mr. Molden?" Adam persisted.

"Because he caused my Mr. Ferrett to change," Bertha replied. "Then last autumn he started bringing *that* woman here."

"What woman?"

"Well, she was hardly more than a girl," Bertha answered. "A very pretty girl. I never knew her full name. Mr. Ferrett referrered to her as Elaine."

"Elaine or Elena?"

"I'm certain he called her Elaine," Bertha said.

"There was a fan belonging to a Miss Elena Phenwick found in Mr. Ferrett's room," Adam mentioned, and watched for her reaction.

"It's a wonder there wasn't more than that found in his room what belonged to her," Bertha declared. "She must have come up here a half-dozen times with Mr. Ferrett's brother. His brother would discreetly leave them alone for an hour or so. After she had been to see him, Mr. Ferrett was different—his attitude toward me changed. He began getting guilty looks as if he were up to something he shouldn't be. Prior to that time he spoke freely with me. Then he became as tight as a clam. In time he complained that I irritated him. I stayed away." Tears had come again to her eyes. "Finally, when I could stand it no longer, I went to call on him in his room. That was when Mrs. Stout said she hadn't seen him in several days. She and her husband broke into the room and found him dead ... murdered. And I'll tell you who killed him."

"Who?"

"It was his brother," Bertha stated, "and *probably* that woman."

"Do you know that for a fact?" Adam inquired. "Did you see it happen?"

"No. But I know as sure as I'm sitting here," Bertha continued, "that that's what happened. Who else could have possibly done it?"

After ascertaining that Bertha Sprague had never owned a fan of any value and that she really had no proof or evidence, Adam and Curtis excused themselves and left.

"Shall we have a glass of Scotch below, before we get back to the Savoy?" Adam asked.

Curtis nodded in approval.

Adam sat in silent contemplation as he stared at the amber liquid in the glass. Curtis observed him for nearly ten minutes. Finally Adam raised his glass and downed the entire contents. A cough and further reaction to the bitter taste caused him to violently shake before the sensation passed. Then he brightened as if he had made a discovery. "Of course!"

"I beg your pardon?" questioned Curtis.

"Of course, that's it! I should have seen it before!" exclaimed Adam. "Come on, lad, let's get back to the hotel and pack."

"Pack?"

"I'm ready to return to Boston."

"Can you tell me what conclusion you've reached?" Tinkersly questioned.

"Not yet. Not yet . . . but soon."

CHAPTER NINETEEN

"Please stop!" Ann Marie Phenwick screamed as the carriage in which she was riding careened around a corner and nearly tipped over. She had been to visit her father at the Medallion office. Upon leaving the building, she had found a carriage waiting. The driver had assured her it was for hire. She had instructed him to take her to Triumph House. Had something frightened the horse? How had the driver lost control of the animal?

From the window Ann Marie could see that they were moving in the direction of Triumph House, away from the city. Then she could hear the malevolent cracking of the whip, as if the driver were racing the animal to his death. But why?

"Driver! Won't you stop? Can't you control the animal?" she called.

After terrible, heated words and name-calling with her cousin the evening before, Ann Marie was intent upon going to Triumph House to have a showdown with Isabelle. Ann Marie had been alone at Edward House when her cousin suddenly had appeared in her room. Annoyed by the invasion of her privacy, Ann Marie had told the other in no uncertain terms what she thought of her. Isabelle had quickly and equally as vehemently retaliated.

Ann Marie had walked away from the argument that was swiftly turning into a battle. After having all night and that day to think about it, she was ready to take on Isabelle.

The carriage was racing erratically, as if it had gone out of control. Ann Marie held onto the straps and screamed incoherently at the driver. By the sound of the horse's hooves, it was going over a wooden bridge. There was a bump. The carriage tipped, joggled, and rocked several times. Ann Marie screamed hysterically as she was pitched helplessly about and the carriage crashed onto its side.

Dazed and panicked, a sharp pain in her side and back, Ann Marie reacted only with the desire to lift herself from the vehicle. She could hear the horse crying in pain, and as it jerked, the carriage lurched. She managed to pull herself to the window. The horse was on its side. There was no sign of the driver.

The awareness of blood spouting from the area of her abdomen caused Ann Marie to lose consciousness.

Black-gray clouds had rolled in from the Atlantic and hovered mysteriously above Triumph House.

Tommy Phenwick praticed at the piano between six and eight hours a day. Critical praise of his playing and a consensus of opinion that he was verging on being a genius of the keyboard encouraged his continual tenacity at perfecting his skill. When he was not at the piano keyboard, he was at the organ. His life at that point was devoted to his music.

During her stay at Triumph House, Isabelle had spent very little time with Tommy. She had no knowledge or apparent interest in music. Where could they have a meeting of minds? Still, the youth had a quiet respect for his distant cousin. Her beauty did intrigue him. Yet, because he knew his mother had hoped to push him in Isabelle's direction, he obstinately cultivated indifference toward her. He was far more interested in Ann Marie, but not enough to forsake his music to pursue a romantic relationship with her.

In the midst of a full keyboard arpeggio in the key of G flat, Tommy could not be distracted by the opening and closing of the door to the music room. His fingers raced over the thirty-second notes, ascending and descending, several times as he perfected his technique. That meant he had to stop and rework the fingering to suit the prescribed speed and to obtain the desired effect.

"Damn!" Tommy shouted, slamming his large hands down on an octave and half of keys. "What the devil do you want? Can't you see I'm practicing?"

The response was a childish whimpering sound.

He had mistaken the intruder for his mother. When he turned to see Isabelle and not Millijoy standing by the door, he tried to control his raging temper. "I suppose I must have a substantial lock installed on that door once and for all, Isabelle, as long as you're prowling around Triumph House and indiscriminately go poking in wherever you damn well please!"

Isabelle had braced herself against the door, a wild expression in her eyes. "She's after me! She's here in this house!"

"What in the name of common sense are you going on about?" Tommy asked.

"I've seen her ghost," Isabelle said frantically. "She keeps haunting me. First she was down on the beach; then she was in my room; and just now, while I was in the solarium, she came at me."

"Who? Who? Who?" Tommy shouted.

"Elena!"

"My God, Isabelle," Tommy said, rising and impatiently moving to her, "don't you remember that Elena is dead? Can't you get that through your silly head?"

"I do know she's dead. I attended her funeral. *That's* all in my silly head, Tommy," she blurted, and broke into crying. "But I know what I saw just now! I know what I've seen! I know my sister!"

"Your sister's ghost, you mean, don't you, Isabelle?"

"Yes. Yes—yes!" Isabelle screamed. "Help me, Tommy! Now that she knows I'm here, I've got to get away."

"You silly thing, don't you realize that Elena is all in your head?" Tommy fired. "It's your imagination being overworked. Now, if you don't mind, I've not finished practicing. The piano is the most important thing in my life. I've no time for crazy notions about ghosts. Go away. Leave me alone."

"Could you just go into town and ask John Phenwick to come to Triumph House?" Isabelle pleaded. "He'll help me. He loves me."

"I know perfectly well that Uncle John loves you," Tommy returned. "But I'm not leaving this house for at least an hour. Besides, look at the sky—it's on the verge of a storm. Go upstairs and take a sedative and try to relax, Isabelle."

"Please go for John."

"I will later." Tommy put his hand to her shoulder to push her from the room. "I have to go into town later anyway, storm or not. The *Twin Dolphins* has returned from London and Adam was to have brought me some music. I'll tell John to come see you at that time." He shoved her from the room and turned the key so she could not return.

Before he reached the piano, Tommy could hear Isabelle's whimpering sound on the other side of the door. He sat angrily and played with bombastic gusto, so loudly that all other sound was completely drowned out. Caden-

222

zas played at triple fortissimo rippled fantastically beneath his touch. Normally he could have put such disturbances as the recent interruption from his mind. Why couldn't he now?

Several minutes later, he pounded both his forearms hard on the keys, knocked the piano stool over as he rose from it, and stomped noisily toward the door.

Isabelle was gone. The house was quiet. But the memory was still in his mind.

Tommy went directly to Millijoy's room on the second floor. She was in the process of dressing and listened to her son's complaints about Isabelle as she watched him through the mirror.

"If you asked me, Mother, she's going mad!" Tommy raved on, when he had not received the response from his mother he had hoped to get. "You know where she should be, don't you?"

"Where is that, Tommy?" Millijoy condescendingly asked.

"In a hospital. A hospital with bars on the windows so she can't get out," Tommy declared.

Millijoy sighed. "I'm afraid you're right, Tommy. I thought perhaps we could help her."

"If Cousin Joseph Ornby can't help her," Tommy said, "how can we? She needs to be where Cousin Joseph can look after her. If she keeps raving on about the ghost of Elena, *I'll* begin seeing her next."

Millijoy turned to face her son. "Have you?"

"Have I *what?*"

"Seen Elena's ghost?"

Tommy swallowed hard. "No, of course not!" He snorted contemptuously. Then, on second thought, he asked, "Have you?"

Millijoy eyed her son through the mirror, then turned about to face him. A peculiar, enigmatic smile came to

223

her lips. She thought a moment before shaking her head. "No. No, of course not."

"Why do you say it that way?" Tommy asked.

"It's just that, the other night when I was getting home late from a concert," Millijoy said, "I did see Isabelle wandering through the second-floor hallway. When she apparently caught a glimpse of me, she ran into the shadows and disappeared. I went to my room and changed out of my dress. Once in my robe, I considered the matter of Isabelle and decided to go in and have a look at her. I found her soundly asleep. The next morning when I mentioned the situation, she claimed to know nothing of it. Doubtless she had taken a sedative Dr. Joseph had given her, and it caused her to forget."

"Mother, you opened our house to Isabelle because you wanted me to become romantically interested in her, didn't you?" Tommy questioned. "Well, since she's been here, I have developed nothing but contempt for her."

"Contempt? But why, Tommy?"

"I hadn't meant to tell you this," the young man said, "but a week or so ago, while I was bathing, Isabelle came into my room. I asked her to leave because I was modestly in the tub. She refused and tried to coax me out, saying that she would dry me off if I did. I insistently remained where I was, and I had to use the scrub brush to beat her away when she came over to the tub and . . . well . . . became indiscreet."

"Why did you resist her, Tommy?" Millijoy asked.

"Why? Oh, Mother! If I'm to be a man, then I must be the aggressor," Tommy stated. "Furthermore, I will pick and choose. And I'm certainly not in the least bit interested in a woman who humiliates me and makes derogatory remarks about me and about my music."

Before Millijoy could question him about such remarks, a knock sounded against the door. "Tommy, be a dear and see who that is."

Tommy opened the door to Victor Samson, the butler.

"You'll excuse me for interrupting, madam," Samson apologized, "but a rather urgent message has arrived by a young messenger. I fear it is quite important."

Millijoy apprehensively went to the man standing at the door. She tried to read a message in his eyes. Quickly she took the paper and scanned it. "Oh, dear! *Dreadful!*"

"What is it, Mother?" Tommy asked, reaching for the paper.

"Ann Marie has been in a terrible accident," Millijoy said as her son read the words. "She is calling for both of us—poor child."

"She's been taken to the hospital," Tommy commented as the paper dangled in his hand.

Samson caught the paper and folded it. "Shall I get the carriage, Madam? Inclement weather is threatening."

"Yes, by all means, immediately," Millijoy ordered. She turned to Tommy. "Will you go with me?"

"Yes, of course," Tommy replied. "Do you suppose it's as bad as it sounds?"

"I—I don't know." Millijoy had grown pale.

Moments later Tommy had changed and ran to join his mother at the carriage entrance. Samson was waiting with the vehicle.

"Maybe we should take Isabelle with us," Millijoy suggested.

"Mo-ther," Tommy moaned.

"You're right. She's doubtless taken a sedative." Millijoy patted her son's leg and called for Samson to start.

Several drops of rain had fallen and Samson had gone back to get rain apparel since he would be exposed in the driver's seat.

"You were mistaken, Mother," Tommy said as the carriage pulled out the drive and it circled around so that he could look back and see the house. "Isabelle is standing at the upstairs window watching the carriage leave."

"Maybe we should go back—"

"Mo-*ther*! If we do, you'll have to choose between Isabelle and me," Tommy stated. He glanced again up at the second floor window and silently wondered why his cousin was dressed as she was.

So much was happening, all in one day. The *Twin Dolphins* had docked at Boston harbor shortly after Ann Marie was found by a farmer on his way to market. He took her to the hospital.

"I can't get off with you this time, Adam," Curtis Tinkersly remarked as the other was preparing to go ashore. He glanced to the sky. "There's heavy wind behind those clouds. I need to stay on board."

"The *Twin Dolphins* will be in Boston several days, won't she?" Adam questioned, briefly looking up at the invading blackness.

"Yes. And we'll have time for a chat or two later on," Curtis remarked, "but I've got to remain aboard for the next twenty-four hours or more." The ship had begun rocking, bobbing up and down. "Makes me suspect a hurricane, this time of the year."

Adam pulled up the collar of his coat. He removed his hat to keep it from being blown away. His dark hair was swept upward and to the side. "I suppose it is hurricane season, isn't it?"

Curtis waved from the top deck. Adam carried only two satchels. The rest of his luggage would remain at the ship's office until he decided where he wanted it sent.

A carriage hired, Adam directed it through the now-wet streets to the Medallion office in Tremont Street. There he was forced to wait a few minutes until Stuart finished with a business appointment.

"Adam!" Stuart exclaimed happily as the two greeted with a warm embrace. "I was expecting you, of course, but I didn't think you would be here quite this early."

"Just anxious to see you, Stuart," Adam replied. "I believe that some very urgent action is going to have to be taken."

"Urgent action?" Stuart was about to lead Adam to a comfortable chair when the door suddenly burst open and his eldest son, Danny, entered.

"Dad, you must come at once!" Danny exclaimed.

"What is it, son?" Stuart knew that Danny would not have interrupted unless it was vitally important.

"Ann Marie! She's been in a terrible accident," Danny informed him. "She's in the hospital. Cousin Joseph has just got there."

"I'll go with you," Adam volunteered. "I had the carriage wait downstairs."

Stuart ran into the hospital with Danny and Adam behind him. Upon learning where Ann Marie had been taken, the three immediately went in that direction.

Joseph Ornby was just coming out of the private room when the three arrived. He wore a grim expression and stared glassy-eyed at Stuart. "I can give you little hope, Stuart." He clasped the other on the shoulder. "She has lost a tremendous amount of blood. We have no idea what time the accident occurred, but the farmer who brought her in said it took him nearly an hour to make it into town."

"Can I see her?" Stuart asked.

"She's unconscious now. I've given her something," Joseph replied. "I've also sent for two colleagues who specialize in working with such cases. They're both very busy men."

"Do whatever you can, Joe. Spare no expense," Stuart ordered.

Stuart went into the room, followed by Adam. Joseph caught Danny and detained him outside. Then he put his arm around the boy.

"I don't believe you want to see your sister as she is now, Danny," Joseph commented. "It isn't a pretty sight."

"Did the man who brought her in know what had happened?" Danny asked.

"He simply found her in the overturned carriage," Joseph explained. "He mercifully shot the suffering horse before he pulled Ann Marie from the wreckage."

"If Ann Marie is as bad as you say she is—"

"Now, now, boy, it's only legal to shoot horses." Joseph thought he was being somewhat humorous; he realized he was not.

Danny would remain at the hospital while Adam accompanied Stuart to tell Ruth about the tragedy. Stuart felt his wife should be informed and should alert the other children. They would return to sit out the ordeal.

As they walked down the corridor toward the front of the hospital, a raucous sound punctuated by a familiar voice caught Adam's attention.

"One moment, Stuart," Adam commented, and quickly went to the door of the room from which the sound was coming. He turned back. "It's John Phenwick."

John was sitting bare-chested while a young doctor was examining him, a stethoscope to his chest.

"There is nothing wrong with my heart or lungs," John complained. "I tell you I'm quite all right."

"John!" Adam interrupted.

"Adam! When did you get back?"

"Ann Marie has been in an accident," Stuart said quietly. "I've got to go tell Ruth and come back to stay with my daughter."

"Ann Marie in an accident, too?" John questioned. "That's odd."

"You were in an accident?" Adam asked.

"Yes."

228

"I'll go, Adam," Stuart said. "You remain here. It'll be best that way."

John submitted to having his wrist bandaged by the young doctor. "It was the darnedest thing, one of those freak accidents. I was leaving court and hailed a carriage. We'd gone no more than two blocks when the rear wheel rolled off. I fell to the side and banged my wrist and got shook up a bit. It was nothing. I was close by, so I came in here. But my coat and blouse were torn, so this idiot started jabbing me with a stethoscope."

Adam related all he could about Ann Marie as he helped John dress and get as presentable as he could with torn clothing.

"Is there anything we can do?" John asked.

Adam shook his head. Then a thought struck him. "What did the carriage driver do after the accident?"

"That's the peculiar part," John said. "He just disappeared."

"Can you describe what he looked like?" Adam asked.

"He was tall . . . had red hair . . . blue eyes . . . freckles," John related. "I would say he was somewhat handsome. . . ."

CHAPTER TWENTY

The wind was pushing with hurricane force. The sky was a dense, swirling mass of black clouds. Although it was still afternoon, the atmosphere was gray, dark, the eerie light of a storm. Giant elms were bent to sixty-degree angles and the red maple leaves were stripped from bare limbs. A huge oak bough snapped outside of Triumph House, near the window of the room assigned to Isabelle.

Shutters slammed in the distance, banging back and forth where they had broken free of the catch that held them in place. Gun shots? The glass doors were blown into the room, tumbling lightweight objects with the invading wind. A china vase was heaved from the table, and crashed into tiny pieces on the floor.

Isabelle was on her back, lying across the width of the bed. She had earlier freed her hair. In that position her long tresses fell to the floor. The wind caught and twirled them, causing a strange sensation to move through her.

A lamp was pushed to the floor, shattering as it fell. The sound alarmed Isabelle and she rolled over onto her front side to survey the damage done. The entire matter struck her humorously and she laughed. Then, rising, she pushed her way against the blast of wind and had to cling to the bedpost to keep her balance. More laughter. She actually wondered what she found so funny about the destructive violence that was taking place.

Her feet crunched over broken glass. Fortunately it was fine and did not not penetrate the soles of her shoes. As she nearly made it to the window, her body was blown back into the room and she fell against a chair. Annoyed and tingling from a smarting sensation that was bound to turn black and blue, she mustered the strength to brace herself. Closing the French doors was another matter. The shutters on the terrace needed to be shut first. That was a task she was ill-equipped to deal with.

Wrestling doors and shutters, she gave up on the latter and settled for firmly closing and locking the doors in a moment when the wind seemed to pause to catch its breath.

Isabelle brushed a trail with her foot through the broken glass and made her way to the door of the room. Her intention was to find a servant to come assist her with the shutters. But when she got to the corridor outside her room, she had difficulty remembering what she had intended to do. Heavy gray hung in the hallway. No light was glowing, and the ominous storm light created a special gloom of its own.

"What did I come out to do?" she asked herself. "It's my mind. It's become so foggy and vague. Insanity, that's what it is! Oh, why couldn't it have been me and not Elena who was killed at Carrickfergus? She had so much to live for, and I so little—now less." She lurched her way around the circular hallway to the balcony above the stairs that led to the round entrance hallway on the first floor. The myriad prismed baubles on the mammoth chandelier chattered noisily due to the restless inpouring of drafty air. Why hadn't the servants seen to locking and securing the windows?

Isabelle braced her arms on the balcony railing and stared down at the chandelier as it swayed. The movement distorted her senses and she began to get a slight queasy feeling. Rain was falling heavily on the cupola and against the glass panes that circled its base. Was Tommy still in the music room? She followed the curve of the stairs with her eyes and focused on the door to the music room. The sound of the storm was so loud, she believed it might have drowned out the noise of the piano. Was that possible?

A lonely, empty feeling came over Isabelle. She mustn't disturb Tommy, she thought. He had gotten all out of sorts with her earlier. Why couldn't she make him understand about Elena? Why couldn't she persuade anyone of the truth of the terrible haunting experiences she had endured? Millijoy had at least appeared sympathetic to her plight. Millijoy? She would go to Millijoy!

Turning back to the inner corridor, Isabelle went immediately to the second-floor sitting room where she knew Millijoy spent much of her time while in the opulent mansion. The door was heavy. She pushed against it and it budged. Perhaps it would be better etiquette to knock first. She did. No answer. Upon trying the door again, she was able to shove it into the room.

The French doors leading to the terrace had blown into that room. With the inner door open, the cross-draft was almost overpowering. Isabelle slid into the room and closed the door behind her.

"Millijoy? Are you in here?" she called in a feeble voice.

A tree limb snapped just outside the French door and landed on the terrace. Isabelle screamed: *"Milli-joy!"* The wind answered her with a fitful roar and blew rain in through the window.

As Isabelle attempted to close the doors in that room, she slipped on the wet floor and fell. Getting to her feet was another matter that took much effort. Satisfied that Millijoy was not present, she managed to escape the room and returned to the balcony.

Was it her imagination, or had the entrance hall become darker? The chandelier was definitely swinging with broader, pendulumlike movements. She cocked her head to the side and asked, "Elena, are you causing that to do that? If you are, you had better stop it. I don't care for your pranks, you know." A chill moved up her back. "Elena? Oh, Elena, *is* that you?"

Thunder exploded like a blast of dynamite. Isabelle squealed and hurried down the curving stairway as fast as she could. She did not stop running until she reached the kitchen. Plunging through the swinging door, she stopped cold in her tracks as a blaze of lightning flashed against the window.

Fire was still smoldering in the stove, and a teakettle emitted a fine stream of steam. No living person was present. A large tabby cat was stretched before the stove. When Isabelle went toward the animal, it suddenly got to its feet, arched its back, and hissed. A moment later the cat had disappeared down the stairs leading to the servants' quarters below.

What had become of all the servants? Isabelle was certain she would have discovered at least old Clara Whiteside, who seemed to never go out. Perhaps the stableman or groom was out in the carriage room or stable. It would take a man, she thought, to—to *what?* Oh, yes, to close the shutters. Why did she have such a difficult time with her memory?

After climbing down the stairs, knocking on doors, and discovering nobody there, Isabelle retraced her steps and went back to the entrance hallway. Her attention lingered briefly on the black marble statues of the handsomely proportioned bodies. But they stood like dark silhouettes in the faintly lit room. Instinctively she knew it was still afternoon as a terrifying thought came to her. "This place will be pitch-black by nightfall. I must find some matches and light the lamps. If I'm caught here in deep blackness, I'll become more frantic than I already am frantic. And there's no doubt in my mind that I could not stand being any more frantic than I am at this very moment." Pause. "Elena? Are you here, Elena? I'm alone, afraid, and quite frankly, *frantic*! Elena?" She twirled around as her voice seemed to echo in the baubles of the chandelier.

"Tommy!" she exclaimed, and hurriedly ran to the music room. The door fell open at her touch.

The music room was modestly furnished. The large grand piano, which had been imported from Vienna, seemed to occupy at least a third of the space. Two light-weight upholstered satin library chairs were placed on either side of a small table. A love seat was arranged so it, too, was facing the piano. Music cabinets were against one wall, and a low bureau was on the opposite side of the room, a brandy decanter placed upon it. The curved east wall, of course, was practically solid glass with three sets of double doors that led out onto the terrace that overlooked the rose garden. On a nice day, there was an exquisite view of the ocean from that room. Now the ocean was obscured by sheet after sheet of water that was falling in a deluge from the sky. Even the rose garden was curtained in darkness.

Isabelle remembered a box of matches kept in the drawer of the small table between the two library chairs. She found three matches, one of which she immediately struck and put to the lamp on the same table. Then she lit candles in a candelabra on the piano.

"At least one room will have light," she said aloud. "I can always curl up on the love seat and stay right here. I don't believe Elena knows about the music room. At least I hope she doesn't."

She sat at the piano and played a simple piece she had

learned as a child. That amused her. But the insistent sound of the storm outside put her on edge. She did not wish to remain in the music room, not until she was certain there was no one else in the house.

South of the music room was the morning room, which was really like a solarium Millijoy had seen while in Europe. It had many plants growing in it. Comfortable wicker furniture painted white comprised most of the decor. Isabelle stopped at the round table and touched the heads of three chrysanthemum blossoms in a large glass vase. Rain peppered against the windows, and with it a bird, probably a seagull, was pitched at it. The poor thing's body made a terrible thud as it hit. It was a wonder it did not break the glass upon impact.

Isabelle went to the window. Perhaps the bird was only injured. Without thinking of the consequences, she jerked open the door. The wind blew her aside, nearly plunging her into a large hydrangea bush that was planted in a tub near the door. "I'll not be thrown around like this!" she declared, and valiantly made her way back to the door. She braced her hands against the door frame. "See! You—whoever you are—will have to break my arms to push me from here now! Do you hear?" Pause. "Is that you, Elena?" By then she was drenched from head to foot and had completely forgotten about the bird that had hit against the window.

As she stood in the open doorway, the inrushing wind overturned several pots and the glass vase with the chrysanthemums, scattering the flowers in all directions. When Isabelle realized what had happened, she managed to close the door and fasten it. Oblivious of the damage caused, she stepped over objects and made her way back to the entrance hallway. How dark it was there, compared to either the music room or the morning room.

Convinced that she was quite alone in the foreboding house, Isabelle removed her clothing as she climbed the

235

stairs, letting each article of apparel drop where she removed it. She had become completely disrobed by the time she reached her room. Barefoot, she drifted into the room. Her hair was wet and dripping water. Crossing to a full-length mirror, she gazed at her naked reflection for several minutes. "Is that you, Elena? I might have thought it was at one time, but I know that is a mirror and I'm gazing at my own reflection. It is *not* my twin—it's *my* reflection! Oh, but Isabelle, how sad and abused you appear . . . and scandalously without clothing. What would Mama say?" She thought a moment. "But what will I wear? Something daring, I should think. I don't own daring clothing. I know . . . Millijoy! I'll borrow one of hers. I must dress appropriately for a storm."

As Isabelle stepped on pieces of broken glass, several bits lodged in her feet. She took time to pick them out. Then she went to Millijoy's bedroom and directly to her closet. Barely able to see the gowns, she took several out to examine. Then, finding a blue dress made from an Empire pattern, she decided upon it. Seconds later she was slipping it over her head.

Finding a match, Isabelle lit two lamps in the room. The sound of the storm only remotely bothered her as she prepared to sit at Millijoy's dressing table.

"Glory be! D'ye know what all this brightness does t' me poundin' head?" a small voice cried from a sewing basket where Millijoy kept yarn she used for needlepoint.

"Moorduke? Is that you?"

"Ay, an' I've got me hat pulled down over me eyes."

"I should hope you did," Isabelle returned. "Here, with me dressing practically under your very nose."

"I did nay see a thin'."

Isabelle stepped to view herself in the mirror over the dresser. She glanced back. "Of course you didn't see a thing, because you don't exist."

"I don't?"

"Not in the least. I've been thinking about you, and I've reached the conclusion that you have manifested in my life because you are part of my decaying state of mind—a figment of my imagination. And do you know where *that* will lead? To complete insanity. You didn't appear until after Elena was drowned."

"I did nay appear before, because I niver chanced upon ye before. An' that's th' truth. I'll take a fairy oath upon it."

"I don't believe you, fairy oath or not," Isabelle said. "So as far as I'm concerned, you can go peddle your malarky elsewhere." Taking a grand pose, still barefoot and with hair streaming with water, she receded from the room.

"Sure an' b'gorra, maybe she *is* losin' her sanity."

Glassy-eyed and feeling oddly omnipotent—and weak at the same time—Isabelle marched to the balcony above the entrance hall. Only faint flashes of light reflected in the chandelier's prisms. "Elena!" she called. "Elena, if your ghostly purpose is to drive me mad, I will readily admit that you are succeeding!" Her voice raised in pitch and volume as she shrieked. "Elena, show your ghost to me now, if you dare! *Elena! Do you hear me?*"

A deathlike silence seemed to envelop the sound of the storm as Isabelle stood in a moment of triumph. Then from some distant place—or was it everywhere at once—came the reply: "*Yes, Isabelle, I do hear you.*" Hollow, haunting laughter.

"Elena!"

"*Isabelle!*"

"Elena?"

"*Isabelle!*"

The chandelier was spinning as Isabelle teetered against the balcony railing. Frantic pulse-beats charged through her. It was all she could do to keep from collapsing.

"*Come and find me, Isabelle!*"

Millijoy was all but drenched before she reached the inside of the hospital. Tommy was dripping water. Samson remained with the carriage. He had worn a slicker and mariner's hat, but he was soaked to the skin.

Tommy was inquiring where they might find Ann Marie Phenwick's room, when Millijoy spotted Danny.

"My sister is resting and unconscious," Danny informed them. "My father has gone to Edward House to tell the others. I doubt if either of you can go in to see Ann Marie now. I believe it is best if you don't."

"It would have been best if we had not left Triumph House at all," Millijoy stated. "But we did, and here we are after several unforeseen incidents. I wanted Samson to turn the carriage about and return to the house, but he said it would be impossible to make the hill in all this storm. We had no other choice but to come here."

Danny took Millijoy and Tommy to where John and Adam were waiting. Millijoy repeated what she had told Danny about the trip.

"Isn't Isabelle with you?" questioned John.

"No. She was a bit under the weather," Millijoy said. "You'll forgive the pun. She is the fortunate one not to be out in all this storm."

"You left her *alone* at Triumph House?" John stated.

"There are servants about," Tommy related. "She knows her way around. Besides, the way she's been acting lately—well, we would have done her a favor to bring her here to the hospital—and leave her. I'm going to speak to Cousin Joseph about her, if I see him."

"What are you saying, Tommy?" John asked.

Tommy explained his impression of Isabelle's mental state. "I know your strong feelings for her, Uncle John, but even you must be practical in this matter. She claims she sees the ghost of her dead sister. She rambles on about her as if she were very much alive."

"It's gotten that bad, has it?" Adam inserted. Then he

238

put his thumb and index fingers to his mouth and pinched his lips. "Hmm."

"I don't like thinking of Isabelle being alone on that hill," John stated.

"It would be foolish of you to attempt to ride up there in all this storm, John," Millijoy advised.

Danny appeared in the room and informed Millijoy and Tommy that Joseph Ornby wished to see them.

Adam was seated with his feet propped up on a table. He seemed to be staring at the rain-covered window pane. But his eyes were not really focusing at all as he gazed into the distance.

"Adam—?"

Adam snapped his fingers. "The name of Kathleen O'Dwyer comes to my mind. I thought I had this thing sorted out and pieced together. Now I'm confused again." As he stared vacantly, his head slowly turned to one side. He removed one foot from where it was resting, then the other, as he slowly sat forward, an incredulous expression on his face.

"What is it, Adam? What do you perceive now?" John asked.

"A little man," Adam replied, holding up his hand indicating about three inches between thumb and forefinger, "about this big. He has side whiskers and is wearing a peculiar green and brown costume. I must be taking a touch of a cold."

"What did you say?"

"I must be taking a touch—"

"No before that."

Adam repeated what he had said. "Maybe Isabelle isn't the only one who is having hallucinations."

"Isabelle? Of course!" John exclaimed. "What's the little man doing? Can you hear if he's saying anything?"

Adam looked curiously at John. "I'm not the only one

who's hallucinating." He stretched. "Fatigue and frustration cause a man's mind to play strange tricks."

"It's Moorduke," John stated. "I'm certain it's Moorduke!"

"Who's Moorduke?"

John explained as best he could about the leprechaun.

"Well, then, why am I able to see it and you're not?" Adam questioned.

"I don't believe that is important, Adam. What is he doing?—I mean precisely."

"He's jumping up and down and pointing out the window," Adam explained. "I get the feeling there is something terribly urgent about what he wants. He's a funny little creature all right."

John said, "Why can't I see him?"

"Whose initials are L.N.A.?" Adam asked. "It seems to me he drew those letters."

"L.N.A.? L.N.A.?" John repeated.

"Say that again."

"L.N.A.?"

Adam jumped to his feet. "No! *L.N.Uh.* Elena! That's it! Of course! And I thought it was Kathleen."

"You're not making any sense, Adam."

"I am to myself, dear John," Adam exclaimed. "Storm or no storm, we've got to instantly get to Triumph House! Are you willing to brave the elements?"

"I'll do whatever you say, Adam."

Adam ran from the room and found Danny in the hallway. He gave him a message to take to the authorities as quickly as he could. Never mind the storm, they were to get assistance up to Triumph House as soon as possible.

CHAPTER TWENTY-ONE

Dazed and not functioning normally, her mind vague and her thoughts troubled with peculiar images, Isabelle traced the sound of the voice that had been calling to her to a stairway that led up to several rarely used rooms on the third floor of Triumph House. The steps were creaky and she had the sensation that she was ascending into dense darkness. Still, as she got nearly to the top, she perceived a faint glow of light coming from the distance.

The heavy part of the storm seemed to be moving away from the house, going north. Wind still whistled and rain fell, but the terrible blackness of the storm was drifting away. It seemed that the dim light was afternoon daylight, a kind of brown amber that hung in the gray.

Suddenly, as if a cloth had been pulled from around a lamp, a blaze of light flashed up, and in the glow of it, Isabelle viewed the likeness of her twin sister. She took several steps forward, staring as if she were hypnotized by the image.

"So you've found me at last, sister," Elena said.

"Why don't you dart away from me as you did in the past?" Isabelle inquired, inching nearer.

"Perhaps I've grown weary of the game of *blindman's buff*. And perhaps there is no longer need to play it."

"Why don't you leap out at me and attempt to terrify with a spooky tone to your voice?" Isabelle asked. "I know I'm quite mad and you're only an illusion. Moorduke told me about ghosts and spirits and things. But I am convinced you're only an illusion, a figment of my imagination—or something like that. I know you're dead, Elena. I saw you in your coffin. Of course your face was covered because it had been mauled by a wild animal."

Elena laughed. "You grieved over the remains of an idiotic Irish girl who was so crazy to know passionate adventure with an itinerant seaman that she walked into a trap and to her own death."

"What are you saying, Elena?"

"That I'm no more dead than you are—at this moment," Elena stated. "In a few moments from now—well, that will be another matter, won't it?"

"I don't understand, Elena, you were drowned," Isabelle said, confusion stirring fantasy with facts.

"I didn't drown, you silly fool. I was prepared for it when the carriage wheel hit the boulder on the bridge in Carrickfergus. I leapt to safety while you were meant to drown."

"I was meant to drown?" Isabelle asked incredulously. She turned as she heard footsteps moving behind her.

Derrick Molden emerged from the shadows. "So you have her now, Elena. Let's get on with it, then."

"There's plenty of time, Derrick," Elena returned. "The storm will continue for another hour or more."

"Can't we get it over with *now?*" Derrick questioned. "Suppose the stableman or groom should work his way out of the ropes—or that old lady."

"You put water on the ropes, didn't you?"

"Yes."

"They won't work out of them."

Isabelle had turned to face the man. "Derrick? Derrick Molden?"

"You're right, she is looney, ain't she?" Derrick commented.

"Will you tell me what this is all about, Elena?" Isabelle asked. "I don't often have discourse with ghosts."

"Will you get it through your head, Isabelle, I am *not* dead!" Elena stated. "The body buried in my place was that of Kathleen O'Dwyer, and—wait." She pulled open the bodice of her dress and lowered the shoulder of it down her arm. "See? Remember the freckles in the shape of a seven?"

"I should imagine that if you had freckles in life," Isabelle said absently, "I should think you would still have them on your ghost body."

"Damn it, Isabelle, *I am not dead!*" Elena shrieked.

"Let's kill her now and get it over with," Derrick interrupted. "This is getting on my nerves."

The word *kill* jarred something within Isabelle and she reacted with uncanny awareness. "Kill? Why kill me?"

"Because I intend to take your place, sister dear," Elena said tauntingly. "I was always the brightest, the cleverest, the one with the most talent, the outgoing one, the one with ambition . . . but you were the one designated to become a Phenwick woman. Well, I can still be me and assume your identity as well. In time people will just presume that shy little Isabelle has blossomed forth."

"I don't understand, Elena. What ever did I do to make you think this way?"

"Something you were unaware of: *You were born first,*" Elena said through closed teeth. "I was still a child when I began to plan for the day I would take your place. The accident in Carrickfergus was meant to kill you. It would have been simple and over with had things gone as planned."

Isabelle turned again to Derrick. "And now you're going to kill me? How was Elena able to persuade you to do such a terrible thing?"

"The same way I persuaded him to kill Kathleen O'Dwyer," Elena interceded. "I held money over his head. A very large sum of money."

"Neither you nor I had access to any large sums of money, Elena. Where would you have gotten it?"

"I already have it, sister. I masterminded a scheme to have it embezzled from Medallion Enterprises in London," Elena related.

"From Daddy's business?" Isabelle inquired as things seemed to be getting less and less fuzzy.

"I played up to one Melvin Ferrett, who was head bookkeeper for Medallion," Elena boasted. "He also, conveniently, happened to be the half brother of Derrick here. When I learned that fact, I put my plan into motion. I compromised Melvin Ferrett. I found his weakness and took advantage of it. Then, when he had done what we wanted of him, Derrick did away with him. It all would have been perfect if you had been killed when you were supposed to be. But we've surmounted those complications, haven't we, and here we are about to dispatch you once and for all, Isabelle."

"What have you done with Daddy's money?" Isabelle asked.

"It's no longer his," Elena said. "But if you really want to know, Derrick and I were on the *Twin Dolphins* when you and Daddy came across. Twice I pretended I was you to Daddy, just to make certain I could fool him. He never suspected a thing. I even gave you a bit of a reputation, sister dear, via a flirtatious assignation with the first mate—a charming and sufficiently experienced man, I might add. I left the ship in the disguise of a sailor. Immediately thereafter, I traveled to New York, where I had the British money exchanged into American dollars."

"You seem to have had this all very well planned, Elena."

"Perfectly, down to the last detail," Elena bragged. "Now you have even brought my goal nearer to me."

"How so?"

"By causing John Phenwick to fall in love with you," Elena said. "Once you're out of the way, I will merely step in where you left off. I'll encourage an early marriage, probably by the time Daddy returns from Savannah. Then I will have achieved that which I was always told would be withheld from me: I will become a Phenwick woman."

"Oh, Elena, I can't believe you capable of doing all this!"

"Can't you, Isabelle? You might be surprised about me and the things I am capable of doing," Elena stated. "Take her away Derrick, and get rid of her!"

"Elena—" Isabelle pleaded. "No last farewells?"

"Not even a parting kiss. Don't be melodramatic, Isabelle, it never did become you. Derrick—"

In the next moment Derrick had his fingers clutched about Isabelle's upper arm. He jerked her down the stairs. Isabelle could be heard pleading as he took her away.

A light rain was still falling as Adam and John Phenwick approached Triumph House on horseback. The ride from town had been hazardous, but the most treacherous part was the last stretch, coming up the steep hill to the house. Several times both horses nearly lost their balance and fell. The last several yards, the men had dismounted and walked the animals.

"Are you certain of what you're talking about?" John asked as they stood at the front door.

"I would be willing to gamble on it," Adam declared. "You just do as I tell you." He reached to pull the doorbell cord. "The first indication that I'm correct will come in just a few minutes."

Lamps had been lit in the entrance hallway. Elena had been waiting. Allowing sufficient time, she opened the door.

"Oh, John, dearest John, you've come at last," Elena said. "I was so terribly frantic and terrified of the storm and being here virtually alone in this terrible house." She kissed him. "Oh, I see Adam is with you."

John kissed her again.

"Not in front of Adam, my darling," Elena stated. She took his hand and led him toward the music room. "You will excuse us, won't you, Adam?"

"Haven't you a kiss for me, too, Isabelle?" Adam questioned.

She stopped. "Should I?"

"Don't you recall our arrangement, Isabelle?" Adam persisted.

"*What* arrangement?" Elena questioned, confused that she had missed a point along the way.

Adam grabbed her by the wrist and pulled her into his embrace. He could tell by her reaction that she was experienced in romantic adventures. However, not permitting her to further object, he pressed his lips to hers. The kiss was so passionate that John became embarrassed and considered breaking the embrace apart. Adam's hand moved to her throat until he caught his fingers beneath the top of her dress. His kiss became more than Elena was able to cope with. She pushed him back. And as she did, he pulled at her dress, tugging it down over her shoulder onto her upper arm.

The action had happened so fast. Elena had not foreseen that eventuality. In the confusion of the moment, she jerked herself free of Adam's hold.

"How dare you molest me this way? John, aren't you going to do something?" she cried.

Adam caught her again tightly in his arms. He kissed her throat and moved his eyes over to her shoulder.

"This is infuriating!" Elena exclaimed.

"My dearest, have you forgotten?" Adam asked innocently. "Don't you recall we agreed that I would make a far better husband for you than John, who doesn't give a tinker's damn for ladies."

"Impossible! That *isn't* true! I recall no such arrangement. And I know that is incorrect about John," Elena sputtered. "I intend to become a Phenwick woman!"

Adam gently kissed her shoulder again. "Do you really . . . *Elena?*"

Elena whitened. She was caught tightly in his embrace and could not possibly get her hands free.

"Do you see the seven in freckles here on her shoulder, John?" Adam asked.

"I do."

"Then would you say this was Isabelle's shoulder?"

"It can't possibly be," John replied coolly.

Adam's attention went to the window in the music room and a tiny light he perceived bouncing up and down on the window sill. He released Elena and went to examine it closer. What he saw—or imagined he saw—was Moorduke frantically trying to get his attention. The wee one seemed to be pointing outside in the direction of the beach.

"We haven't time to waste with Elena, John," Adam stated as he left the window. He grabbed John by the wrist and dragged him from the room.

As they left, Elena rubbed her arm and prepared to sneak from the room.

"If'n I was ye, I would nay plan steppin' a inch from this here room, lass."

"What? Who said that?"

" 'Tis me," Moorduke replied, enlarging himself so that he could be clearly seen by the lady.

Terrified by the sight of the small creature, Elena

backed from him into one of the library chairs and abruptly sat. "Who—who or what are you?"

"Me name is Moorduke an' I'm a leprechaun. Ye see it started wif yer mither when she kicked over the toadstools in me fairy ring. An' there do be a legend an' a warnin' among us wee folk concernin' mortals. Once we befriend one o' them, we kin expect t' be plagued wif them fer years t' come. First, it's th' mither, then th' datter, then th' granddatter—it goes on like that. 'Tis a sad curse fer th' likes o' me. That's why we little people rarely show our faces."

"No . . . no—it can't be!" exclaimed Elena. "Such things don't exist. I know that for a fact."

"Do ye now?" Moorduke executed the steps of a jig and made a directing gesture with his hands. "Ye're under a fairy spell now, lass, an' ye're me prisoner. Jus' ye try t' budge from that spot."

Elena exerted as much energy as she could muster, but she discovered she could not rise from the chair. Moorduke found her actions amusing and rolled over with laughter.

Part of the path leading down to the beach had been washed away, making it difficult for Adam and John. A light rain was still falling, and in the west streaks of sunlight penetrated the horizon.

Derrick had pulled Isabelle out into the turbulent surf. Four different times she had managed to escape his hold, but each time he had caught her again before she could get away. Frantic with fear and fighting for her life, Isabelle clawed at the man as she felt his leg wrap about hers and trip her. She went down. Seconds later his hands were at the back of her neck in a firm hold, sustaining her head under water. She struggled, kicked, and tried to pull his hands from about her throat. He had amazing strength, and she had so little.

An instant before Isabelle was certain she was about to

lose consciousness, the fingers were released from around her throat. Had he presumed her to be dead? In the next moment two strong arms were gripped about her and she felt herself being tugged upward.

John was wet, but he was the most beautiful sight Isabelle had ever seen. Weakly she gazed into his face. Then, with all her remaining strength, she lunged her face forward and upward. Their lips met as they mutually went to each other.

"Now I know I haven't lost my mind, dearest John," Isabelle gasped. "I was so certain it was happening. Oh, John, love me back to complete sanity. Please love me back, John, please love me!"

Breathless and emotional, John squeezed her to him and gently led her from the surf. When they stood on the sand, he embraced her again. "Elena—I spoke with Elena."

"So did I," Isabelle whispered, a faint, weak feeling coming over her. "Derrick was going to kill me. Elena instructed him to do so."

"We know, we know. Adam and I know, dearest Isabelle," John said as he kissed her again and held her with his cheek tightly next to hers. "You can't imagine the way I worried about you and the terrible things I was forced to think about your condition. How could I have ever had doubts about you? How?"

"Because I had doubts about myself," Isabelle replied.

"Do you have doubts about me?"

"None whatsoever, dearest John, none whatsoever."

Derrick Molden had temporarily eluded Adam after sharply kicking him in a painful area. But Adam quickly sprang back, ignored the smarting ache, and scurried to wrestle Derrick to the ground. Using tactics he had learned from his Indian friend, Jamatu, Adam soon had the advantage; and, before he knew it, Adam had removed Derrick's belt and had secured his hands with it.

"I know some other tricks," Adam stated as he gasped for breath, "which will be very painful experiences for you if you force me to use them."

"She made me do it," Derrick blubbered. "It was all her idea."

"I do believe you, Molden. Elena is being detained by a leprechaun."

"By a *wot*—?" Derrick gasped incredulously.

CHAPTER TWENTY-TWO

Ann Marie Phenwick never regained consciousness. She slipped from life the following morning. Stuart was grief-stricken. Ruth tried to console him, but she was incapable of dealing with his emotional reaction. His son, Danny, came close to comforting him, but the young man, too, was deeply distraught.

Adam stayed near his old friend, Stuart, and was able to give him more solace than anyone else.

In the meantime, under heavy interrogation by the authorities, Derrick Molden confessed to being responsible for the accident that ultimately caused Ann Marie's death. He, furthermore, admitted to having attempted to jeopardize the life of John Phenwick in a similar carriage mishap. Since the authorities were armed with information about the man's background, Derrick also signed a confession stating that he had personally and in cold blood killed his stepbrother, Melvin Ferrett, and a young Irish girl by the name of Kathleen O'Dwyer.

"I cannot possibly prosecute my own sister," Isabelle said two days later. By then she had regained her strength

251

and was fast on the way to getting her mental attitude into a positive frame. "After all, Elena is my twin."

John understood. "Very well, but what is to become of her?"

"I believe she should be sent back to London and dealt with by my parents," Isabelle stated, looking lovely and comfortable in a soft blue afternoon gown.

John kissed her. "Yet, back in England, Elena is apt to be prosecuted along with Derrick Molden."

"Only because she brought it upon herself," Isabelle related.

"Well, I shall personally see that she is never permitted to set foot back in America," John commented.

"I fear Elena will reap her own destruction," Isabelle sighed. "Hate and greed do such terrible things to a person, don't they?"

"And love does such beautiful things," John whispered as he moved his face to hers.

The sailing of the *Twin Dolphins* was detained due to the death in the Phenwick family. Adam was to make the sea voyage to see that Derrick was delivered to the authorities in London. He was also to accompany Elena, who would be confined to her cabin for the entire trip. Hence, Adam wished to remain in Boston to be with Stuart as long as he was needed.

"I'm fine now, Adam," Stuart assured him. "I will survive."

"Are you certain?" Adam questioned lightly. "We can always wait for another crossing."

"No, no, I'm quite all right," Stuart insisted. He took Adam's hand. "I don't know how to thank you for all you've done."

"You've already thanked me enough," Adam replied "However, if you wish to do something special for me give young Alexander a special amount of love for me

I'm very fond of that boy—but then, which of your children doesn't mean a great deal to me? I consider them my family, too . . . as I consider you."

Stuart embraced his friend and wished him well.

"I've decided not to take my captaincy commission at this time," Curtis Tinkersly stated as Adam went aboard the *Twin Dolphins.* "I figure you'll need a hand with those two, and I want to be around to help."

"That's very kind of you, Curtis," Adam remarked. He sighed. "Do you know, I'm looking forward to this journey and a time of relaxation."

Curtis showed Adam to his cabin.

"I'll just relax a while before the others come to say farewell," Adam announced. He thanked Tinkersly for his assistance and expressed his pleasure at seeing him aboard.

Alone in his stateroom, Adam sorted a few personal items and washed his face. Afterwards he stretched out on the bed. He was about to doze off when he heard a peculiar sound.

"Saints b' praised! What in th' divil am I doin' here?"

Adam raised his head. "Who is it?"

"Glory be, an' I'm nay alone."

"Who is it, I say?" Adam braced himself with his elbows.

"Ay, lad, it 'pears as if'n I'm headed back t' th' other side o' th' world, don't it? Oh, do nay look so perplexed. I'll make meself a mite bigger so ye kin see me." Moorduke grew larger. "I know fer a fact that ye ain't got any wee ones o' yer own—an' chances are, ye won't—so I'll not be doomin' meself t' further torment in th' years t' come by showin' me face t' ye."

Adam stared at the leprechaun, shook his head and fell back on the pillow. "Moorduke, what have I done to deserve you?"

"I kin nay think fer th' moment, but it musta bin somethin' good."

Millijoy and Tommy were at the wharf to see the *Twin Dolphins* off. After all, Adam was her very good friend—and Tommy felt quite close to him. Stuart was there with Danny. Ruth and the other children had remained at Edward House. Stuart stood close to his eldest son, aware that if he weakened, Danny would be there to give him support.

Isabelle and John Phenwick were among the family. At first Isabelle had had a desire to have parting words with her twin sister, but at the last minute she became convinced that she had said all there was to say. In a way she was sad, thinking of Elena being taken back to London, virtually as a prisoner. Yet the memory of what she had put Isabelle through, not only in Boston but from the time of the accident in Carrickfergus, was still indelible in her mind. She had forgiven, but Elena nor what she had caused would never be forgotten.

"The wind is at our backs," Captain Keswick announced, "I believe we had better get on with it."

The guests were cleared from the ship and the anchor was hoisted. Adam stood at the railing, eyes clouded with tears as he waved good-bye.

"Here," Curtis Tinkersly said, handing Adam a handkerchief. "These things always have a tendency to be a little damp. But you'll be back, Adam. I've never seen a man loved as much by any family as the Phenwicks love you. And if I think about it much longer, I'll have to take my handkerchief back and use it myself."

Adam smiled up at his friend, used the handkerchief and handed it back to him. For one of the few times in his life, he could not find adequate words.

The ship was out in the harbor, going toward the sea. None of the Phenwicks were any longer able to see

Adam. They spoke among each other, then disbanded to go their separate ways.

"Dear Isabelle," Millijoy exclaimed in parting, "you know you are welcome to stay at Triumph House until your wedding. I'm certain it will be different now."

Isabelle exchanged glances with Tommy and smiled. "Thank you, Millijoy . . . Tommy . . ."

"And when will that day be?" John asked, when they were alone.

"*What* day, John?"

"Our wedding day." He squeezed her hand.

"Mama, Alexandria, and Bertie will want to be here," she said, "and—well, and Daddy. And there are other Phenwicks in London who might wish to come. Then there's your mother and brother Thadius, and the Phenwicks in Greenfield, and—"

"And the Phenwicks in Portland," John added. "I know, I know, I know! My dearest, whenever it may be, it will be the happiest day of my life."

"Of *our* lives, wonderful John, of *our* lives," Isabelle exclaimed, and glanced about her before she leaned her face against his shoulder. In proper Boston even that was considered a familiarity. "I'm frantically in love with you, you know."

The door was stoutly locked. Elena had tried it. The small compartment was passably comfortable, but certainly not to her liking. She paced like a prisoner. Confinement was terrible punishment for her.

"What could be worse than crossing the Atlantic in a dreadful hole like this?" Elena said aloud as she fumed.

"What could be worse, lass?" a tiny voice came from a luggage rack. "Wal, d'ye want me t' tell ye, er would ye prefer seein' it first hand as it happens? Ye know, we leprechauns do have a' impish way about us at times."

"No! No!" Elena fumed. "I could have gotten away if

it hadn't been for you. Get out! I don't want you around me!"

"Ye'll excuse me fer sayin' so, Elena, but th' door do be locked. 'Twould seem ye're stuck wif th' likes o' me— fer a while anyway." Moorduke laughed.

Elena beat her fist into the palm of her other hand. An ultimate feeling of defeat came over her.